Winner of the TSB/Peninsula Prize for fiction, this
novel represents the remarkable debut of a major
fictional talent. Valerie Maskell has created a superbly
vivid evocation of life in a small south-coast town in
the years between the wars. Yet FANCY WOMAN is
far more than a period piece: it is an enthralling story
of love and loss — and of a woman's unconquerable
resolve.

A successful playwright, Valerie Maskell grew up in
Kent, then attended RADA. She now teaches drama in
Newbury, Berkshire.

GW00320299

Also by Valerie Maskell in Warner Books:

SHOPKEEPERS

VALERIE MASKELL

FANCY WOMAN

WARNER BOOKS

A WARNER BOOK

First published in Great Britain in 1992
by Little, Brown and Company
This edition published by Warner Books in 1993
Reprinted 1996

Copyright © Valerie Maskell 1992

The moral right of the author has been asserted.

*All characters in this publication are fictitious
and any resemblance to real persons, living or dead,
is purely coincidental.*

All rights reserved.
No part of this publication may be reproduced,
stored in a retrieval system, or transmitted, in any
form or by any means, without the prior
permission in writing of the publisher, nor be
otherwise circulated in any form of binding or
cover other than that in which it is published and
without a similar condition including this
condition being imposed on the subsequent purchaser.

A CIP catalogue record for this book
is available from the British Library.

ISBN 0 7515 0120 4

Printed in England by Clays Ltd, St Ives plc

Warner Books
A Division of
Little, Brown and Company (UK)
Brettenham House
Lancaster Place
London WC2E 7EN

To Maureen Duffy
with love and thanks

CHAPTER 1

Lilian Watts stood in the doorway of Rosie Timms's kitchen at number 9, Shelley Street, and faced her future.

The room was small, square and half-filled by a deal table, covered with a shabby cloth of dark green plush. The wooden tea-tray was ring-marked by years of wet cups, and of the two standing on it now beside the brown teapot, only one was complete with saucer. There were some lumps of sugar on a different, second saucer near a cracked white china jug containing milk. Lilian understood that Rosie was doing her best.

'Sit down dear, and make yourself at home. I thought we'd have a nice cup of tea, and then I'll show you round. Your things have come. They're all upstairs except the baby's bath; that's in the scullery. You can put her down on the couch if you like, she won't hurt it. We're used to babies here.'

She moved to take Sylvia from her mother's arms, but Lilian clutched her child even closer. The battered chaise-longue, with its stained, threadbare, once plum-coloured upholstery was no fit resting place for Sylvia May Watts. But she would come round to it. She would

1

have to, left here all day with this woman while her
mother was out at work.

Lilian sat down on a kitchen chair jammed sideways
between the table and the pea-green distempered wall,
and arranged the baby more or less comfortably on her
lap. Mrs Timms was gabbling nervously as she poured
out tea.

'Lovely hair you've got dear, I always wished mine
was that colour. Is it what they call auburn?'

'It's just ginger I think.'

Lilian glanced at her landlady, surprised that she
should have any aspirations at all as to appearance. Her
hair, which seemed to be of no particular colour, was
pulled back into a tight bun, and her face was lined and
tired. Yet there was something strong about her, a brisk
positiveness that had no doubt seen her through many
troubles, and would probably help her to cope with
many more.·

'So much of it too, and naturally curly. No wonder Mr
Fitzgerald took such a fancy to you. Ooh, I shouldn't
have said that, should I?'

She replaced the teapot on the tray and covered her
mouth with her hands, looking anxiously at Lilian. But
she soon recovered. 'Still, no good trying to keep secrets
when you live in the same house, is it? And you with
that little bundle of trouble. I see you're not wearing a
ring. Well, why should you? What business is it of
anyone else's? Nobody's perfect, that I do know. I've lit
the fire in the front room for you. Mr Fitzgerald said you
was to have a sitting-room to yourself, but I daresay you
won't be there much. You'll always be welcome out here
when you feel like a chat. I'm mostly on my own in the
evenings. Neddie and Albert never get in till after
eleven, Lord knows where they get to, and my eldest

girl Dollie, she's as bad. Pretty, she is, though I says it as shouldn't, too pretty for her own good. And lovely hair, too. Not so fair as it was but plenty of it, and curly. I said to her yesterday, "You look out, my girl" I said. "You'll get yourself in trouble one of these days, and I doubt if your Mr Leeson in soft furnishing is the marrying kind." She works at Collingham's, you know, on the haberdashery. Girls these days, you've no idea what they get up to.'

Lilian smiled. 'I daresay I have.'

'Ooh, my Lord. Whatever have I been saying? You'll have to forgive me, I always was a chatterbox.'

'Don't worry about it. How many children have you, Mrs Timms?'

This was more than just a polite enquiry. Lilian was anxious about the number of people the little house would have to hold. How many would be washing in the scullery when she needed to fetch water? How many would be using and waiting to use the outside lavatory?

'Oh, Rosie. Do call me Rosie, please. I was always Rosie when I was in service, and you get fed up with being Mum all the time. Six, I've got now, six. It would have been seven but Willie was killed in France in 1917.'

'I didn't know. Oh, I am sorry.'

'Yes, he was a lovely boy, my Willie, really lovely. So now there's just the six. Nell's at my sister's, of course, you've seen her.'

She had not realized that the exhausted little maid-of-all-work at Mrs Denning's High Class Boarding Establishment, where, after her mother's death, she had lived until eight months ago, was a niece of the proprietress.

'Then there's Ned, he's in window-cleaning, and Albert, he's looking round at the moment, and Dollie, and Nance, and then this young rascal.'

She turned to where her youngest child was squeezed into a high chair rather too small for him, stolidly sucking at an almost empty feeding bottle. Rosie sighed, took the bottle and refilled it with milky tea.

'This is Georgie. Loves a nice cup of tea, don't you, my chook? Like his mum. Eh? You're like your mum then, aren't you?'

She stroked his wispy hair fondly, and Lilian saw that despite his sticky face, stained, dribble-soaked, towelling bib, and the unpleasant smell emanating from his person, this child was beloved. She was surprised. She herself would find it quite impossible to love anything so unattractive. Supposing Sylvia became like that? It must not happen. She would go on bathing her every morning, and top-and-tailing her every evening just as Nurse had shown her, and she would tell this little woman that Sylvia must not have tea, only boiled milk, and she would find someone nearby to do her washing, for there was obviously not room to do it here.

'My husband was in the Navy, you know.' Rosie Timms was saying with some pride. 'On the *Suffolk*. That's a cruiser. Got torpedoed, just before the war ended.'

'How dreadful for you.'

'Oh, well, he wasn't killed then, no, the torpedo only blew a bit off the end of the ship. No, it was the TB that killed my Arthur. Course, he picked it up while he was in the Navy, I make no doubt about that, he was a war casualty just the same as Willie, but you see he didn't pass away till a year ago last Christmas, in and out of hospital he was for three solid years, and because of that you see, I don't get no pension. Still, we've kept going.' She turned to her little boy. 'We've kept going, 'aven't we, my love, and when you're a big boy you'll buy

Mummy all those things your dad never 'ad time to get.'

No wonder the place looked poverty stricken! What on earth would her bedroom be like? Still, so long as it was clean.

Raising her white china cup to her lips Lilian caught sight of herself in the spotted, greenish mirror on the opposite wall. Tilted downwards, it foreshortened her face, which, as it was rather long, seemed an improvement. She was still wearing her deep-crowned, wide-brimmed hat, pulled well down over her springy red hair. It was quite an old straw hat but she had recovered it with dark blue silk and trimmed it with a pearl buckle at one side. She had on her navy jumper dress, loose fitting and calf length, over a white blouse, and her spring coat with the velvet collar. These clothes were not new but, bought in more prosperous days, they were of good quality, if not now in the latest fashion. Her image seemed out of place against the background of the dingy room. She thought that she looked rather like Lady Bountiful, but she was not on a visit. She was hard up, very nearly penniless, and she had come to stay.

Luckily, perhaps, she was prevented from brooding by Georgie, who chose this moment to demonstrate his favourite game. This consisted of holding the tray of his high chair up in front of his face for several seconds, then letting it go so that it crashed back into its normal position. His mother ignored him. The crashes grew more frequent but came at maddeningly irregular intervals. Eventually Lilian said, 'Perhaps I could see our room.' She had no wish to see it. She wanted never to see it, but short of jumping up and strangling her landlady's child, she could think of no other course of action.

On the way through the narrow hall Rosie Timms

opened the door to the front room that was to be Lilian's sitting-room, revealing little more than a quantity of thick yellowish smoke, and closed the door again, quickly.

'That fire smokes something chronic,' she said, 'but it'll be better when it's burnt up a bit.'

Lilian followed Rosie up the steep linoleum-covered stairs, noticing as she did so the sagging brown tweed skirt and dreary knitted cardigan, both of which looked as though they had been made for someone consider-ably larger than their present wearer. At the top there was a square yard of landing and three brown painted doors. The paint, though chipped, was clean, and in fact the whole place was reasonably clean, but Lilian was struck only by the dinginess and the poverty.

There was just enough room to open the door into the front bedroom, almost the entire space being filled by an enormous brass bedstead covered with a white honey-comb quilt. Sylvia's cot, one of Will Fitzgerald's extrav-agant presents, stood undraped in the corner by the window. The iron rod at the head, with its projecting arm over which the pink muslin canopy would hang, had a sinister look. It reminded Lilian of a miniature gallows.

'Your things are here, so I'll leave you to get settled in. If there's anything you want, just give me a call.'

Rosie paused in the doorway, looking round the bleak little room. 'I know it's not what you're used to, dear, but we'll make you as comfortable as we can, and you've got your little one. Funny thing, really. When you find out they're on the way you'd give anything to be rid of 'em, then when they're here you'd sell your soul to keep them safe. Funny really.'

Lilian placed her daughter in the middle of the sur-

prisingly white counterpane, and squeezed her way
round the end of the bed to the window. She stood
gazing down into the street of mean little dwellings that
alternated door, window, window, door, all the way to
the main road. This was what it had come to. She
remembered the crisp lace curtains and the little front
garden with the laburnum tree, and how her mother had
told her so often not to eat the seeds because they were
poisonous that she had been afraid to go near it, and
waited to feel ill if she accidentally brushed against the bark.

She thought of her front upstairs room at Mrs
Denning's, with the two long windows overlooking the
green where the church stood, and the view of the sea
beyond. It was to this room that Will Fitzgerald had
so often come on Sundays, after he had been to
St Austin's, for he was a good Catholic. Then she
pictured the room in the cottage at Sturry where she had
given birth to Sylvia, Nurse Tebbitt's cottage, pretty and
comfortable, and Nurse Tebbitt so kind. The months
there had been happier than she could have believed.
But all good things come to an end, and Nurse had
needed her room for another young lady in difficulties.
Then Lilian realized for the first time that she was one of
a succession of unfortunate or unwise young women,
who provided Nurse Tebbitt with a useful addition to
her income.

So now this, the poverty-stricken back street
bedroom, where the house opposite had two broken
windows filled in with cardboard, and grubby children
played in the gutter.

Surely Will could have found her something better
than this? The area known as Poet's Corner was notor-
ious in Culvergate. But of course it had to be a place
where there was someone who could take care of Sylvia

and it could not cost too much. Nurse Tebbitt had been expensive, but that was over; now she had to manage on her own wages, which had been raised a little to help with her new circumstances.

At least the surroundings didn't worry the baby. She was sleeping peacefully, wrapped in her white shawl in the middle of the big bed.

Lilian opened her father's old black tin trunk, and took out the drapery and bedding for the cot, thinking that it might help to see the infant in her usual surroundings of palatial splendour, but it did not. The pink lace-trimmed muslin canopy and frills only made the damp-stained brownish roses of the wallpaper appear more squalid. When Sylvia was settled again she stripped the bed, inspected the mattress, which seemed to be perfectly clean and fairly new, and made it up with her own linen. Out of various bags and baskets she took the small things that she hoped would make the place seem more like home. A framed photograph of her parents which included herself at the age of six she placed on the yellowish chest of drawers that was wedged between the bed and the wall on the window side. She looked at the three set faces.

The sepia studio portrait was mounted on grey card and framed in dark wood. It showed her father seated bolt upright, pince-nez in place, moustache fiercely pointed, with her mother standing beside him. She looked young, round faced and tightly corseted. In front of her stood the child Lilian, hair loose for the occasion, with no pinafore to conceal her best black velveteen dress. Mother and father looked reproachful, accusing even, though she knew that this was due more to their having had to keep their heads still for a long moment than to the state of their emotions at the time.

Realizing that the picture could evoke few happy
memories and quite a number that brought no pleasure
whatever, Lilian opened the top drawer of the chest,
meaning to put it out of sight. A stale unpleasant smell
wafted from the shallow drawer, despite the fact that it
had been freshly lined with newspaper. How could she
put her clothes and private things into this unattractive
receptacle, redolent of someone else's life, some other
woman's femininity? She would like to have given the
whole thing a good scrub, but how was it to be done
without offending her landlady? She would have to await
her opportunity and in the meantime keep her own and
Sylvia's underwear in a suitcase. Now there was the
whole question of personal cleanliness to be gone into.
Easing herself past the cot she gave her attention to a
small wash-stand that was the sole remaining item of
furniture. The pink china jug was badly chipped, and
when she lifted it to inspect the basin in which it stood
she saw that although this had been wiped clean, a dark
crack ran two thirds of the way across it. It would be
remarkable if it continued to hold water. Next, the soap
dish. This was covered by a suitable though not matching
lid, but the operations of the cleaner had not extended to
the inside. In the grimy dish lay a slither of grey soap, and
adhering to this was a tightly curled black hair. Remembering her mother's houseproud ways, remembering Mrs
Denning's complaints if Nellie's work fell short of perfec-
tion, remembering Nurse Tebbitt's standards of hygiene,
Lilian succumbed to depression. She lay down on the
bed, meaning to think, to take stock of her situation and
decide what was to be done, but having walked from the
station with Sylvia in her new and splendid perambulator, she was tired out. Soon she was asleep.

*

Waking slowly half an hour later, the first thing she saw was the photograph, still on top of the chest. She considered the plain little face, framed by the masses of curly hair, of the child she had once been. She looked at her own small hand resting on her father's knee. The photographer had placed it there, she remembered, embarrassing them both, because they were not that sort of father and daughter. Going to tea with Phyllis several years later, she had seen her climb all over her father, tweak his nose and whisper in his ear and she had been amazed. Surely it was only with mothers that you could behave like that? Not that she would have tweaked her mother's nose, but she often whispered in her ear. It was necessary, life being so full of shameful private things.

But perhaps Dad would have been different if she had been more like Phyllis, small, pretty and cuddly with winning babyish ways, and a sort of flirtatiousness, even then. Whereas, as far back as she could remember, Lilian had been thin and lanky, with a nose too big for her face. She lacked Phyllis's saucy manner that seemed to please people so much, and on the one occasion when she had tried to copy it, at the wrong moment, with her father in the wrong mood, she had been angrily snubbed. It was dreadful to be so unattractive. Though she hadn't quite realized just how unattractive she was until that first time Phyllis came to tea at forty-four York Road.

Mum had got out the best tea-service, the one with the gold-edged cups that were decorated with pansies, which Lilian thought silly and unnecessary. After all, Phyllis Fitzgerald was only eight, a child like herself. What was more, they lived in a flat over a shop, not a proper house at all. She pointed this out to her mother.

'There are flats and flats, Lilian, and theirs is more than twice the size of this house, and it's on two floors, anyway, with attics as well. More of a maisonette, really. You wait till you've been there. You won't say "just a flat" then.'

'Do you think I ever will go there?'

'Perhaps. If you're good.'

Alice Watts spread a lace cloth over the chenille one that covered her grandmother's round table, and placed three small, pretty plates and three knives equidistant from each other upon it, and went out to the kitchen. She returned with two plates full of thin bread and butter, one of white bread, one of brown.

'Why are we having tea in here and not in the kitchen? We usually have it in the kitchen when it's just you and me.'

'Well, it's not just you and me, is it? Phyllis is coming.'

'I mean when Dad's not here. He's not going to have tea with us is he?'

'No. He'll have his later as usual. He'll be back about half-past six, I expect. It's early closing.'

Lilian felt depressed. She liked to be safely in bed before her father returned from his long day's work at Fitzgerald's. Her mother had worked there too before her marriage to Harold Watts, and she loved to talk about those apparently halcyon days. Fitzgerald's was really two shops on the stretch of esplanade known as the Fort with nothing on the other side of the road but the promenade, and then the sea.

If there had ever been a fort there, no trace of it remained, and Fitzgerald's was a luxurious establishment that sold silverware and jewellery in one shop, and delicate porcelain and cut-glass in the other. Alice had worked there in old Terry Fitzgerald's time, and it was in the jewellery department that she had first met her husband, a pale, tense, anxiety-ridden man, fastidiously neat in his black bow-tie and uncomfortable collar. She had thought she understood him, and could help him to enjoy life. Occasionally, it seemed to Lilian in later years, she had succeeded.

He had fallen in love with her voluptuous body and curly red hair. He wanted her so much that he dared not propose for fear of putting paid to his hopes. In fact he became so desperate that he decided to emigrate. One morning, standing illicitly in the china department watching her dust a Worcester vase, he told her of his intention.

'I've been and got my ticket,' he said, showing it to her. 'Look, Australia. In six weeks' time. There's no point in my staying here.'

He did not know that Alice's heart sank. She said, 'I'm sorry you're going.'

'Well,' he replied angrily, 'if I stayed here, you'd never marry me, so what's the odds?'

'How do you know I wouldn't? You've never asked me.'

Then of course he did ask her, and they both lived happily ever after, or so Lilian was given to understand, for she liked to hear this story. It seemed to make her father almost human.

So, of course Alice knew quite well what the flat was like, and remembered when Mr William, as they had called him in his father's day, had taken over the business and got married, soon after she had left to become Mrs Watts. His bride was the imposing Louisa Pickford, whose well-to-do family owned Pickford's Brewery.

Phyllis was a year younger than Lilian, and this was
the first time she had ever come to tea. By straining their
finances to the utmost the Watts were sending Lilian to
the same private school as Phyllis, so Alice had
suggested to her daughter that they extend the invitation. Phyllis, she said, would be a nice friend for her to
have. Lilian tried to explain that she hardly knew
Phyllis, who was still in Form 1, while she herself had
graduated to Form 2A, but her mother seemed not to
understand the importance of this. So pretty, bright
little Phyllis had been delivered by the Fitzgeralds' maid,
with instructions that she was to be home by seven, and
could run along the front by herself.

This surprised Lilian, who was never allowed to go
further than the sweetshop at the top of the road unless
accompanied. She thought her mother looked disapproving.

The visit was a success, despite Phyllis's lack of
maturity. After tea the little girls played in the back
garden, and Alice brought down the dressing-up box.
They pretended they were ladies, in old straw hats, with
a feather boa for one and a moth-eaten velvet cloak for
the other. Lilian freed her hair from its plaits, and
Phyllis tried unsuccessfully to do it up in a bun,
admiring as she did so its colour and quantity. It had
never before occurred to Lilian that it was in any way
enviable, and even now she had her doubts, remembering how the boys from the rough school called
'Carrots' after her in the street.

Alice hurried out soon after six to collect the dressing-
up clothes, putting an untimely end to their game of
Ladies Going Out to Tea. It would not do, she told
Phyllis, for the garden to be littered with clothes and
shoes when Mr Watts came home. Lilian was cross and

sulky, and confided to Phyllis that she hated her father. Phyllis, who saw him sometimes in the shop, said she thought he was quite nice. Lilian could not agree, and was glad when he was apparently delayed by a late customer, so that they were able to play snakes and ladders peacefully in the dining-room until nearly a quarter to seven. Alice sat sewing near the window. The room was gloomy although it looked out onto the small oblong garden, for the light was cut off by the projecting wall of the kitchen. Lilian thought her mother looked pretty, though her bright hair had faded to sandy, and her high-collared best dark blue silk dress was too tight. Prettier than Phyllis's mother who wore lots of beads and talked in a very grand voice. Mrs Fitzgerald was old, too, older than her husband. Lilian knew this because her parents often talked about it.

With her usual sinking of spirits she heard her father's key in the door. Alice hurried out into the passage.

'Oh, Harold,' she said as he hung up his bowler hat on the hall-stand, 'do you think you could just walk to the corner with Phyllis and see she gets home safely? Or I'll go if you don't mind waiting a minute for your tea. I don't really think she ought to go on her own, there's that man about ... he's been ... up ... to several little girls lately and ...'

'Yes, I'm surprised at Mrs F. letting her out alone. Well, let Lily go with her. He wouldn't go up to two together.'

'Well, he might. And anyway Lilian would have to come back on her own.'

'She'll be all right. No one's going to bother about her.'

As he spoke he entered the dining room, greeting

Phyllis quite cheerfully, and asking if she'd had a good tea. She said 'Yes, thank you, Mr Watts' very primly, and then giggled. Glancing at Lilian he said curtly, 'Sit up straight for Heaven's sake. You'll get curvature of the spine if you sit like that. I'll have to get you some braces to hold your shoulders back. Look at Phyllis, how straight her back is. They don't have to tell you to sit up, do they?'

Phyllis murmured 'No, Mr Watts,' and lowered her eyes, becoming very interested in the interrupted game.

Lilian felt a sob rising in her chest. This double insult was too much. The first one she scarcely understood, though she remembered it years later when knowledge increased her bitterness. The second one was commonplace and perhaps justifiable up to a point. She did try to hold herself up straight when she remembered, she didn't want to be like Hunchback Harry who swept the streets, but her long back soon tired.

Alice said, 'I'll put the kettle on, and then pop down to the corner with you, Phyllis. I expect your daddy will be looking out for you.'

Lilian slid off her chair. 'I'll come too.' She struggled to undo the buttons of her pinafore. Normally she would have gone out with it on, but Phyllis was not wearing one. Alice fetched the guest's pretty white hat from the front room and took her daughter's tam off the hall-stand.

'No point in you going, you can stay with me.'

But Lilian had no wish for her father's company. 'I want to go with Phyllis,' she said, untruthfully.

She went out into the passage before he could say any more, and she and Phyllis waited safely on the front path, while Alice moved the kettle to the hottest part of the kitchen range and fetched her own hat from upstairs.

When they reached the corner Alice said they might as well go the rest of the way, so they walked on among the throng of summer visitors, all elegantly dressed, the women in fine materials with elaborately trimmed hats that were heavy with flowers and chiffon and fruit and feathers, the men in smartly striped blazers and straw boaters. They were hurrying from the bandstand to their hotels for dinner, for at this hour only the well-to-do visitors were about. The others, those that looked after their children themselves without the aid of nursemaids, were already finishing high tea in their boarding houses.

Arriving at the Fort Restaurant, they could see Phyllis's father standing on the pavement outside his shop, looking in their direction.

Phyllis ran towards him, and Alice and Lilian, instead of turning back, followed her.

Will Fitzgerald was tall and thin, with straight dark auburn hair. He smiled kindly down on Lilian and said to Alice, 'Well, Miss Hewitt, it's a long time since we met. Why do you never come into the shop?'

She answered almost pertly, 'Well, I don't work there any more, do I? I can't come in for nothing. And I'm Mrs Watts. It's ten years since I was Miss Hewitt.'

'Nonsense. As far as I'm concerned you'll always be Miss Hewitt, the best assistant we ever had. They don't make them like that any more. Why you wanted to get married I don't know. You could have been here in the shop in a smart dress all day doing clean work, handling beautiful things, and something to show for it at the end of the week.'

Lilian, listening avidly as only children do, was anxious. Would Mum rather not have got married? Rather not have had her? You couldn't have babies unless you were married. She knew that.

Alice laughed and pulled her daughter forward, holding up the child's hand clasped in her own.

'I've got this to show for it now.'

Will Fitzgerald looked at Lilian. 'What wonderful hair,' he said. 'Absolutely pre-Raphaelite. Where did you get a pre-Raphaelite child, Miss Hewitt? Who does she take after?'

'My hair used to be that colour.'

'So it did. I'd forgotten. Well you'd best get back to your husband. Can't keep my manager waiting for his tea. Say goodbye, Phyl, and thank you for having me.'

Goodbyes were said, and Lilian and her mother retraced their steps. The child skipped a few yards, then took Alice's hand.

'He liked my hair.'

'No good you getting vain about it. I expect it'll go off as soon as you have a baby. Mine did.'

Lilian didn't skip any more. They walked home in silence.

There had been a return visit, of course, and subsequent invitations on both sides, but she hadn't seen a great deal of Phyllis. They weren't friends in the way that she and Mabel were. For one thing, Phyllis changed school when she was ten and went as a weekly boarder to an even more select establishment a few miles along the coast, so the meetings only took place in the holidays. Arranged as a duty on both sides, these occasions were nevertheless enjoyable to the participants. Lilian found Phyllis an exciting, sometimes even disturbing companion.

It was Phyllis who invented the smelling-salts game. Bored with cutting figures out of old fashion books in the dining-room over the shop, they were on the way upstairs to inspect the latest additions to her wardrobe when she paused on the first landing and pushed open the door to her parents' bedroom. Lilian drew back.

'We shouldn't go in there.'

'Of course we can. They don't mind.'

Lilian, though unconvinced, was curious enough to allow herself to be propelled into the big shadowy room. It was the same size as the drawing room underneath, which Lilian had never seen, though its windows were smaller. With holland blinds half drawn, lace curtains, and dark velvet ones as well, there was not much light though it was only three o'clock on a spring afternoon.

'What about your mother?'

'She's out. She's playing bridge with Mrs Farmiloe.'

Lilian was impressed. The Farmiloes were bakers, owning several shops and supplying bread to nearly everyone in Culvergate. Feeling safer, she advanced towards the huge bed. The white counterpane was similar to the one at home, but this one was partly covered by a pink satin quilt. The dressing-table, with its many and fascinating little drawers and its load of silver brushes, stood between the windows. Phyllis advanced towards it. They looked at themselves in the dim glass, two young girls, one rosy-faced with dark curls, one pale with ginger plaits. Phyllis took up the silver brush and passed it over her hair.

'You mustn't do this,' she said. 'I can, because it's my mother's. Has your mother got a silver brush?'

'Yes.'

It was true, though Phyllis seemed sceptical.

'This is my mother's hair.'

Lilian looked with some distaste at the little glass jar. It had a silver top with a round hole about an inch across, in the middle, and was filled with dark hair-combings.

'I know.'

Then Phyllis took up a cut-glass bottle, quite small, filled with dark green crystals. 'Smell!'

Obediently Lilian sniffed. The pungent strength of the salts took her breath away. Her eyes watered and she found her handkerchief, burying her face in it.

'You beast!'

'Fancy not knowing what smelling salts are. You don't know anything, do you? They're for headaches. I don't mind them. Look,' and she took a long sniff of the bottle, holding it close to her nose. She had over-estimated her own resistance to the power of ammonia.

'Ow! Ow! It's awful! Save me!'

Hands over face she stumbled to the bed and flung herself across it, face downward. Lilian stood anxiously by, wondering if any real harm had been done. But in a few moments Phyllis recovered. She went back to the dressing-table and held out the bottle.

'It's your turn.'

'I don't want to.'

'Go on, I dare you. It's quite nice in a way, sort of blows your head off. Oh, come on, Lily, don't you ever do anything?'

Lilian took the bottle, hesitated a moment, then sniffed violently. She too found her way to the bed, and buried her face in the pink silk, caring for nothing but an end to the agony. At last she raised her damp red face to see her friend with the bottle in her hand.

'I'm going to do it again.'

Somehow it became a sort of competition. In turn they sniffed, rushed squealing to the bed, writhed and moaned in real if exaggerated anguish until the burning, exploding sensation subsided, and then returned to the bottle for more.

'My head nearly blew off that time, I swear it hit the ceiling.' Phyllis was enjoying it more than Lilian.

'Mine did too.'

When they were tired of it, Phyllis put the cap back on the bottle and straightened the crumpled quilt.

'It's got a wet mark on it. You must have done that.'

'I didn't. It was you.'

'Well, I don't suppose she'll notice, it'll dry. Look, this is my Mum's nightdress. I bet yours hasn't got one like this.'

Lilian said 'Yes, she has, lots,' but it was a lie, for Alice possessed nothing like this froth of crêpe de Chine and lace.

'My Dad doesn't wear anything in bed. I bet your Dad wears a night-shirt, doesn't he?'

Lilian admitted that he did.

'Well, my Dad doesn't. He doesn't wear anything at all. Once when he was getting out of bed I saw his thing, sticking right up. Have you seen your father's thing?'

Not knowing what she meant Lilian said yes, of course she had, heaps of times, but Phyllis saw through this feeble pretence straight away.

'Of course you haven't. I bet you don't even know what it's like. It's like a banana.'

'How can it be?' Lilian tried to assume a decent pretence of curiosity, but really she just wished Phyllis would stop.

'Well, it is. It sticks out just like a banana and when you were born he stuck it right up inside your mother and then you came out.'

'Don't be silly.'

Lilian felt hot and embarrassed. She wished she had stayed at home drawing or reading or dressing up, and not come to tea with Phyllis.

Just then they heard the voice of Ivy the maid. 'Miss Phyl! Miss Phyl!' There were hurrying footsteps on the stairs. Ivy called again just outside the bedroom door, and then went on up, still calling.

'Quick! Quick! She'll tell Mum.'

'But you said . . .'

'Oh, come on!' Phyllis pulled Lilian out of the room; they half fell down the stairs and were seated innocently at the dining-room table when the maid caught up with them, having searched the upper floors. What had happened after that? The clear memory stopped there with Phyllis's innocent, 'We've been here ages, Ivy,' and the maid's disgruntled, 'That I know you haven't, Miss Phyl. If your mother knew what you got up to the moment her back was turned . . .'

They must have had tea, Lilian supposed, and played some more, before her mother had come to fetch her home. Or perhaps if it had been early closing day she would have walked home with her father. That had happened sometimes if she'd been invited to tea on a Thursday. She remembered how once, at closing time, he had come up the stairs from the shop, entered the dining-room and spoken to Phyllis. They'd been drawing and he'd looked at Phyllis's designs for ball-gowns and admired them lavishly. Emboldened, Lilian had held up her own modest work of art for his inspection.

'And what's that meant to be, then?'

'It's Blackie.'

Blackie was the Fitzgeralds' cat.

'Then you'd better write Blackie underneath, so we'll all know what it is, eh, Phyllis?'

Lilian remembered how Phyllis had quietly taken back

her drawing book saying only, 'Does Lilian really have to come now, Mr Watts? Couldn't she stay a bit longer?'

Her father had answered irritably, 'No, we must be off,' and to Lilian, 'Get your coat and hat.'

He had followed his daughter out of the room and waited for her at the foot of the stairs.

They walked all the way along the front without speaking. When they reached the corner Lilian could stand it no longer. She started running, running away from him and home to her mother. He'd be cross with her for that, she knew, but then he was already cross. Phyllis hadn't laughed when he said that about Blackie's portrait, that was why. He wanted Phyllis to like him. He didn't care whether Lilian liked him or not. Well, she didn't. She hated him and hoped he would die. Soon.

Sometime after that she had gone to tea with Mabel, her real friend, Mabel Wright, who sat next to her in school, played with her in the playground and always walked the long way round to her own home so as to keep Lilian company.

Mabel wore steel-rimmed glasses, and had frizzy mouse-coloured hair. She had a depressed widowed mother, an uninteresting brother, and was not very good at anything, except perhaps for sewing. She was afraid of Lilian's father who clearly did not admire her as he admired Phyllis, and often on the way home from school they would invent humiliating experiences for him, giggling together as they imagined him wetting his trousers in church or being sick in the street. After these occasions Lilian always felt ashamed and disgusted, yet she would join in eagerly enough the next time.

That particular tea-time had not been very lively. Mabel seemed boring after Phyllis and when Lilian told her about the smelling-salts game she just said it was

silly. After tea they worked on their scrap-books. Mabel
collected pictures of the royal family which she cut out
of magazines, and Lilian spent most of her pocket
money on picture postcards of ballet dancers and
actresses. She loved sweet large-eyed faces, and cloudy
hair, and longed to look like that herself. But that afternoon, having nothing new to add, she could only rearrange the contents of her scrap-book.

Mabel, apparently sensing her boredom, had
embarked on a more than usually scatological invention
concerning Lilian's father, which Lilian found so repug-
nant that she told her friend to shut up, and left to go
home half an hour earlier than usual. But they'd made it
up the next day.

'And we're still friends' thought Lilian, recalled to the
present as her baby stirred and whimpered in the frilly
cot. Mabel had stood by her, travelled to Sturry to visit
her regularly, and sewed and knitted dozens of
garments for Sylvia. And Lilian was grateful, truly fond
of her. 'Dear Mabel,' she said aloud. The trouble was,
she didn't really like her, now that they were both
grown up. Perhaps she never had.

Sylvia began to cry in earnest. It was time for her
feed. A few weeks earlier Lilian would have felt the milk
flooding into her breasts at the thought, but that happy
time was over. Sylvia had been weaned onto boiled
cows' milk, so that anyone could feed her, and Lilian's
breasts were encouraged to dry up. Nurse Tebbitt had
bound her tightly with belladonna plasters and rigor-
ously limited the amount she drank, while Sylvia had
screamed and refused her bottle, suffered fearfully from
wind and stopped gaining weight. It had been miserable
for both of them, but the objects had been achieved.

Sylvia began to do well again, and her mother could go
to work without fearing that the milk would leak and
soak through her dress. Still, it wasn't right. The infant
had been let down, deprived of another of her natural
rights, the first being the love and care of a legitimate
father.

Lilian wondered if Will would grow to love the baby,
take an interest in her. He had paid for their stay with
Nurse Tebbitt, bought the pram and the cot, but of
course he could not acknowledge his child. Not that he
seemed to care if people guessed the truth. Rosie Timms
and her sister Mrs Denning knew, Nurse Tebbitt herself,
and how many more? If only Mrs Fitzgerald would die
and he could marry Lilian, then Sylvia could take her
rightful place as the daughter of a town councillor and
leading business man.

Telling herself that it was wrong to hope for somebody to die, Lilian carried the baby downstairs. She had
brought fresh milk, and her special little saucepan and
would make up this feed herself, boiling the milk,
cooling it, adding a little sugar and then testing it on her
hand – but would Rosie do the same? Would she clean
the saucepan and feeding-bottle properly? The worries
were endless. Rosie didn't seem very particular, but at
least she had the right attitude to babies.

Lilian was only somewhat reassured to be told that
she would be meeting no other members of the Timms
family that evening. Their mother had instructed them
to keep away from home until bedtime in order to give
the new lodger what she described as 'a chance to get
settled down'. Even twelve-year-old Nance had been
banished to the kitchen at Victoria Lodge where she
would no doubt give her sister a hand with the washing
up. But would the early morning, when they were all

rushing to get ready for work, be a better time to make
their acquaintance? It seemed unlikely. But they would
have to be faced, if only because the outside lavatory
could only be reached through the scullery.

Lilian returned to bed as soon as Sylvia was settled
for the night, and slept fitfully. The house seemed full of
movement and subdued voices, and mysterious muffled
thuds. Waking not long after five she decided to go
down and make Sylvia's early morning feed and to slip
out to the lavatory while the milk came to the boil. In
dressing gown and slippers she crept downstairs into
the kitchen. As she passed through into the scullery, a
groan from the corner of the room startled her. It was
followed by creaks and a muffled swear-word, and she
realized that someone was sleeping uncomfortably on
the ancient chaise-longue. When she was ready to go
back upstairs with the baby's bottle she opened the
scullery door a crack, and stood listening. Supposing the
kitchen contained a half-dressed man? Supposing he
thought she was a burglar and knocked her down? All
was silent. Averting her eyes from the inadequate couch
she passed through into the room and out into the
passage. How dreadful. Should she have to do this
every morning?

Soon after seven Rosie brought hot water to wash in,
and a little later a tray burdened with a plate of lumpy
porridge, and a cup of strong tea to the door of her
bedroom, apologizing for her failure to provide a fire in
the front room downstairs. Since Lilian had no wish to
have her breakfast in a smoke-filled room she said truthfully that it didn't matter. From her window she saw
them all leave the house. Only then did she go downstairs herself, place Sylvia in her pram in the kitchen
where it was extremely in the way, and set off for work.

She hated leaving the baby and counted the hours till she would see her again.

In the past she had eaten dinner with the Fitzgerald family while the shop was closed at lunchtime, but from now on she intended to hurry back to Shelley Street to attend to Sylvia again. Even if she walked as fast as she possibly could she would have barely twenty minutes indoors, but she could not leave the baby all day in someone else's hands. Not at first, anyway. She wished she had not sold her bicycle, and wondered about getting another.

The walk from Shelley Street, at the back of the town took her up the hill, along by the park, across the main street and down York Road to the esplanade.

Trying not to worry about Sylvia, or about how she herself would be received at the shop, she set herself to review the circumstances and actions that had brought her to this pass. After all, she had been well brought up, well educated, attended church occasionally, been christened and confirmed. Was it her own fault?

CHAPTER 2

It had begun, she thought, after her father died, and Will Fitzgerald had offered her employment. Up till that time she had simply stayed at home, helped her mother in the house, done a little war work and practised her elocution. This was her great talent and source of pleasure. She'd enjoyed reciting at the family parties that had come to an end when her grandparents died, then at school concerts, and at fourteen had begun lessons with Elise Faraday, a retired actress. Long poems by Alfred Noyes and Henry Newbolt, scenes from Shakespeare, Sheridan and Congreve, selections from Tennyson, she learnt them all easily and performed them with a confidence and vitality that eluded her in all other areas of life. Miss Faraday even hinted that she might stand a chance on the professional stage, but of course her parents would not hear of that. Nevertheless she began to acquire a limited sort of local fame, invariably winning the elocution class at the music festival that was for some reason called the Eisteddfod, although they were on the south-east coast of England, as far from Wales as they could be. Sometimes she was asked to perform at

charity concerts and finally her parents were asked to
take her to one of the Fitzgeralds' musical evenings.

Lilian did not believe that her father loved her, but
sometimes he was proud of her, and then he behaved as
though he did. She hoped he would be pleased with her
that Sunday evening, as they waited outside the shop
door for Ivy to admit them. She came at last in her best
black with a lacy cap and apron and greeted them
unsmilingly. It was clear that she felt that her employers
were lowering themselves, inviting an employee and his
family to one of their select evening At Homes.

Harold was tense and irritable, afraid that his women-
folk would let him down. Alice reflected his anxiety, so
they both continually admonished Lilian, seventeen
years old though she was.

'Don't do your piece until Phyllis has done hers.'

'Don't do more than two pieces whatever anyone
says.'

'Don't laugh too loudly and don't whisper while
things are going on.'

'. . . and don't eat too much, just one sandwich . . .'

'. . . and speak up so that we can all hear.'

Lilian never answered this kind of thing. She had long
since given up trying to defend or justify herself, since
this was invariably described as 'answering back' and
not allowed. She had often as a child wondered what
kind of answering wasn't 'answering back', and also
wondered why her father was allowed to insult her
freely, while she might not be even mildly critical of
him. On this occasion, however, her mother answered
back on her behalf, for which she was grateful.

'Oh Harold, there's no need to tell her that. She
always speaks up so beautifully. You can hear every
word.'

'So she should. What do we send her to that woman for? It costs enough.'

Then Mrs Fitzgerald came out of the drawing room to greet them, and took Lilian and her mother up to the bedroom to leave their coats. The room seemed to have become smaller since the time of the smelling-salts game, but it was still a splendid apartment. There stood the wardrobe with the long mirror set in the door, the huge high bed, and the dressing-table loaded with silver. There were pink shades on the gasolier, and a warm powdery feminine scent in the air. In the soft light it was mysterious and intimate, this room in which Phyllis's mother slept with Mr Fitzgerald. Lilian remembered how, when she was a little girl, he had admired her hair, and was glad she had taken special pains to arrange it becomingly.

'Would you care for one of these?'

Mrs Fitzgerald, tall, full bosomed, beaded and plummy voiced as ever, was holding out to Lilian what seemed to be a tiny book.

'*Papier poudre*,' she said, making it sound very French indeed, 'so useful when one comes in from the cold. Just take a leaf and rub it on.'

'Oh, I don't think ...' Alice was doubtful but Lilian boldly tore out a leaf and rubbed it over her nose, afterwards peering anxiously at herself in the mirror. It was not an improvement. The pinkness caused by the cold wind was disguised, but it now looked unnaturally white and larger than ever.

'We have to let them grow up,' said Mrs Fitzgerald. 'Not that I could stop Phyllis if I wanted to.'

'No, indeed,' said Alice vaguely.

'It's all right, Mum. Do you want some?' Lilian offered her mother the tiny page.

'Oh, no dear, thank you. I'm past worrying about that kind of thing.'

'My dear Alice, you are years younger than I, and I still worry about that kind of thing, so why shouldn't you? We mustn't give up, must we?'

It certainly looked as though Louisa Fitzgerald worried about that kind of thing, judging by the number of silver-topped pots and mysterious, expensive-looking jars that were neatly grouped among the brushes and mirrors.

'I'll have a bedroom like this one day,' thought Lilian. Passing the great bed as she left the room she thought of Phyllis's parents lying in it, side by side.

If the bedroom was impressive, the drawing room was magnificent. Though Lilian had taken tea with Phyllis once every few months for several years she had never entered this room. It spanned the width of the two shops, and faced the sea. Three french windows, now curtained in blue velvet, led out on to the fretwork-trimmed balcony. At one end a fireplace was surmounted by a gilt-framed mirror, and at the other stood a 'baby grand' piano. Phyllis was seated on the duet stool, turning over some music. There seemed to be several settees and a lot of light-looking chairs. The room shimmered in a confusion of crystal chandeliers and polished silver. The leaping flames brought answering lights from the brass fender and fire-irons. There were hothouse flowers and a pleasant buzz of conversation.

'The girl we've been waiting for!'

Will Fitzgerald rose as they entered the room, grace-fully introducing them to the other guests, finding them seats, taking Lilian over to Phyllis.

'What are you going to give us tonight?'

'I haven't decided yet.'

This was quite untrue. Lilian had made up her mind over a week ago that it was to be 'The Highwayman'.

'Oh, Lily, shall we play a duet?' cried Phyllis, and though Lilian, a very indifferent pianist, was forced to refuse, she was grateful for the friendliness of the suggestion. So Phyllis played a Chopin waltz while Lilian sat beside her and turned over the music.

After Mrs Fitzgerald had boomed out a contralto solo from *Merrie England* it was Lilian's turn. 'The Highwayman' was very well received. The small audience, having so far hidden their usual boredom under a polite show of appreciation became absorbed in Alfred Noyes' dramatic story of Bess, the landlord's daughter and her outlaw lover, and afterwards applauded enthusiastically.

Mr Francis Pickford and his wife were most complimentary, and Phyllis hugged Lilian with unaffected delight, saying, 'Goodness, Lily, you nearly made me cry.'

Lilian glanced at her father. He disliked hearing her called Lily, but did not seem to mind it from Phyllis.

'She's had professional training, of course,' he said proudly to Agnes Pickford, and moved up to make room for his daughter on the chaise longue.

'Come and sit next to your old father.' He patted the space next to him, but she pretended to be unaware of his invitation and resumed her place beside Phyllis at the piano. A buzz of conversation broke out and Louisa Fitzgerald asked her husband to ring for Ivy. Lilian was impressed by this. It seemed so peremptory. Would the dignified Ivy really come running up the stairs at the sound of a bell? She appeared at the door after a remarkably short interval, slightly out of breath, and it seemed that refreshments were imminent. Despite the alcoholic connections of the Pickford family, tea and lemonade were the only drinks offered, but the tiny sandwiches and almond biscuits were delicious.

Mr Fitzgerald rested his arm round Lilian's waist in a paternal way and said,'What made you go in for that kind of thing?'

Surprising herself with her own lack of maidenly modesty she answered boldly, 'You did.'

'Me?'

'Don't you remember that book you gave me?'

'I ... no ... at least ... which one?'

The Fitzgeralds always gave Christmas presents to the children of their employees, and Phyllis and her father had shopped together for something to 'send to Father Christmas' for the jewellery manager's little girl.

At forty-four York Road no one was allowed to open any parcel until after breakfast. The Watts did not have a tree, because the rooms were too small. Instead the parcels, and there were really quite a lot, were piled on the sideboard. Lilian kept up the pretence of believing that Father Christmas had called since her parents seemed to require it of her, though this was difficult in view of the fact that all the gifts were clearly labelled. Inscriptions such as 'To dear Little Lilian with love from Grandma' or 'From your loving Auntie Edith and Uncle Tom' seemed to obviate the need for any supernatural agency. The book 'from W. Fitzgerald and Phyllis' looked just like any other picture book on the outside, but between the covers what enchantment was in store! From the centre pages a theatre ... a whole three-dimensional theatre sprang into being. Elaborately cut out, intricately folded and fitted together, the stage, the orchestra, the boxes and above all the actors lifted themselves up and ranged themselves in their exact places for her delight.

Cinderella in her white lacy ballgown, about to step
into her pumpkin-coach raised a delicate paper foot as
the fairy godmother held her star-tipped wand on high.
For hours that Christmas Lilian had sat in front of this
magical scene, staring and dreaming, becoming Cinderella on her way to the ball, and at the same time hearing
the frantic applause of a crowded audience.

She had seen more than one pantomime at the Hippo-
drome Theatre in the square, but the actuality, though
enthralling, had never enchanted her in the same way as
the paper-cut-out. Now she understood why. She had
been on the wrong side of the curtain. She wanted to
stand there at the end, in the centre of the row of fairy-
tale characters, blowing kisses and curtseying while
everyone shouted and clapped. She would hold out her
arms to the packed rows of people and receive their
admiration. Their admiration and their love.

She knew that Phyllis's appended name was just a
matter of form. It was from Mr Fitzgerald: Mr Fitzgerald, who had admired her hair.

She described the book, explaining how the pictures
stood themselves up and he said he remembered it.
Then she found herself telling him how, ever since, she
had wanted to go on the stage, and had persuaded her
father to let her have lessons from Miss Faraday, who
said she should go to a London drama school, but her
father had forbidden it.

'Well, perhaps it wouldn't be quite the thing, leaving
home at your age. Besides, we don't want to lose you.
You must come again and do something else for us. To
tell you the truth we have enough of singing sometimes
don't we, Phyl?' He and his daughter exchanged
conspiratorial smiles.

'I've still got the book,' said Lilian.

That night in her bedroom she took it down and reread the inscription. 'From W. Fitzgerald and Phyllis.' She put her thumb over the words 'and Phyllis' and sat staring at the page for several moments, before going to sleep with the book under her pillow.

At breakfast the next morning her happy memory of the previous evening was somewhat soured. Expecting her father's good temper to last the night she had come downstairs cheerfully, saying as she sat down at the breakfast table, 'It was fun at the party, wasn't it? I'll have to ask Miss Faraday for something good for the next time. It's my lesson this afternoon.'

'You're always ready to make a fool of yourself.'

Both Lilian and Alice looked at Harold in amazement.

'What do you mean? She didn't make a fool of herself. Everybody enjoyed what she did. You enjoyed it yourself.'

'What on earth made her put that stuff on her face?' Lilian looked at her mother, knowing that anything she could say would come under the heading of 'answering back'.

'It was Mrs Fitzgerald, she persuaded her. It was just a little powder, that's all. I didn't think it really looked ... common, or anything.'

Daringly Lilian murmured, 'Phyllis uses it.'

Her father looked at her with distaste. 'It's all right on her. It just made you look like a clown.'

Lilian made an effort to continue eating her porridge as though it was not choking her. She tried to blink away her tears without using her handkerchief. He should not have the satisfaction of seeing that he had hurt her. By the time he left the house she had regained control of herself and was able to ask Alice quite calmly, 'I didn't really look like a clown, did I, Mum?' but the answer to her question was not as reassuring as she could have wished.

'Well, it was a bit whitish to begin with, but anyway the room was so warm that it soon wore off.'

So she could console herself with the thought that when she had ceased to resemble a clown, she had looked hot and shiny. Yet her performance had easily been the most popular of the evening. Everyone had seemed to like her, and they had asked her to go again.

But there weren't any more parties for many months, because the war started. Mr Fitzgerald believed that Culvergate was a dangerous place, too near the French coast for comfort. He spoke of aeroplanes coming over and dropping bombs, which Harold and Alice thought absurd, and when he sent his wife and daughter to relations in Ireland and talked of closing the shop they thought he was a scaremonger. But during the third year of the war no fewer than nine high explosive bombs descended on Culvergate. A system of air raid warnings was devised and the Watts family, like most others, spent many hours sheltering in their cellar.

Passing forty-four York Road Lilian was surprised by the absence of lace curtains, and the untidiness of the once-neat little front garden. So clear had been her memory of herself and her mother and father huddled in the ice-cold cellar listening to the drone of aeroplanes overhead that it was a renewed shock to remember that other people lived there now, that the war had been over for nearly four years. As she turned into the alleyway that ran behind the row of shops along the Fort she wondered what her parents would have thought of the way she lived now. Entering her place of employment by the back door she hung up her coat and

hat in the passage and opened the kitchen door to greet
Elsie, the cook-general who had superceded the austere
Ivy. She was a bright cheerful girl, delighted to see
Lilian.

'Miss Watts! You're back then! Well, I never.'

'Hello, Elsie, how are you?'

'Mustn't grumble, Miss, but how about you? We've
missed you something awful, no one to get round Mr F.
when he's in a bad mood. Like a bear with a sore head
he's been lately, but still he'll be all right now you're
back. And how about your poor Auntie? Passed on, did
she? Mr F. said she was very old.'

So that was the story he had told them without ever
consulting her. For a moment Lilian was tempted to say
casually, 'There's no Auntie, and never has been. I've
had a baby, a little girl. Illegitimate.'

But she did not. She saw that she must keep up the
fiction of a sick relative as the cause of her prolonged
absence. Really, Will might have mentioned that he'd
saddled her with a dying aunt.

'Yes, she was very old. Now tell me what you've been
up to.'

She glanced at the watch on her wrist. Nineteen
minutes past eight. Time enough to drink the cup of tea
that Elsie was pouring out for her. Passing the tea, Elsie
was carefully displaying her other hand, pushing it close
to Lilian's face, and grinning broadly. 'Well, I never did.
I thought you'd have heard. Well?'

Lilian saw the ring with its tiny diamond. 'Why, Elsie,
you're engaged. Congratulations. Who is it?'

'Well, it'd have to be somebody who worked here,
wouldn't it? Since I'm here all the blooming time, so I
give you two guesses.'

Two guesses. Jim Smallwood, the watchmaker, and

manager in his employer's absence, and Charlie Finch the handyman. Jim was short, pale, dumpy, wore glasses, and had permanently sweaty hands which were a nuisance in his work. He was continually wiping them on a small towel which he kept near him for the purpose, a habit which Lilian found repellent in the extreme. On the other hand he had clean-looking brown wavy hair, and was well-spoken. Charlie was a big, raw-boned simple man of about forty, who unpacked the china from the big straw-filled crates, put up the shutters, washed the windows and the front step, and did anything else that was required of him.

Lilian stared at Elsie. Her cheeks were red and shiny from hanging over the black range, her hands were rough, and she was rather too plump, owing to her habit of eating bits and pieces throughout the day, but her round face was good-humoured and her eyes were a very bright blue. She was uneducated but not stupid. She could not marry Charlie, who had dirty nails, always needed a shave, blew his nose on grubby bits of rag and hardly ever spoke. No, even Elsie could not marry Charlie. Yet what would her life be, without a husband? No one wanted to be a cook-general for ever, and Charlie had his own house, a three-room cottage near the harbour left him by his mother. After years in this dark kitchen, with the pea-green paint peeling off the walls, the view of the back yard filled with packing-cases, and the temperamental black-leaded range, perhaps Charlie was better than nothing.

'Well, I expect you're doing the right thing, Elsie. He's a very lucky man.'

'Who is?'

'Well ... Charlie ...'

Elsie stared at her, the red cheeks growing redder.

She smoothed her none-too-clean morning apron over her full bosom, and said nothing. Lilian swallowed nervously.

'Isn't it Charlie?'

'No, it's not. It's Jim. I'm engaged to Mr Smallwood.'

'Jim!' Lilian quite failed to keep the note of amazement out of her voice.

'Yes, you thought it couldn't be, didn't you?'

'No, of course not, it's just . . .'

'Just that I'm a servant and you didn't think Mr Smallwood could marry a servant, not after being sweet on you for so long. Well, I shan't be a servant when we're married, shall I? I'll be Mrs James Smallwood, and we're getting a house in Station Road, and Jim's painting it up.'

She had risen, shaking and tearful. Lilian thought that the right thing to do would be to put her arms around her, but she remained seated.

'Then I think Jim's very lucky . . . getting a wife who can . . . cook . . . and everything . . .'

Elsie was now completely dissolved into tears. 'He's not marrying me because I can cook . . .'

'No, no. Oh, dear, don't cry please, Elsie. Look I must go into the shop, it's getting late . . .' Lilian stood up and gave Elsie a small pat on the shoulder.

'But do you think we'll be all right, Miss? Mother says there's no good comes of marrying out of your station in life. But he does really want to, and I'm ever so keen on him. Ever since he first came here I've liked him, only of course I didn't stand a chance when you were here, then after you went away, he started to take a bit more notice, like . . .'

She really did look very unattractive, snuffling wetly into the corner of her apron. What on earth was Jim thinking of?

'Of course it will be all right. Jim wouldn't be
marrying you if he didn't want to. Now I must be
getting into the shop, it wouldn't do to be late on my
first morning back.'

'He wouldn't say anything to you,' said Elsie, sniffing,
but Lilian had gone out into the passage and into the
shop. She had to pass through the jewellery department
to reach the china section and as of old she paused at
the counter for a moment, surveying herself in the large
mirror placed there to enable customers to judge the
effect of earrings or necklaces they were considering. It
was a need for reassurance rather than vanity that
prompted her to do this. Though her mouth and eyes
were pleasing, her face was too long and her nose too
large so it was important that her hair was right and her
collar properly arranged. Jim turned from the shop
window where he had been replacing the valuable items
that were kept in the safe at night. He closed the door
that opened onto the display with care and came slowly
towards her. Lilian had always known that he admired
her and had deliberately kept her distance, but during
the last few anxious months Jim Smallwood had come to
represent something along the lines of an insurance
policy. If the worst came to the worst, if Will cast her off
and she could not cope with life and Sylvia alone, then,
she thought, with a little encouragement this not
entirely impossible young man would probably ask her
to marry him. And of course he would be so pleased to
get her that he would gladly accept her daughter as well,
and even be a good father to her. Now she saw that she
had been wrong. She stood in front of the counter,
tweaking up her hair that had been pressed down under
her hat.

'You're back.' His tone was not welcoming.

'Aren't you pleased to see me?' She heard her own voice, cheaply flirtatious, and was disgusted.

'And Mr F? Is he pleased? And what about Mrs F?'

So he knew. What a fool she had been to imagine that he did not. But he had not shared his knowledge with Elsie, unless she had been making a polite pretence about the sick aunt. Or a sneering one. But no, Elsie was not like that. Jim had guessed the truth, but he had kept it to himself.

'How is Mrs F?' she asked guardedly. The staff always referred to their employers as Mr and Mrs F.

'All right, I suppose.'

So he was not going to gossip, although Mrs F, her snobbery and her extravagance, had once been a favourite topic of conversation between them.

'And Mr F?' Lilian felt bound to ask, although she knew that he was well, having seen him only three days earlier. He had come to the cottage at Sturry, settled Nurse Tebbitt's account, and given her Rosie Timms's address, adding that he would expect her at the shop as soon as she had settled in.

Jim answered with another curt 'all right' then added, 'Elsie and I are engaged.'

He made the statement baldly, defiantly, almost.

'I know. Congratulations.'

'She's a good girl. Respectable, I can rely on her.'

Lilian felt her face grow hot. In the mirror she saw it redden. 'I'm sure you can.'

The unspoken condemnation hung in the air. Trembling, she walked away through the archway into the china department. Her special duster was still in its old place at the back of a drawer, and she took down a Worcester figure; but her hands were so unsteady that she feared she might drop it. Replacing it carefully on the shelf, she stood, trying to regain control. Jim Small-wood, daring to despise her. That little whipper-snapper. A shop assistant, no more. Who did he think he was? He'd found his mark in Elsie. And at least she, Lilian, had a real man, a man of standing, a councillor, ex-mayor, leading business man. One who had been to public school, sat on committees and made important decisions. At tall, broad, handsome man in the prime of life, a well-educated man who could appreciate music and art and poetry, a man who had raised her to terri-fying heights of physical passion which Elsie would never know existed. She'd done a lot better than Jim Smallwood.

At that moment Will Fitzgerald came briskly down the stairs and into the shop.

'Good morning, Mr Smallwood,' and a moment later, 'Good morning, Miss Watts.'

He took his hat from behind the office door, and went out. She had expected no more than this, but still the brief impersonal greeting depressed her. She reminded herself of other mornings when he had passed her without a pause or a look. The more passionate their encounters on Sundays, or on the occasional weekday evening, the less notice he took of her in the shop on the following day. It had been a joke then, but there was something frightening about his coolness now. It seemed too real.

'I must be calm,' she told herself. 'I must think what to do.'

Slowly, carefully, she began to dust the precious china.

At one o'clock the shop closed for an hour and a quarter, as did all the other shops in the town, to enable staff and owners to partake of a midday meal. Jim, having washed his hands in the kitchen and combed his hair with a greasy little black comb, went upstairs to partake of the Fitzgerald dinner. It seemed to Lilian that it would be awkward for him to be waited on by his fiancée. She smiled to herself, the French word seemed so unsuited to the plump, capable Elsie. Her own dinner-hours would be different from now on, mostly taken up with the walk to and from Shelley Street.

On this first day she heard Sylvia's enraged screams as soon as she turned the corner. She ran along the road and into number nine. In the kitchen she found her landlady almost as distraught as the child. The baby was scarlet-faced, rigid with fury and refusing to take her bottle.

Thankfully handing her over Rosie said, 'I'm ever so sorry, dear, I just don't know what can be the matter with her. I thought I knew all about babies, but I've never had such a morning.' Sylvia, immediately quiet in the familiar arms, sucked at the rubber teat as though it was the one thing she'd been waiting for.

'There, look at that. Well, it was your auntie you wanted, wasn't it, my love?'

'Auntie?' Lilian looked up, surprised.

Rosie was apologetic. 'Well, we'd better start as we mean to go on, hadn't we dear? And she can't very well call you anything else, with you not wearing a ring, I mean. Not that talk really worries me, mind, but well, we don't want to ask for it. Not with Dollie and everything.'

'But I'm her mother.'

This was an aspect of the situation that Lilian had not previously considered. At the shop no one need be told about the existence of Sylvia May, and what Shelley

Street thought concerned her not at all. Now apparently, Rosie had feelings that must be taken into account.

'I can't wear a ring. But you can say I'm a widow if you like.' She held the baby closer. Poor little thing, she had so little, how could her own mother deny her? It was unthinkable.

'Well, I suppose that will be all right. No one's likely to see you much after all. I'd better get your dinner. Have it in here, will you? The boys have been in and had theirs and Nance has gone back to school.'

Lilian sat down at the table. It was now covered by a clean, pretty lace-edged cloth, obviously designed for afternoon tea, and undoubtedly Rosie's best. Probably a scarcely used wedding present. Because the food at Mrs Denning's had been very good, it seemed likely that Rose would at least be a competent cook, by reason of being the boarding-house keeper's sister, but this was not the case. The stew that was placed in front of Lilian was decidedly unappetizing, even to one who had walked the mile from the Fort in under twenty minutes. Alice Watts had reared her daughter on simple, econom- ical but well-cooked food, and her stew had been delicious, with meat and vegetables cut up small, an entire absence of gristle, and thick flavoursome gravy. The meal that seemed to defy Lilian from its thick white plate consisted of untidy lumps of meat, quartered onions, chunks of carrot and some greyish glutinous objects that appeared on further investigation to be dumplings, all partly submerged in pale thin liquid. She scarcely touched it, saying that the need for haste had taken away her appetite, and she left the house hungry, if comforted by the knowledge that Sylvia, now clean and fed, was safely asleep in her cot. But she would not see her again for hours, and what sort of a state would she be in by eight or nine that night? And in the summer, the holiday season when the shop would remain open until ten o'clock, she would scarcely see the baby.

Will should have done better for her than this. She should have shown firmness, been harder to please, but it was not too late. She would ask him for the money, her mother's money that she had lent him, and perhaps it would be enough to buy a small cottage. She should have done that after Alice had died, and the house in York Road, still mortgaged, had been sold. Instead of accepting Will's suggestion of investing her money in Fitzgerald's and going to live at Mrs Denning's, she should have made a little home of her own. Then perhaps she could have taken a lodger, or taught elocution, or both, and somehow scraped by without having to leave Sylvia. Indeed, if she had followed that course, the baby might never have appeared on the scene, for it was to Mrs Denning's that Will had come that Sunday morning, barely a week after she had moved in.

It had all happened so quickly. One moment, it seemed, she had been living securely, a young girl at home with two parents, and the next a woman alone, waiting for her lover in the big front bedroom at Victoria Lodge. Yet much had happened to bring the change about. The war itself had not really affected the Watts family very deeply to begin with, at least not as far as their daily life was concerned. Alice worried about her youngest brother, who had enlisted, and she spent most of her spare time knitting dreary colourless garments for him or writing long letters that were supposed to cheer him up. When Harold had been called up in 1918 despite being nearly forty-one years old, Lilian found herself happier than ever before. She and her mother were companionable at home, and also had more social life

than in peace-time. Lilian would have liked to become a
Red Cross nurse, but this idea was vetoed by her father,
so she contented herself with giving recitations at
charity shows, working for bazaars, and going to tea
with Mabel. Fitzgerald's never actually closed down, but
contracted its business premises to one of the shops,
and its staff to a young girl assistant. After a while, Mrs
Fitzgerald and Phyllis returned from Ireland, reopened
the big drawing room that had been under dustsheets
during their absence, and began to hold musical
evenings once more.

When the war ended people said to Lilian, 'How glad
you'll be to have your father safely home,' and Lilian
would concur, trying to look pleased at the prospect.
Her uncle would not be coming home at all, having lost
his life on the Somme, but Harold, in the Pay Corps,
had never left England. When they were summoned to
the military hospital where he lay ill with pneumonia
she did her best to share Alice's anxiety, but she could
not honestly look forward to a resumption of their
former relationship. The telegram had been sent from
the Cambridge hospital, and they hurried to London by
train, crossed the city in a taxi, and took another train to
Cambridge. At the hospital they were met with blank
stares and complete ignorance of the whereabouts of
Corporal Watts, because the message had come from the
Cambridge Military Hospital at Aldershot. Alice in her
haste and anxiety, had not read it properly. She wept,
partly with exhaustion, all the way back through
London to Aldershot, reaching the huge grey hilltop
building twenty minutes after Harold had, as the nurse
told them, passed quietly away. Thinking of his loneli-
ness at the last, even Lilian wept then.

Nevertheless, once the funeral was over she looked

forward to the peaceful companionship that she and Alice had shared during the few months that Harold had spent in the Army, but she was soon disillusioned. Alice was stricken by the death of her critical, autocratic husband, and in an effort to live up to his standards she herself became hard to please. If Lilian went out looking smart she accused her of trying to attract men, if carelessly dressed she was letting herself down.

Six months after Harold's death Mabel invited Lilian to a dance. It was no grand civic affair such as the Fitzgeralds regularly attended, but a modest occasion in a church hall, and Mabel and her mother had helped to organize it.

'How can you think of such a thing? It's far too soon.'

'I know, Mum, but I haven't been out at in all this time. What difference does it make?'

'What difference? You may well ask,' said Alice cryptically.

Lilian tried again. 'Mrs Wright will be there. I'll be with her and Mabel.'

'But you don't know anyone else, you don't know any men. Who will you dance with?'

'Mrs Wright will introduce me.'

Lilian spoke with a confidence she did not feel. Who, after all, would she dance with? But she wanted to go.

'Mum, I'm twenty-three, and I've never once been to a dance.'

'We are not that sort. Your father and I never went to dances. We didn't need that kind of thing. All we needed was our own little home.'

Lilian interrupted quickly, 'Well, I won't go, if you really don't want me to, but I could wear my mauve dress, the one you made. I've never once worn it and it does seem a pity.'

Presumably it was the thought of the wasted dress that changed Alice's mind, and Lilian became quite excited as the day drew nearer. Perhaps after all she would 'meet someone'.

The dance was as successful as any dance can be in a draughty church hall, with a violinist accompanied by a slightly out-of-tune piano to supply the music, and a very small proportion of young men.

Mabel danced every dance, the waltz, the Veleta and the newer foxtrot, but Lilian was a wallflower until she was dragged, protesting, into a Paul Jones. Then she was forced to dance with whichever of the men came to a standstill in front of her when the music stopped. The dancers moved in concentric circles, facing each other, and hope was superceded by dread as reasonable part-ners passed by, their places taken by a succession of elderly churchgoers, some fat, some bald, and all of them embarrassingly gallant. Sometimes there were girls left over when partners were taken, and usually they made the best of things by dancing together, but when Lilian saw that her fate was to be a dance with Mabel's mother she excused herself, and flopped down on a chair, in pretended exhaustion, trying to laugh.

Apart from the Paul Jones she danced once with Mabel's spotty brother, and at half-past nine she put on her hat and coat and walked home alone. Up in her bedroom she stared at herself in the mirror on her dressing-table. To be honest the mauve frock was not a great success. The plain boat-shaped neckline did not become her, and the simple cut of the bodice empha-sized her thinness. But her face was not bad really, apart from her nose which was only a bit too large, and not red tonight, and she thought her hair was beautiful, if not everybody's favourite colour. Anyway, Mabel was no prettier. But Mabel knew what to say to boys. She could laugh and tease and give them playful pushes and scream in mock outrage, in a way that Lilian envied while it embarrassed her. But the boys liked it, what boys there were left.

After this Lilian went to no more dances, but she began to accept invitations to recite again. Better to be admired and congratulated by grateful audiences of old people or hospital patients than to be ignored by weedy youths like Mabel's brother. These engagements, however, brought in no financial reward, and Alice in her widowhood found her small income insufficient for their needs. After some thought she decided to approach her former employer. It was nearly twenty-five years since she had gone out to work, and times had changed, but still, Harold's place at the shop had not been filled, and she would soon pick up the threads. It was true that Harold had, nominally at least, been the manager, but with business so slow and a staff reduced to one young girl, there was very little to manage. A competent senior assistant might be just what was needed at this stage. So said Alice to her daughter as she put on her rather shabby black coat, and her black hat with its trailing widow's veil in order to call on Will Fitzgerald. Lilian watched her go from the front window, sincerely wishing her success. It would be nice to have the house to herself all day. She would make things comfortable and pleasant for her mother to come home to, and perhaps they would get on better. But she had her doubts. Fitzgerald's was still a smart luxurious shop, in spite of the war, and her mother seemed such a dowdy, middle-aged figure, depressing in her widow's weeds.

Alice was back within half an hour. Lilian met her eagerly in the passage. 'Any good, Mum?'

Alice took off her gloves and laid them carefully in the glove-box that was part of the mahogany hall-stand, then she slowly removed her hat.

'Mum, what did he say?'

Still Alice did not answer. She took her coat, hung it up, and went out into the scullery. She half-filled the kettle, took it back into the kitchen, and lit the gas. She took down the teapot, and one cup and saucer from the dresser.

'Mum ...' Lilian saw dislike and distrust on her mother's face.

'He doesn't want me. I suppose I'm too old.'

That faint emphasis on the word me, had it meant anything? She dared not ask.

'He'll take you, though. If you want a job.'

'Me? A job?'

New worlds opened out for Lilian. Since she had given up hopes of becoming an actress she had never envisaged herself as anything but a daughter-at-home.

'What did he say? Shall I go and see him? What do you think? Oh, Mum!'

'Go if you like. We could do with the money.'

It was not until Lilian was leaving the house next day, her ginger hair brilliant under the turned back brim of her stitched black velvet hat, that Alice said, 'And don't let him take any liberties with you!'

'Liberties? Mr Fitzgerald? With me?'

'I know what he's like. Just you keep your distance. I'll say no more.'

Not at all put off by this conversation Lilian walked briskly down the road. The thought of working among the jewellery and fine china was delightful, and she felt confident of being equal to anything that might be demanded of her. Since she left school her life had been dismally circumscribed, and it seemed to her that freedom was now in sight.

'If I get this job,' she thought, 'I'll have my own money and I'll do whatever I want.'

And who could be nicer to work for than Mr Fitzgerald, her friend Phyllis's charming father, who at all their previous meetings had really seemed to like her?

CHAPTER 3

She enjoyed the work from the start. In two months she was doing almost everything that her father had done, though, being a woman, for little more than half the money. She dressed windows, served customers and learnt the trade. In the china department she learned to tell Worcester from Coalport, to appreciate fine porcelain and take pleasure in the graceful lines of the statuettes and in the glowing colours of the decorated tea-services. Behind the jewellery counter she became interested in gems and learned which were precious and which were semi-precious. Though lacking her father's long apprenticeship she made up for it by a keen eye and an ability to learn, and was soon able to distinguish between the genuinely good quality and the often convincing imitations that people sometimes brought in for valuation or sale.

On one such occasion a man brought a ring into the shop.

'How much for this?' he demanded curtly.

With a professional air Lilian peered at it through a

watchmaker's eyeglass, seeing the flawed stone, examining the hallmark.

'Only nine carat gold, I'm afraid, and the stone's poor quality. Mr Fitzgerald wouldn't be interested. I'm sorry.'

And she was sorry. The man's face showed some desperation.

'I'll see the boss.'

Her pity evaporated. 'You'll be wasting your time, I'm afraid.'

'I want to see someone who knows what they're talking about.'

She'd noticed the shabbiness of his clothes, heard by now his dreadful cough, but his rudeness antagonized her. She put the ring down on the counter and hurried to the little office at the back of the china department.

'I've got a man in the shop who wants to sell a ring. It's absolute rubbish and he won't believe me. In fact he was very rude.'

Her employer nodded briefly and she returned to her place behind the counter. 'Mr Fitzgerald is coming,' she said coldly.

The man stood holding the ring on the palm of his hand. Will Fitzgerald glanced at it briefly. 'Couple of quid any good to you?'

'It's not worth more?'

'Afraid not, old man. Look, I'll put it by for you and you can buy it back when times improve.'

Two pound notes were handed over. The man touched his cap as he left.

'Thank you, Guv'nor.' He closed the door carefully.

'That thing wasn't worth ten bob, let alone two pounds!'

Lilian had gained confidence working in the shop. Apart from little Rene, the junior, there were no other staff, and she spoke her mind.

'Poor devil. Did you hear his cough? Gas, I should think.'

'Well, we shan't make our fortunes like that.' But she was ashamed. She had been hard.

'Don't look like that. You haven't murdered anyone. You did right.'

He was kind, too, to the gypsy woman who came selling sprigs of white heather. Lilian had been working in the shop for nearly a year when the gypsies came and set up their colourful, squalid camp on some waste ground at the back of the town. By this time, with the place recovering from the Great War, business had improved considerably, and Fitzgerald's had acquired the services of a young man called James Smallwood, in the capacity of watch-repairer and deputy manager. Lilian, feeling quite capable of managerial duties herself, was hardly welcoming. She had enjoyed working in the jewellery department, and found that she was henceforth chiefly to be concerned with the glass and china. She would enjoy that too, as she always had, but she was proud of her increasing knowledge of precious stones and hallmarks, and now it seemed that this was to be wasted. Also she believed that she exercised a restraining influence on her employer who continued to be over-generous and too kind-hearted for his own good when poor-looking men or women came in to try to raise money on cheap trinkets.

'Anyone would think we were running a pawn shop,' she told him after another of these incidents.

'Thank the Lord I've got you to keep an eye on me,' he said and he patted her on the shoulder twice, letting his hand rest there for a long moment.

Lilian felt herself grow hot. Was this one of the

liberties her mother had warned her about? If so, it was the first in over a year. She thought about it all day.

In fact the thought of him was often all she had, for the presence of Mr Smallwood, soon in the absence of customers to become Jim, meant that the proprietor was less often in the shop. He could give more time to his council work, to being a Justice of the Peace, and his preparations for taking office as Mayor.

It was soon after the mayor-making that the two gypsy women came into the shop with their baskets of white heather. One was a thin young girl, silent, who wore a shabby black coat over a grubby grey cloth skirt and a flowered apron, with a scarf tied over her head. The older woman was taller, and in spite of her shabby clothes an imposing figure. She wore a broad-brimmed hat trimmed with faded silk flowers, beneath which her thick braids of black shiny hair were twisted and coiled, and the apron that showed below the man's jacket she had on was crisply clean. Her dark eyes were circled with brownish shadows. Jim was serving a customer and called Lilian from her shelves of porcelain to deal with the intruders.

'Buy some lucky white heather, lady.'

Her servile gypsy whine was at odds with the majestic figure.

'Not today, thank you.'

The dark eyes were on a level with Lilian's own. Taller than average, she was not used to this, and felt at a disadvantage. The gypsy persisted. 'I've got a sick child at home, lady.'

She stood her ground, not even troubling to make this claim sound true. Lilian wished that Jim would come to the rescue, but he did not. The woman looked her up and down slowly and said, 'I hope you never need luck, lady.'

With dignity she moved to the door followed by her silent companion.

Lilian felt as though she had been cursed. She stood, undecided, wanting to get rid of them, but also wanting to call 'wait', to fetch her purse and buy a sprig of the wretched stuff. Then Will Fitzgerald turned briskly into the entrance and opened the door, causing the women to move back.

'What's all this?'

'Buy some lucky white heather, sir. We all need luck.'

'Indeed we do.' He pulled a handful of silver and copper out of his pocket and poured it into the woman's outstretched palm.

'Thank you sir. You're a lucky man and a good one too. You don't know what you've done, sir.'

He took the sprig of dry-looking heather she offered him, and held the door open for them in as courtly a fashion as he did for customers. Lilian walked back to her department, trembling, and a moment later her employer passed through on his way to his cupboard-like little office.

With her back to him, duster in hand, she said, 'You shouldn't encourage them. They'll keep coming back.' Lilian's voice was angry. She felt humiliated, publicly shown to be mean, and not only mean but unimportant.

'What does it matter? They do no harm.'

'It is I who will have to keep saying no when you're not here.'

'Then tell them to come back when I am. Or get her to tell your fortune.'

'Tell my fortune? In the middle of the shop? Anyway, I don't want my fortune told.'

'Please yourself. Here you are, take this. Perhaps it will bring you luck.'

He held out the sprig of white heather, on the palm of his hand. Lilian took it, her fingers brushing his skin. She would forget it had come from the gypsy woman.

They stood still, Lilian looking at the heather, as though it had suddenly become interesting. In the silence they heard Jim close the shop door behind his customer.

'Well, Miss Watts, there's that box of Goss to price up. We want it on sale tomorrow.'

'Yes, Mr Fitzgerald. I'll get on with it straight away.'

She spent the rest of the morning pricing the cheap souvenir china with the cost price in code and the selling price in plain figures. There was a ready sale for these ugly little ornaments, variously shaped into the likeness of flat-irons, chairs, cottages, almost anything in fact, and all bearing the Culvergate coat-of-arms in bright red and blue. Though why the shape of an iron, for instance, unpleasing in itself, should become attractive when reproduced in shiny white pottery, no one in the shop could understand. Old Terry Fitzgerald, said Alice, would never have stocked such objects, but times changed.

As she worked, Lilian wondered whether she had been over-familiar with her employer, but he hadn't seemed to mind and after all it was by no means the first time she had spoken frankly. And he had given her the heather, a token of ... what? Approval? Goodwill? Or was it just because he didn't want it? She put her hand in the pocket of her skirt and touched the brittle, dry sprig. Perhaps after all it would bring her luck. But what form could this take? She thought she was quite lucky as things were. She was happy in her work, and that was the main thing in life. Not quite so happy as home, though, with her mother so bad-tempered and critical.

Perhaps a change for the better would come there.
Possibly the patent medicine she had been taking for
some time to ease the pain in her stomach would begin
to take effect.

When Lilian arived home that evening the change had
already begun. Alice, deciding that the Vitadatio tablets
were not effecting a cure, had been to the doctor.

Opening the front door, not needing to use her key
because it was never locked if someone was at home,
Lilian called 'Mum', as she always did. She took off her
coat, damp with the shower through which she had
walked and called again, but the house was silent. She
went into the dining room still holding her hat which
she feared had been spoilt by the rain.

The room was almost dark, lit only by a dying fire. At
the table sat the small hunched figure of an old woman.
Lilian stared, seeing her mother in a new way.

'Mum! All in the dark? Why haven't you lit the gas?
And the fire's nearly out. Honestly!'

She was cold, she missed the welcoming warmth and
the tea that her mother usually had ready. This part of
the evening was often quite a companionable time.
Putting her hat on the table she found the matches,
turned on the gas and lit the two fragile white globes
under their glass shades that projected on brackets one
each side of the fireplace. They gave out a yellowish cold
light, and Lilian saw that something was very wrong.

Alice sat at the table with her coat on. Her greying
sandy hair was untidy, her nose and eyes red.

'Mum, what's the matter? You've still got your coat
on. It's wet, you'll catch your death of cold.'

Alice laughed but said nothing.

'Has something happened?' Lilian racked her brains.
A death in the family? But there was hardly anyone left.

Aunt Annie was the only relation who still lived in Culvergate and she never seemed to want to see them. Had they lost all their money? An absurd idea, they had none to lose.

'Sit in a comfy chair, Mum. I'll make some tea.'

'Tea!'

'What is it, Mum? Don't you want any?'

Alice rose stiffly. 'I'll get it. I'm not an invalid yet.'

'What do you mean, not yet?'

'It's nothing you need worry about.'

For several days nothing more was said on the subject. Alice seemed almost cheerful, and though she went to bed early she rose as usual to get breakfast before her daughter left the house. Then one evening, an evening when they had been laughing together over Lilian's stories of strange and unreasonable customers, she said abruptly, 'I've got to go into hospital.'

Lilian's heart seemed to sink like a stone. It really does that, she thought. I felt it go. Her hand shook as she replaced the cup of cocoa in the saucer.

'Mum.'

'It's nothing much. You're not to worry, but you never know with these things so I've made a list for you just in case.'

'Just in case what?'

Lilian's voice was sharp with terror. Alone in the world. She would be alone in the world.

Alice placed a sheet of paper in front of her. It was a page from an old school exercise book, roughly torn out. The list was short:

£103.15s.6d in the Post Office.
£390 paid off on the house. (£210 still owing)
My jewellery. Diamond engagement ring £22.

Grandma's gold bracelet, £7.10s 0d
Brooch with aquamarine, £2.2s.0d
£37 pounds cash in drawer upstairs.

Lilian read the shaky handwriting through twice, trying not to cry. That her mother had done all this, when she was ill and knew she was going to die. She wanted to put her arms round her as she had so often done in childhood, though less frequently as she grew up, and since her father's death not at all. Alice had seemed not to wish for gestures of affection. So there was nothing she could do until she was able to control her voice.

'Oh, Mum, you'll get better, I'm sure ...'

'You'd better keep that carefully. Mr Huxtable in the High Street, he's our solicitor. He'll do everything.'

'But Mum, you're only going into hospital, don't talk like this.'

She paused. She knew she must make some enquiry as to the nature of her mother's illness, but feared the answer. Was it, could it be the dreaded disease of which the name was never spoken above a whisper, as though it were some malignant god? Surely not, for here was her mother sitting beside her, talking sensibly, drinking cocoa. When she spoke again her voice was rough, unsympathetic. 'What's wrong with you then?'

Perhaps her mother would shield her again, would say 'Nothing for you to worry about' as she had before.

Alice's voice was calm, matter-of-fact. 'A blockage. In the back passage. They're going to try and take it away.'

'And then you'll be all right?'

'We'll see.'

We'll see. Whenever, as a child, she had wanted something very much, whether it was a friend to tea, an afternoon on the sands, permission to go on the school outing or any other small treat, the answer had always been 'we'll see'. How she hated the innocuous phrase, how she longed for a definite yes or no. On this occasion, of course, 'we'll see' was infinitely preferable to 'no' but still the old phrase had power to irritate her. With an effort she refrained from pressing her mother further, but it was difficult to make a show of optimism when she felt that its falseness must be so apparent.

On the day of the operation she went to work as usual. Will Fitzgerald telephoned for her at the appointed time. Alice had come through.

Accompanied by the rarely seen Aunt Annie, Lilian went to the hospital that evening. It was known as the Cottage Hospital, and the building was surprisingly small and domestic-looking, but the strong antiseptic smell that pervaded the long green corridor seemed ominous, redolent of illness and suffering. When they reached Saxby ward the Sister, intimidating in her starched apron and flowing white cap, took Lilian aside and explained the nature of the surgery her mother had undergone. Lilian was appalled. Surely no one could live like that? The body's private functions even when normal were hard enough to live with, but this! She did not want to go into the ward, and when she did, followed at a safe distance by her aunt, her main feeling was one of embarrassment. Her mother was sleepy, her eyes scarcely open, and she smelt of anaesthetic. She looked very old, not like herself at all. Overcoming her revulsion Lilian bent close, trying to comprehend the mumbled words. They were 'Where's Daddy?' Tears sprang to her eyes. The sister led her away and gave her a cup of weak lukewarm tea. Afterwards she did not know whether she wept for her mother or for herself, that in spite of her devotion she had not been loved the best.

Three weeks later Alice was sent home and the months of nursing began.

Lilian tried unsuccessfully to smother the memories of that dreadful time. Once her sister was out of immediate danger Aunt Annie retreated to her reclusive life in the old family home. More distant relations wrote kind letters, and acquaintances, for Alice had no friends and rather disapproved of friendship, sent flowers, but the actual nursing had to be done by Lilian herself with the help of a visiting district nurse. Almost overwhelmed by repugnance she somehow maintained a cool detached manner as she discharged her duties. Worst of all was the application of hot fomentations to the wound in Alice's abdomen.

Before she acquired the knack of wringing out the boiling cloth until it was almost dry, she scalded the raw flesh, making her mother scream with pain and fury, giving her more agony to bear. When applying it too cool she encouraged the sepsis which lay in wait for the right conditions. Outside the sickroom she wept with pity for her mother and herself, and with anger too, for Alice in her terrible distress shrieked filthy names at her daughter, words that could barely have entered her knowledge and never been used or thought of till now. Being a competent young woman Lilian eventually got it right, but the frequent dressing of the wound was still something to be dreaded by them both. Exhausted and miserable, Lilian would ask herself how long this situation could continue, afterwards becoming prey to pangs of conscience, feeling she wished to shorten her mother's life.

Then Will Fitzgerald changed everything. He did the only thing that could have restored their dignity and their relationship. He provided a full-time, living-in, trained nurse.

Arriving with flowers and grapes one afternoon he was met at the door by Lilian, pale and untidy. He was not invited in because she was ashamed of the house, which was now grubby and pervaded with the nauseous smell of the sickroom. When he spoke kindly she broke down. Taking her tears as a sign of anticipatory grief he tried to share with her his comfortable faith in an after-life. Although she would miss her mother, who would undoubtedly be with God, sorrow passed in the end. She would find joy in Alice's release from pain.

'It's not *then*,' whispered Lilian. 'It's *now*!'

The next day Nurse Pratt arrived in a taxi with a suit-case, engaged, instructed and paid for by Will Fitz-gerald.

A week later, when he called again, the benefactor was invited in. The house was fresh and clean, the invalid tidy and hopeful, and he was even allowed a brief word with her from the doorway of her room. Lilian's gratitude was beyond bounds, she had no thought of doing other than accept the release he offered. Alice demurred at first, then told herself that the whole family had worked hard for Fitzgerald's in their time, and it was only what any decent employer would do.

Before the long weeks came to an end there were some rewarding moments. Moments when Alice, freshly cleaned up and made comfortable, would chat to Lilian of her childhood, of Christmas at home with her brothers and sister, of Arthur killed in the war, and Edwin who died in childhood. She told of how they had danced to her father's fiddleplaying, danced and quar-relled and played tricks, and how she, Alice, had been such a tomboy, climbing trees and rocks, exploring caves. Yet Lilian was an only child, they had wanted no more. Why had her mother deprived her of all this fun? How her own childhood had been dreary by comparison. And how Alice had changed. How had the reckless child become a staid adult, worrying about what other people thought, keeping herself to herself. It was a mystery.

Now of all the family there would soon be only Aunt Annie left. Little mouselike Annie whose loathing of all things physical had kept her a spinster, and separated her long ago from her only sister who possessed one of those repellent objects, an infant daughter, a creature only slightly less disgusting than an infant son. Poor Annie, Alice called her, though it was she who lay in bed, and Annie who crept in just once with a small bunch of flowers and left as soon as she decently could.

'Poor Annie, she's missed so much,' sighed the invalid when Lilian returned from seeing her aunt out.

'She never once held you when you were a baby, and once she came in when I was changing your napkin and was sick. Yet she was such a naughty little girl, the worst of us all, though she was always shy.'

So the stories went on, slower, feebler, more often unfinished as the days passed, until Alice talked no more, lying semi-conscious for a few days before she died.

Will Fitzgerald saw to everything. He arranged the funeral, sold the house which Lilian could not afford to keep, disposed of the furniture, showed Lilian how much she had in the bank at the end of it all, which was amazingly nearly four hundred pounds, and helped her to move with her clothes, books, her mother's silver brush and comb set and the best of the household linen into the big front bedroom at Victoria Lodge, an Exclusive

Boarding Establishment which was personally supervised by the proprietress, Mrs Violet Denning.

Aunt Annie, dressed in unrelieved black, with her sandy frizz of hair scraped back to avoid any hint of frivolity, attended the funeral and afterwards tentatively offered a home to her niece, which was the right and proper thing for her to do.

'Lilian, if you want to come and live at Prince's Crescent, I shall do my best to make you welcome. After all it was your grandparents' home, so you have every right. I don't eat meat, I expect you know that, and of course you couldn't have mother's and father's room, and you see Arthur and Edwin shared the attic, so it wouldn't do for you to sleep there, but there's room for a bed in the boxroom, I cleared out most of the stuff in there some time ago, it was only collecting dust ... and really if you don't need things ... I like to wash in the scullery, it saves taking water upstairs, but we could take it in turns.'

She paused nervously, then, staring fixedly down at her feet, went on, 'I don't use a chamber pot. I find if I go out the back last thing at night I can nearly always wait till morning ... You'd soon get used to my ways, I'm sure.' Lilian quickly put her aunt's mind at rest. She could not imagine a worse fate than to share a home with poor Annie, who was really getting very funny. She thought she would sooner starve.

A week later she was back at work, though it was some time before everything was settled and she was able to leave forty-four York Road, with all its depressing associations, and make a new start.

'Here you are then,' said Will, putting down her largest suitcase. Lilian had already seen and approved Mrs

Denning's first floor front with its brass bedstead, white curtains and clean faded carpet. She had looked with pleasure at the comfortable armchair, the round table, and the vast wardrobe with the mirror set into the door. A full-length mirror was a luxury that her old home had never afforded.

The little maid who had shown them up disappeared quietly, and Lilian went to the window. Though the house was on a main road in the middle of the town there was an open view across to the church which stood on a green mound a hundred yards away, and beyond it lay the sea.

'It's lovely,'

'You'll be all right here, then?'

'Oh, yes. And thank you ... thank you for all you've done.'

When he put his arms round her she embraced him in return. With her cheek against his she looked over his shoulder at the big bed. For one brief moment she heard Alice's voice 'Don't let him take liberties. I know what he's like.'

But this was not a liberty and she knew better than anyone what he was. He was kind and good and understood how to do everything. He had protected her and looked after her interests, and was, she believed, fond of her. He was also married and had a daughter her own age. She was just twenty-five, which made Phyllis twenty-four.

So why, that night when she lay in the wide bed, did she pretend to herself that Mrs Fitzgerald had suddenly died, and he had come to her lonely and wept with his head in her lap, while she stroked his fading auburn hair? She tossed and turned as the fever of longing built up, and finally went to sleep flat on her back on one side of the bed, imagining that if she put out her hand she would find him there. In this dream, naturally, they were married.

Waking to cold grey daylight she remembered all this, and was ashamed. She was assailed by a sense of fear and loss, of being adrift and homeless. Had she done the right thing in selling the house? Should she have tried to keep it? Too late now. Had she been thinking clearly? Her mother's death, though expected, had nevertheless shocked her. On Friday morning she had wakened as usual in her own familiar bedroom, risen and gone down in her dressing-gown to make a pot of tea, then dressed herself before preparing breakfast for herself, the nurse and the patient. She'd tidied the house, shopped, sat with her mother for an hour while Nurse Pratt took the air, and done all the things that had become habitual in recent weeks. A day of dull routine, or so it had seemed, but by nightfall her mother was dead.

She'd tried to look on it as a happy release, as the doctor advised, and to treasure the memories of the times when Alice, blessedly free from pain for a while, had enjoyed her company. Then the excitement of moving and of returning to work had carried her through. Dressing herself quickly in this cold room with the alien sounds of strangers moving about the corridors, pulling chains, calling for hot water, she realized how alone she was, how unprotected. Supposing she were ill? Who would take care of her? What about the small physical problems she had always confided to her mother, not 'coming on' at the expected time? Who could she talk to now? Aunt Annie was out of the question. Mabel perhaps, her old school friend? Married now, with her own little semi-detached home,

Mabel made a point of inviting Lilian to tea every week
on early closing day. Even during Alice's illness, the
visits had continued once Nurse Pratt was installed, but
since the wedded Mabel had hinted at delights that her
friend could not dream of, Lilian, embarrassed and
repelled, had kept the conversation on a less personal
level.

No, she would have to worry away on her own, and
go to the surgery if things got really bad. She had never
visited a doctor by herself, or even seen one on her own
account for several years, but she could hardly hope that
it would never be necessary.

Her breakfast was served in the dining room at one
end of a long table. No one else was there when she
entered the room, but several people, most of them men,
had taken their places before she had finished. She
returned their greetings politely, but her aloof manner
forbade any attempts at conversation.

At the shop all was as usual. Elsie was ready with a
cup of tea in the kitchen when she arrived, Jim Smallwood in his cubby-hole at the back of the jewellery
section, Rene the junior, dolefully examining her spotty
face in the mirror, and her employer not descending
until all was uncovered and polished and ready for
customers. Then he entered briskly, glanced around,
fetched his hat from his little office and went straight
out for his constitutional walk and his morning paper.
Returning, he paused near Lilian before going to open
his letters.

'Everything all right?'

'Yes, very nice, thank you.'

'Think you'll be all right there then?'

'Oh, yes, I'm sure I shall.'

'That's good. My wife's having one of her do's on

Thursday evening. We've missed you lately. Got something new for us, have you?'

'I'll find something. Thank you very much.'

Lilian had not attended a musical evening in the big first-floor drawing room since before Alice had been taken ill. She'd wondered whether she would be invited again. Would it be all right for her to go alone, unaccompanied by her mother? Evidently it would. She must send a card to Mabel, cancelling her usual visit. Mabel would understand that an invitation from her employer could hardly be refused. Then what should she choose for her recitation? Months ago, under Miss Faraday's tuition, she had been learning a dramatic monologue about a young woman who, through the many vicissitudes of an ill-starred love, was too proud to show her feelings. It was called, 'I Don't Care', and had, she thought, a very telling final line, 'God knows how much I care!' She imagined herself delivering it with a break in her voice while an admiring audience could scarcely restrain its applause. As she dusted, she tried to go over the words in her head but found it difficult to concentrate, wondering who would be there. Pickford relations of course, and a sprinkling of useful and important townspeople, and Phyllis. She and her fiancé would be the only other young people, but that didn't matter, because he would be there.

'No use you getting sweet on Mr F,' Alice had once said, with the uncomfortable perspicacity of mothers. Lilian was indignant. He was older than her father would have been, as well as being married. It was simply, she said to herself, but now aloud, that he was kind, made her feel important and attractive, was knowledgeable about jewellery and porcelain and appreciated her interest and flair.

But on that Thursday evening as she ironed her best
blouse in the kitchen at Victoria Lodge by special
permission of the proprietress she admitted it to herself.
She was sweet on him. Suddenly the whole outlook was
brighter, she had something to look forward to, a reason
for living. Of course he must never know, she would
keep it a secret for ever. Walking briskly back to the Fort
at half-past seven her eyes were bright, her cheeks
flushed, and she was happy for the first time that year.

The evening went well. All the guests were particularly kind and appreciative, knowing that she had
recently been bereaved, though Phyllis, after an initial
effort to be more serious than usual, gave up, and
became her own giggly frivolous self. Her fiancé, a tall,
self-assured young man, was the son of local business
people who had set themselves up in a large house on
the outskirts of the town and pretended to be gentry.
They had two farms and owned all the dairies for miles
around. Phyllis had done well for herself, and would be
marrying money, though she told Lilian that she was
doing the Harrington family a favour, diamond rings
being superior to milk, and Worcester vases more beautiful than lumps of cheese. She was delighted to have
Lilian back and promised to resume her clandestine
visits to the shop for the discussion of the latest fashions
and other interesting topics, which invariably took place
while her father was out at the mysterious meetings and
committees which took up so much of his time.

In these pleasant surroundings Lilian felt an uprush of
confidence. Here she was, independent and self-
supporting, invited to this elegant party on her own
account. She forgot that she was a shop-assistant,
almost alone in the world, and that the man she set her
heart on was married. She was here in this room, in her

white lace blouse and dark green skirt, about to enter-
tain this distinguished gathering with her rendering of 'I
Don't Care' with perhaps a speech of Portia's for an
encore. For once it didn't matter that her nose was too
big. Alice had always said it gave her face character and
perhaps it did. She was tall and slender and elegant, and
her brilliant hair, her pre-Raphaelite hair, made up for
her deficiencies, of which her flat chest was one.

Louisa Fitzgerald was particularly kind. She made
Lilian sit next to her, instructing her husband to bring
one of the frail little drawing room chairs near to where
she held court in a wing armchair by the fire.

She asked how she liked her 'digs', patted her arm
sympathetically and called her a brave girl. Lilian felt
guilty for a moment because she was happier now than
she had been for months and months and was not being
brave at all. Trying to keep her attention on her hostess
she watched Will. No longer was he Mr Fitzgerald in her
mind and certainly not Mr F as he moved about the
room, refilling glasses with the sherry that had superceded the lemonade, chatting easily with this one and
that. Presently he rescued her.

'Come along Lilian, you have to earn your keep, you
know. Help Phyllis hand round the grub.'

'Really, William.' His wife smiled indulgently.

It struck Lilian as wrong somehow that he should be
calling her by her Christian name while she had to
address him formally. But of course he had known her
since she was a baby, and he always called her Miss
Watts in the shop. And the next morning she was Miss
Watts again. In fact his behaviour towards her was
circumspect. Lilian remembered her mother's words
again, and feared that she was not sufficiently attractive
to deserve 'liberties', and it was summer before events

proved her wrong. She'd become used to living at
Victoria Lodge, doing her work as well as she knew
how, reciting at two or three more musical evenings,
visiting Mabel on all the Thursdays and was wondering
if this was to be her life forever. Sometimes on Sunday
mornings she considered going to church, just for something to do, but her parents had never been churchgoers. Any mention of his employer's Roman
Catholicism or his regular attendance at St Austin's had
called forth some scathing remark from Harold Watts
concerning hypocrites and humbug, and his wife would
remind him of the presence of Lilian. His daughter had
never understood what he meant, but she retained a
certain respect for his opinions. She was lonely at times,
but not lonely enough to go to church.

So that Sunday she had lain late in bed reading a
novel from the library, and had not risen until the
splendid fragrance of roasting beef escaped from the
basement kitchen and wafted about the upper floors.
She had a very good wash, using the lukewarm water
that had been piping hot when Nellie left the brass can
at her door two hours earlier. She stood in front of the
long mirror, considering her reflection. She looked nice,
she thought, with her hair loose, and it was a pity she
couldn't wear it like that all the time, hanging down her
back like a fairy-tale princess. Well, there was something to be said for spending Sunday morning in this
way, lazing about, pretending to be a lady of leisure.

Her mother would have disapproved strongly of such
behaviour, but where was the harm? It was pleasant to
be here in this sunny room, wearing the lace dressing-
jacket that Mabel had made her for Christmas. Better
still perhaps, if there had been someone to admire her.
She daydreamed a little, inventing a sudden and painless

death for Louisa Fitzgerald, after which Will would
confess to her that he had never loved his wife, it had
been a marriage of convenience, and all he wanted was
for Lilian to be at his side for always. They would live
over the shop, Phyllis would soon be married and they
would have it to themselves. She would be Mrs Fitzgerald, wife of Alderman Fitzgerald. She would open
bazaars, preside at important meetings, and give At
Homes. Perhaps she would have a baby, and there
would be a nursemaid to wheel it along the promenade
in a high pram.

There was a knock at the door. She thought it must be
little Nellie, who, knowing she did not come down to
breakfast, sometimes managed to bring her a cup of tea
during Sunday morning.

'Come in.'

Will Fitzgerald entered, closing the door quietly
behind him. Lilian had been so carried away by her
inner vision that she almost flung herself into his arms.
Then it struck her that only some crisis could have
brought him to her on a Sunday morning.

'What's happened, is somebody ill? What's the
matter?'

He stood there in his dark Sunday clothes, holding his
hat and gloves. He has come straight from St Austin's.
He was serious, unsmiling.

'Nothing's wrong. I came to see you.'

'I'm not dressed.' She pulled the dressing-jacket
together in the front.

He flung his hat on the bed.

'Don't hide those beautiful breasts from me.'

To Lilian's amazement he came towards her and took
her in his arms. He held her close for a moment and
then releasing her a little began to fondle her breasts

through the lawn camisole. At twenty-five her ignorance
of love-making was almost complete; she had not even
realized that breasts played a part in it. Her face grew
hot, while at the same time her legs seemed to turn to
water, making her incapable of movement. She sagged
against him and he supported her in his arms.

'No,' she whispered. 'No, don't.'

'You must have known, surely?'

There was a trace of irritation in his tone, making her
afraid, deepening her confusion. He was her employer
and also her befriender, the strong and generous man
who had helped her through the bad time preceding and
following her mother's death.

'I don't know. I don't know anything,' she whispered,
ashamed of not knowing, pressing her face against his
dark worsted jacket.

'But you like me, don't you?'

'Oh yes.'

That 'yes' was heartfelt. She clung to him when he
kissed her.

'Get on the bed,' he whispered.

What was going to happen next? He was taking off
his jacket, unfastening his stiff collar, removing his tie.
With his black and white silk braces exposed he looked
less than dignified. Had he read her thoughts? He was
slipping them off his shoulders, and stepping out of his
well-pressed trousers. Perhaps he was afraid of creasing
them. Then he was on the bed beside her, taking off her
precious lacy jacket, pushing down the straps of her
camisole and exposing her small breasts.

He wants to lay his head on my bosom, she thought.
She had read of such a gesture, and only wished she
had a more respectable bosom to offer. He went on
drawing away the embroidered lawn garment until her

nipples were exposed, which seemed to her unnecessary
and embarrassing. She tried unsuccessfully to cover
them as he kissed her lips. When he transferred his
mouth to her right nipple her astonishment was overwhelming. She thought only babies did that. Her sense
of weakness and openness grew. When a few minutes
later he drove into her, two separate thoughts flitted
through her mind. The first was that her father had been
wrong all those years ago when he said no one would
bother about her. The second was that it really wasn't
much like a banana.

And so it went on, Sunday after Sunday. That was how
she became one of Will Fitzgerald's fancy women. But
no one knew, unless Mrs Denning suspected, for she
must have seen him entering or leaving her house. At
the shop, preserving a formal distance was part of the
fun. Happy, desperately in love, and believing herself
loved in return, she had no feelings of guilt in the face of
Louisa Fitzgerald's pleasant if patronizing manner
towards her. After all, Louisa was over sixty, and must
have been past that kind of thing for years, while her
husband was in his early fifties, young for a man.

Lilian still attended the evening parties, recited when
asked to do so, and helped to hand round the refreshments like one of the family. She was invited to Phyllis's
wedding, the grand reception and wedding breakfast at
the Metropole Hotel. Her intention afterwards was to go
straight back to the shop, knowing it to be inadequately
staffed by Jim and Rene. Phyllis and her new husband
had departed in a shower of confetti on the London
train, seen off at the station by all the wedding guests.
As the engine puffed away she found Will beside her.
Staring straight ahead after his departing daughter he

said, 'Go straight home.'

Did he mean his home? Mrs Denning's wasn't really anyone's home.

'Home?'

'To your room. Wait for me there.'

Lilian walked slowly away from the station. Knowledgeable now, after six months of being his mistress, she realized how the festivity, the wine, and the veiled jovial hinting at the trial his daughter was shortly to undergo must have aroused him. So he thought he could have her just when he liked, did he? Never mind about how she felt.

The wedding reception had not had the same effect upon her. Seeing Phyllis standing at the altar in her pearl-embroidered cream lace dress, and long parchment-coloured veil had brought home to her the fact that she would never now be the central figure in such an event. She had no mother to help her prepare, no father to give her ceremonially away, no eligible young man to provide her with a home, a social position, or children. She was not even sure that she had a good reputation. If people hadn't already started talking, they no doubt soon would. Long ago her parents had whispered about Mr F's fancy women and now their daughter was one of them. For the first time she allowed herself to speculate about the others. Mrs Denning, very likely, perhaps Phyllis's music teacher, the flamboyantly arty Miss Woolley. But not the gypsy woman, for all appearances to the contrary, not the tall dark gypsy who continued to visit the shop from time to time. She could not and would not believe that anything had ever happened between Will and Ruth Smith.

'Tell him it's Mrs Smith to see him.'

How arrogantly she would give the order, and Lilian

would be forced to carry it out and to return with a message to the effect that she was to go through into the office. Sometimes she would remain there for upwards of twenty minutes, during which time Jim Smallwood's face would be a thundercloud of disapproval, and Lilian tried to carry on normally.

'If I had my way I'd throw her out onto the pavement and her basket of heather after her,' said Jim on one occasion.

'She's just begging,' but Lilian lowered her eyes before the withering look he gave her. Walking away to her own department she resolved to have as little to do with Jim as possible. He had a nasty mind.

The incident returned to her unwelcomed as she left the station, so instead of going up the hill to the main road and Victoria Lodge she continued along the front. On the Fort she stood at the railings staring out to sea.

'He shouldn't have,' she thought. 'He's ruined my chances.' But what chances had there been. Jim Smallwood? Only chances she did not want. All the young men she might have met, might have loved, had been killed in the war. And who was to say that they would have wanted her? Mabel was more their sort.

At least she wouldn't be an old maid. Old, perhaps but not a maid. Thinking of all she had learned during the last six months in Mrs Denning's first floor front she smiled at the thought. Her mood changed. She became worried in case her lover arrived to find her absent. He would be angry and disappointed. She might lose him. Hurrying away from the front and up York Road she passed her old home without even a glance. She almost ran into Victoria Lodge and up the stairs. He was not there, as she had expected, but perhaps he had been and gone. She waited for over an hour, agonized, desperate, cursing herself for not doing as he wished. When at last he came, flushed and jovial, with a bottle of champagne, she almost wept with relief. He was all she had or ever would have. She surprised herself with the passion and freedom of her response. Looking back, it seemed as though that long glorious afternoon might have been the beginning of Sylvia May.

Thinking now of her baby, Lilian arrived back at the shop.

'You're late.'

Jim Smallwood spoke curtly. Working in their different departments all morning, they had scarcely exchanged a word that was not strictly necessary in the way of business. Lilian resented his tone. Who was he to tell her she was late?

'I've got a long way to walk,' she said shortly. She might have added 'and a baby to attend to,' but did not. If Jim chose to pretend ignorance he could get on with it. However, having been brought up in a tradition of punctuality and hard work, she felt a little guilty. Lost in the reconstruction of her past life, she had probably dawdled without realizing it. She must walk more briskly in future. In the absence of customers she returned to her never-ending task of dusting the china. Tedious as this might have seemed, Lilian enjoyed it. Worcester vases with their dream landscapes, Staffordshire flowers, each delicate petal a dust-trap, and figurines of all kinds, some clothed elaborately in miraculous lacy garments, some not clothed at all. All of these expensive pieces were beautiful. There was one she had always liked particularly, still unsold after many months: a young naked woman, with long hair, gilded drapery concealing the lower part of her body. She was poised by a tree-stump, leaning forward as if wondering whether or not she was being observed. Once, as Lilian had stood, one hand on the bed post, feeling for her slippers, Will had been reminded of this figure of Milton's Sabrina, and quoted the line about 'the loose train of thy amber-dropping hair'. They had found the poem in her Oxford Book and he had read it to her in his pleasant light voice that still kept the Irish inflection he had brought over from Dublin as a small child.

The next day Lilian had hurried to work, eager to examine the statuette and found Sabrina disappointingly flat-chested. But still she was beautiful, a work of art. Lilian moved her to the back of the shelf out of the sight of customers.

Would he ever be her lover again? Were those times over? He had said nothing about continuing their affair, but then there had been so many practical things to discuss, and in any case the difficulties were immense.

Rosie Timms's front bedroom was not a fit place for making love; she would never let him come there even if he wished to. But where else was there? Sometimes Louisa Fitzgerald went away to stay with one of her sisters but the idea of using the marital bed in that huge shadowy room was appalling. Also there was the risk of another Sylvia, something he had promised her could never happen, but there she was in Shelley Street with Rosie Timms, crying perhaps, or needing her napkin changed.

Lilian replaced Sabrina at the front of the shelf. She had proved a snare and delusion and the sooner she was sold the better.

Taking up another porcelain figure she decided to ask for the return of her small capital that she had so willingly, at her lover's request, invested in Fitzgerald and Son. She would do it that very afternoon.

Will did not appear downstairs until after Jim had disappeared into his watchmaker's cubby-hole. Then he walked straight through into his office. Lilian followed him.

He was already seated at his roll-top desk, and looked up impatiently, just as if she had been a mere shop assistant. Though this had always been his way, it unnerved her.

'Will . . .'

'Shut the door. What is it?'

She stood beside him but he did not look up. Drawing some invoices towards him he studied the top one carefully.

'Will, I'm afraid I don't like it very much at Mrs Timms's.'

'You haven't been there five minutes. You'll get used to it.'

'I don't want to get used to it. Why should I get used to Shelley Street?'

Anger helped her to say what she had come to say. 'I want you to . . . give me back my money, so that I can buy a little house or something . . .'

'My dear girl, it's not nearly enough for that. And it's better where it is. You invested it. It's still yours.'

'But I thought . . . if money was invested you got some back. Interest.' She was pleased with herself for remembering the right word.

'But you are getting some back. I'm paying you, aren't I?'

This confused her. Did being paid a salary preclude her receiving interest on her money? Perhaps it did. She wished she understood financial matters.

'Look, we're just surviving at the moment. It's too

soon after the war, but when business improves, if we have a good season, I'll see what I can do. At the moment I can't pay you interest on top of your salary. The money just isn't there.'

'I see.'

Dispiritedly she moved away.

'Lilla.'

She turned eagerly. He had never used this pet name in the shop.

'Yes?'

'It was worth it, wasn't it? We had fun.'

'Worth it for you. I've got Sylvia to worry about now.'

'A beautiful baby. You wouldn't be without her, surely. Someone of your own to love. I'll look after you both. I have so far, haven't I? Just give me time.'

She smiled at him, of course. And went back to work. It was typical of him, spending money on the luxurious cot and perambulator, while they had to live at Rosie Timms's. But it was true that he had looked after her. When she'd finally in great distress told him that she was expecting his child he hadn't been at all cross. He'd made all the arrangements with Nurse Tebbitt, and paid for everything. Easy enough, said a small voice inside her, since he had all the money. She quelled this disloyal thought firmly. He was a kind man and things would improve. Meantime she must make the best of Shelley Street.

Back in the showroom she decided she had thought enough about the past. It seemed to her that she had gone over everything that mattered and yet she still could not understand why she, Lilian Watts, had become a 'fancy woman' while girls as different as Phyllis and Mabel and Elsie could get respectably married. Quite unable to solve this conundrum she resolved to dwell on it no longer, and fortunately at this point several customers entered the shop and enabled her to keep her resolution.

CHAPTER 4

That evening she hurried back to Sylvia, eager to see how the baby had survived the motherless hours, but considerably less eager to meet her landlady's family. To her surprise she found Sylvia asleep in her cot, reasonably clean and perfectly contented. Another surprise was the bright fire that burnt in the little black fireplace in the front sitting-room. Apparently the wind had changed direction, making this possible. Rosie brought her supper on a tray; a boiled egg, with some white bread, thickly spread with foul-tasting margarine, and for second course a slab of spicy damp bread pudding, which Lilian, after the first dubious mouthful, ate with appetite if not actual enjoyment. Then with the firelight and flickering gas-mantle disguising the poverty of the bleak, sparsely furnished little room she tried to read, but worrying thoughts kept intruding. Most of the time, as her eyes followed the print, she was wondering again if her affair with Will was over. Had he lost interest in her? Was the elaborate equipment he had bought for the baby in the nature of a parting gift? In any case, how could they go on with it now? What could take the place

of those sunny Sunday mornings on the big brass bed
which had resulted in Sylvia May? He had said he loved
her, had always wanted and had waited for her to grow
up. She had style, he said. Style and elegance and
dignity and brains, all he wanted in a woman. He wasn't
a man who liked soft cuddly girls, easy game.

Had she still got style and elegance? Lilian wondered.
They'd be pretty out of place here if she had.

Sounds from the kitchen led her to believe that the
entire Timms family was now at home. She had
resigned herself to facing them when she went through
to the scullery to make up Sylvia's ten o'clock feed, but
now another problem began to make itself felt, and
rapidly became pressing. She would have to 'pay a visit'
in the near future, but how could she walk through a
room full of strange people, and everyone of them
knowing the nature of her errand? And afterwards come
back the same way? Shifting uncomfortably in her chair
she tried to forget her need for the time being, but then
came a knock at the door, and Rosie put her head round.

'I've just made a pot of tea. Would you like to come
and have one with us? Or I can bring yours in here if
you'd rather.'

'Thanks. I'll come and have it with you.' Lilian
accepted the invitation eagerly. Once in the kitchen she
could perhaps slip out to the back unobtrusively.

They were all there, eager to meet the new lodger. A
thin youth in his shirtsleeves sprawled full-length on
the couch, another stood on the hearthrug. In one of the
wooden armchairs by the fire sat a young girl, with
fairish hair in plaits, and a somehow old-looking face.
She was nursing Georgie, who was now fairly clean and
in a nightgown. And at the table sat Dollie, who worked
at Collingham's and was, it seemed, no better than she

should be. She had a clear skin, pleasing if rather coarse features, a lot of pale brown curly hair and large dark-fringed grey eyes. Her black dress with its lace collar was fashionable as well as neat.

'This is my eldest girl,' said Rosie with understandable pride.

'Lo.'

Dollie glanced casually up from her magazine.

'Have a cake,' she said, offering Lilian a paper bag. 'I got six pennorth of stale fancies at Bowketts on the way home. They're all right. Only yesterday's.'

'Thank you.'

Lilian accepted a cube of yellow sponge, coated with very bright pink icing, and having no plate on which to put it, bit into it straight away. Dollie picked up her cup which rested saucerless on the newspaper that protected the plush cloth and drank from it with enjoyment.

'Been dying for that.'

Rosie poured out tea into a cup with a saucer for Lilian, and passed her the sugar. This time it was granulated sugar in a twist of dark blue paper. Lilian looked for a spoon, found only one that had already been used and decided she preferred her tea unsweetened.

'Now that is Ned, and this is Albert, and Nance you already know.' With the exception of Dollie who was once more absorbed in *The Red Letter*, Rosie's children stared at Lilian.

'And I'm Lilian.'

She had not meant them to call her by her Christian name, intending to keep her distance, but it was plain that she would not be able to live with them like that. She would have to become one of the family, for there lay what seemed her only hope of survival.

'I've seen your baby. She'd ever so nice.'

Rosie glanced affectionately at her younger daughter.
'Nance loves babies. Real little mother she is.'

'More fool her.' Without looking up, Dollie took
another cake out of the crumpled bag.

'I'll have to fetch her down for her bottle soon,' said
Lilian, wondering how she could get out of the room to
the back yard.

'I'll fetch her if you like,' offered Nance.

'Well, perhaps I'd better carry her downstairs, but do
come with me, if you'd like to. I'll um ... I'll just go and
see about her bottle.'

Rather precipitately she rose and went out into the
scullery. On the table there she found the candle in a
candlestick and the matches, pointed out earlier by
Rosie in anticipation of such expeditions. There was no
toilet roll in the cramped water-closet next to the coal-
shed, only newspaper cut to size and hung up on a
string.

The floor and the wooden seat were suspiciously
damp. Some people, it seemed, didn't bother to take the
candle.

Returning, she murmured a little prepared speech
about its being rather early for Sylvia's feed after all, but
no one seemed to have noticed her absence or her
return. The boys were putting on jackets and caps,
preparing to go out.

'Mind you shut the front door properly,' called Rosie
as they departed. Turning to Lilian she added, 'I've
packed them off out. More trouble than they're worth,
they are.'

'I've turned you out of your room, I'm afraid,' said
Lilian, making conversation with Dollie.

'It's Mum you've turned out. Mum and Nance and
Georgie.'

'Oh dear, I am sorry.'

Lilian glanced at Rosie in time to see her frown quickly in her daughter's direction.

'Don't you worry about that dear. You see, Mr F said as how you were to have the front room, so me and Nance have shifted into the back that used to be the boys' room and Dollie's come in with us, so they can take turns in the little room.'

'Take turns?'

'That's right, the one whose turn it isn't sleeps on the couch down here.'

So that was it. Whichever boy had just got to sleep on the hard horsehair chaise-longue had been disturbed by her before six that morning. No wonder neither lad seemed particularly pleased to have her as a lodger. She hoped they would stay out for the rest of the evening. She had met so few young men, and none of this type who hitherto had only existed for her as errand boys, railway porters and the like, people of a lower order. She did not know how to talk to them, what manner to adopt, and their presence made her uneasy.

'Tell us about your Mum and Dad, dearie. Where was it you lived before they passed away?'

Rosie's voice was kind, not curious. Dollie and Nance looked up expectantly. These people, so different from all those she had known before, were interested in her, wished her well.

She said, 'I . . . we . . . lived in York Road . . . forty-four . . . It's about halfway up . . .'

Suddenly a clear picture of that once familiar dining room rose in front of her, with the table tidily laid, and her mother in her dark blue dress. She smelt the lavender water that was the only perfume that Alice had ever used, saw her capable hands busy with sewing and heard her voice. The sense of grief and isolation that she had firmly controlled all the time she had been at Mrs Denning's now overwhelmed her. She felt her mouth go square as the tears started to her eyes. Covering her face with one hand, groping for her handkerchief, she rose, pushing back her chair which grated loudly on the oilcloth. She hadn't known she felt like this.

'There now, don't go upstairs and cry all on your own, you don't want to wake the baby. Never mind us, we understand. You've been through a lot.'

'Yes. Yes, I have,' murmured Lilian. 'I have been through a lot.'

Rosie patted her shoulder and stroked back her hair, while Nance poured more tea, and Dollie looked on, her grey eyes wide, munching her stale fancy.

It soon began to seem quite natural for Lilian to join the Timms family for the evening cup of tea, and as winter deepened the front room and its unsatisfactory fireplace were abandoned altogether. Sylvia, with the help of various potions, some commercial, some home-made, known to Rosie, survived nappy-rash, teething, and thrush, while her mother without help of any kind recovered from chilblains, neuralgia and colds in the head. Rosie was kind, Dollie a lively if somewhat outra-geous companion, and Nance was devoted to the welfare and comfort of Sylvia. But for the uncomfortable presence of the boys and the careless way in which they used the lavatory, Shelley Street became quite tolerable. Lilian was able to improve the cooking a little by offering to help on Sunday mornings and by doing bits of shopping on her way home. Rosie, encouraged by the presence of a lodger who was very superior, as lodgers went at Poets' Corner, and having a little more money to spend, remembered some of the domestic niceties she had learned in service. The blue paper sugar bag was replaced by a china bowl, tablecloths were used regularly and the roller towel in the scullery replaced at more frequent intervals. The early morning remained a difficult time, with Ned and Albert shaving, when Lilian was forced to slip through to the yard, but for the rest she managed to live with the family without embarrassment. Although for the first week or two Rosie had taken a breakfast tray up to the front bedroom it soon seemed easier and more natural for her to do as the others did, hacking a slice of bread from the large loaf on the kitchen table, toasting it at the old kitchen range and eating it spread with dripping or margarine. Like the others she would pour her own tea and take her turn for a second cup.

She did not go as far as to eat walking about, half-dressed, like the boys, or to stuff her mouth in the intervals of pinning up her hair like Dollie, but she sat in the corner of the couch sipping her tea, cuddling Sylvia, and wishing she did not have to leave her all day. Even when Rosie changed Georgie's napkin in full view of the company she only averted her eyes, and tried to ignore the smell. It was Dollie who said, 'Mum! Can't that wait till we've gone?'

To which Rosie replied, 'He'll get sore, poor mite. No good being squeamish when you've got a baby in the house.'

'I'll make sure I never have any in my house. I hate babies.'

'Well, you're going a funny way about it my girl. If you don't want babies you'll have to mend your ways.'

'Oh, Mum, you don't know anything. You needn't have babies if you don't want them, not these days.'

'I wasn't born yesterday and I know things can go wrong.'

Lilian listened, though she kept her face turned towards Sylvia. If Dollie knew so much about how to avoid babies, she felt she would like to share that knowledge. A day might still come when it would be useful.

It was months before the acquisition of such knowledge became a practical necessity. The days passed quickly as she worked long hours in the shop, hurried to and fro, and pushed the pram round to Mabel's on early closing day. Mabel's cosy clean little home was a haven of quiet order. They would sit up to the table and eat boiled eggs and thin bread and butter, and afterwards they would settle Sylvia to sleep in the pram so that Lilian could stay to supper. Mabel and Jack would both escort her back to Shelley Street at half-past ten. Jack was a tall handsome man with a heavy black moustache, who worked in the Council offices. He was always rather quiet in Lilian's presence, and Mabel would chatter endlessly, trying to cover up for him. Lilian knew he disapproved of his wife's friendship with her, but she sometimes caught him looking at her with a speculative eye and wondered if he fancied his chance. He would not be the only one. By now Lilian's equivocal social position was common knowledge, and her naturally cool and aloof manner was her only protection when confronted with certain gentlemen in the course of her day in the china department. There were several middle-aged councillors and local business men who found it necessary to call on Will Fitzgerald at his place of business at fairly frequent intervals, when they would find time to engage his tall red-haired shop assistant in unwilling conversation. Sometimes she was rescued by a curt summons from Jim.

'Miss Watts! Could you spare me a moment, please?'

and then she could make a dignified withdrawal into the cubbyhole.

It would have been nice to have a giggle about these silly hopeful old men, but that was not Jim's way. Indeed, he always seemed angry on these occasions, as though it were her fault.

Lilian asked herself whether, if they had not all been married, she might have been able to overcome her disgust, and by a judicious blend of encouragement and circumspection, find herself a husband. After all, she must marry somebody. How else was she to provide Sylvia with a proper home? How else could she pay school fees? The idea of Sylvia attending the council school with the rough, grubby children from Poets' Corner was appalling. Her main hope was that Louisa would die. It was a hope she could not stifle, wicked as she felt it to be, because only then could her past be vindicated by marriage. But supposing this desirable death took place, could she be sure that Will would ask her to marry him? She had every right to expect him to, but what was their relationship now? He hardly seemed to know her, scarcely addressed her except in the way of business.

It was in a perfectly business-like tone that, one Friday evening in the spring of 1923, he told her, as she leaned for a moment against a shelf in the china department, that she was looking tired, she needed a long weekend and could take the following Monday off. Lilian was delighted. A whole extra day with Sylvia! She would give her bedroom a good clean, wash some baby clothes, and spend the rest of the day with Mabel, who would be pleased.

It was the custom on Friday evenings for each of the staff to go in turn into the office for their wages, just before closing time. Without glancing up Will handed Lilian the usual small envelope, saying quietly, 'There's a train to Warne Bay at two fifty-five on Sunday afternoon. Be on it. I'll meet you at the station.'

Surprise and joy suffused her body. She heard him say loudly, 'That's all then. Goodnight, Miss Watts.' He turned away to lock the safe and she left the office.

She could not wait to tell Dollie. Having listened to many a detailed description of her outings with Mr Leeson from soft furnishings she felt she could now expect an interested audience. She hoped Rosie had no plans for Sunday, since it would be necessary for her to take care of the baby. Well, Nance would be at home, she could do everything for the ten-month-old Sylvia, even bathing her, under supervision, and she would be glad of extra pocket-money.

Dollie's response was more than satisfactory.

'There's a lovely hotel at Warne Bay, the Granville. I bet he's going to take you there. You'll have to dress for dinner.'

'A hotel? Do you think so? He didn't say. Then I suppose we'll be staying the night.'

'Of course you'll be staying the night. Were you born yesterday?'

'Oh dear.'

'It'll be all right. He'll sign you in as man and wife. I've done it heaps of times. Only don't go and put Lily Watts in the book, will you? You're daft enough.'

Rosie too was enthusiastic. No, it would be no trouble to take care of Sylvia. She spread the old scorched ironing blanket on the kitchen table, and covered it with a piece of sheeting so that Lilian could iron her best clothes, and helped her to wash her hair at the scullery sink, afterwards rubbing it vigorously with a rough towel.

'Don't eat too much,' warned Dollie, as they sat down

to the midday meal on the Sunday. 'You'll be having late dinner tonight.'

Lilian had begun to wish that Dollie would be a little less free with her advice. It seemed to drag her genuine love affair with a distinguished and important man down to the level of Dollie's own carry-on with the upholstery buyer, who could have married her at once if he wanted to. It was her own fault for becoming too friendly. Perhaps she should have kept the whole thing to herself, pretended she was going to visit a relation.

Just then Dollie said, 'I say, Lil, old thing, I've got ever such a pretty silk camisole my Arthur bought me that time we went to Brighton, you can have a lend of it if you want.'

Dollie might be common but she was a real friend. Ashamed of her previous thoughts, Lilian accepted the offer gratefully.

At Warne Bay station Will was waiting on the platform. He seemed to have complete faith in the separateness of Warne Bay from Culvergate, behaving as if they were at the other end of the world. He took her suitcase, smiling and charming as only he could be, and they left the station arm in arm.

When they entered the Palm Court of the Granville Hotel at teatime Lilian's last doubt vanished. This was real life. Smartly dressed people were seated at little round tables, and waitresses in dark green with frilly coffee-coloured aprons and big moiré bows across the backs of their heads hurried to and fro with loaded trays. A little orchestra of ladies in black lace dresses played something from Gilbert and Sullivan, and there was a pleasant odour of toasted teacakes. Big bay windows overlooked the promenade where a few elegant couples were strolling.

Lilian saw herself reflected in the palm-fringed mirror, tall, slender, suitably escorted. Her best black silk dress, bought for mourning but now enlivened by a diamanté buckle, became her.

She smiled at her lover as the waitress pulled out her chair. When the girl had taken their order for tea and pastries she leaned forward, her elbows on the table. 'This is lovely,' she said.

Will smiled. 'Make the most of it then.'

He spoke kindly, but Lilian felt there was something very wrong with this advice, though she was not quite sure what it was.

After tea they walked along the promenade, arm in arm, among the other early holidaymakers. Warne Bay was an exclusive little resort, it did not encourage day trippers from London, and all the women strolling were smartly dressed, all the men looked prosperous. There were children too, enjoying a breath of healthy sea-air before bedtime. Some walked sedately with their parents, others were pushed in big shiny perambulators. They were mostly dressed in white, and all of them were smocked, frilled, and curled to such an extent that the actual child was scarcely visible. The baby girls wore ruched bonnets, the headgear of the boys was only slightly less elaborate, and many of them were propelled in their chariots by crisply-uniformed nurses. Naturally Lilian's thoughts turned to her own baby, probably now occupying the high chair in the kitchen at nine Shelley Street. Perhaps Nance would be there, spoon-feeding her with bread and milk, and later giving the already replete child her bottle. She knew she could rely on Nance to make sure that the milk had actually boiled, and to cool the bottle under the running tap, and see that the teat was clean. Rosie was kind, but slapdash,

and overworked. Some kind of present must be taken
home for Nance, and perhaps for Rosie too. And of
course she must include Dollie. Perhaps if she lent her
the new dark green velvet dress she had bought for the
evening to come, that would count as a present. It
would be too long, but she could probably pull it up and
let it blouse over the belt a bit more than the designer
intended. Dollie had done Lilian's hair for her, arranging
it round her face and into a rather low chignon that was
both becoming and fashionable.

Before dinner Will and Lilian returned to the luxurious
bedroom in order to change into their evening clothes.
Luckily they had allowed plenty of time, for their
preparations were to be lengthily interrupted. Lilian was
anxious. Suppose she were less desirable than before.
She felt sure she must be. Her breasts, which had been
so delightfully rounded when she was feeding Sylvia,
were now flatter than ever. At first they'd had a
withered look which was not at all attractive, as though
the skin was too much for what it contained. They were
smoother now, but still inadequate. Then, the area of
her body she referred to mentally as 'down below' must
be permanently stretched. She knew her tightness had
been a source of pleasure for Will, and now it wasn't
there. Only years later did she marvel at her own
subservient attitude. It was he who had brought about
these changes; why then should she feel shame and fear
because of them?

Ever since their arrival at the Granville Lilian had
been eager to make use of the well-appointed bathroom
she had glimpsed as they passed along the corridor. The
huge white bath with its gleaming mahogany surround
invited her. At York Road there had been a small cold
apartment where a terrifying geyser heated water for

each member of the family to take a bath once a week. At Shelley Street a zinc 'bungalow bath' hung on a hook outside the back door. It was very rarely used, because the whole process of lighting the fire under the brick built 'copper' that took up half the scullery, baling out the boiling water with an enamel jug, and then adding cold from the tap, was exhausting, dangerous, and expensive. Afterwards the bath had to be emptied with the jug into a bucket, which in turn was emptied into the sink. When only an inch or two of water remained the bath could be carried out into the yard and the last drops poured down the drain before it was returned to its hook on the wall. This final operation needed two people and was extremely awkward, the bath which was four feet long and eighteen inches wide being one of the most unwieldy objects ever made. In Lilian's early days with the Timms family, Rosie had felt obliged to offer the doubtful luxury of a soak in the scullery every week or so, and after Lilian had gone upstairs in her dressing-gown Dollie, Nance and finally Rosie herself would take advantage of the opportunity to immerse themselves in cooling scummy water.

But as time went on the intervals between the bathing sessions grew longer, and longer, until Rosie eventually gave up offering to make the necessary preparation, and Lilian, knowing what a trouble it was, did not like to ask. She made do with carrying extra hot water up to her bedroom once a week and washing all over, but it wasn't the same.

So she announced her intention of taking a bath before dinner, but Will had different ideas.

'Haven't we got better things to do? Haven't you missed me?'

'Yes ... but let me have a bath first.'

She might not even be properly clean. She knew she smelled sometimes, under her arms and between her legs; at least she must have a wash, and she could not do her private washing with him in the room.

'No, Will.' She drew away from his embrace. 'There's plenty of time. I ... don't feel clean. You know what it's like at Rosie's, and we've got the whole night.'

'You'll be clean enough for me. You smell like a real woman. I don't want it all washed away. You can have a bath in the morning.'

A real woman. Hadn't she been a real woman all along? For some reason her mind was suddenly filled with the image of the gypsy, full-bosomed, swarthy, with heavy braids of black greasy hair.

He was freer with her than he had ever been before, kissing, sucking, licking every part, doing things that it had never occurred to her anyone would ever want to do. Did wives enjoy these outlandish caresses, she asked herself? Would Louisa permit him to explore her most secret crevices with his tongue? Or was it only mistresses, like herself and Dollie, that were expected to surrender every last shred of themselves in this way? She worried too, about the possibility of 'falling for a baby' as Rosie called it.

'Don't fall for another baby, love. Make sure he uses something,' Rosie had warned her, but Lilian did not know what she meant, what it was he ought to use. She could have asked Dollie, as she had for some time intended, but the opportunity for private talks were very limited in that small over-populated house, and none arose before she had to hurry away to catch her train.

Will always left her a split second before the stuff came, which was often the last thing she wanted at the time. But it was the stuff that made you have babies.

Better to feel it spurt warm and sticky onto your stomach than let it reach the dark mysterious place inside where babies started. But she already had Sylvia, so on at least one occasion he had not been in time.

When they went down to dinner she felt conspicuous, wondering if anyone would notice her crushed lips, and the awkward gait that was due to the bruised and swollen feeling between her legs, but still she was happier than she had been for months, for obviously he still loved her. Perhaps she and Sylvia would not be living at Rosie's much longer. After all, as soon as business was brisker, when the summer visitors came in full force, she really would ask him for a little house of her own, just a tiny cottage, where he could come as often as he liked and where Sylvia as she grew up would have a garden to play in, and nice children to play with. Then when Louisa died, and after all she must be getting on for seventy, and had nearly used up her allotted span which was all anyone could expect, then they could get married.

Over dinner Will told her about the art galleries he had visited in London, and about the ballet he had seen, something else she would enjoy. He would arrange a couple of days, he said, in the autumn. Meanwhile he chose the wine with care, translated the menu for her, and treated her with courtesy and respect.

After dinner there was more music in the Palm Court while they drank their coffee, then Will astonished her by disappearing into the card room for the rest of the evening, in order to play bridge. Lilian was left with a magazine to listen to selections from *The Mikado* and *The Vagabond King,* feeling cross and neglected, until it suddenly occurred to her that she could be enjoying the bathroom. At the door of the card room she tried to catch Will's eye, but he was absorbed in the game, so it was useless to try and signal her intention.

Well, let him find out. All the better if he sought her in the lounge and in the bedroom and wondered if she had run away. But nothing of the sort happened. When at last he came upstairs she was sitting at the dressing-table, buffing her nails, and enjoying the sole possession of so much luxury.

He kissed her casually, stroking her shoulders. 'Pity you don't play bridge,' he observed. 'You ought to learn.'

Lilian knew that the Fitzgeralds often gave or attended bridge parties, and Alice and Harold had been fond of a game of whist, but she herself was bored by card games, which seemed to her a pointless waste of time, when you could be reading, or talking about something interesting.

'Why don't you take it up? Louisa would teach you. We often need somebody to make up a four.'

Impossible man. Suggesting his wife teach her to play bridge. For someone so fastidious and sensitive he appeared to be devoid of fine feelings.

'I can't be bothered with cards.'

'You don't know what you're missing. Do you want a drink? You've only to ring the bell.' Lilian did not really want anything, which seemed a pity when so much was available. After some discussion they ordered a bottle of wine. A waiter brought it, pale gold and sparkling, in a bucket of ice. It was almost as good as champagne.

They rose late on the Monday morning. After a hasty shopping expedition and an excellent lunch, Will put Lilian on the train for Culvergate. He would take a later one himself. At the station he kissed her, and told her not to be late for work the next day. They'd had a

splendid time and would have to repeat it before too
long. He even stood on the platform waving, as the train
drew out. He was still her own beloved Will, the kindest
of men and the best company in the world. Happily she
settled back in her 'Ladies Only' compartment, seeing
herself in a few years' time. Mrs Fitzgerald, Phyllis's
stepmother! That would be a joke. She supposed she
would have to become a Catholic, and found she rather
liked the idea. It was true she had only once been inside
the Roman Catholic Church of St Austin, on the
occasion of Phyllis's wedding, but the elaborate ritual
had appealed to her sense of theatre.

Then she wondered about Sylvia whom she had never
before left for a night. In a little over an hour she would
be with her baby again. It was strange to be looking
forward to the kitchen at Shelley Street after her brief
taste of luxury, but it would be pleasant to hold Sylvia
on her lap and chat peacefully to Rosie over a cup of tea
before the others got home. Rosie's admiration and
respect always gave Lilian a pleasant sense of super-
iority which Dollie, friendly and interested as she was,
would not allow her. They were on a level, as far as
Dollie was concerned. But of course, she was wrong.

CHAPTER 5

So began a pattern that endured for nearly three years. Years in which Lilian never really knew where she was. On her return to the shop on the Tuesday morning after that first weekend all was as usual. After her cup of tea with Elsie she began her routine of dusting and checking stock. If she expected a warmer than usual greeting from Will she was disappointed. His 'Good morning Miss Watts,' as he went into his office was briskly impersonal, and for most of the day he was off the premises. During the following week he spent an unprecedented amount of time upstairs, or closeted with Jim in his cubby-hole. Lilian remembered how he had said 'We must do this again,' and decided he had changed his mind. Did his wife suspect? Since Louisa Fitzgerald seldom did more than pass through the shop on her way out it was quite likely that she had not noticed Lilian's absence from work on the previous day. But if they were found out, would not Will be forced to give her the sack? Perhaps not, for surely then he would have to return her money. It no longer seemed possible that he might provide her with a home of her own, however small. In

fact he was so aloof that she could not imagine herself
so much as referring to the situation between them.

Gradually, however, he modified his attitude, becoming more relaxed and friendly, discussing business
matters freely, once even asking after Sylvia and
promising to come and see her, when Jim was out of
hearing. This was Lilian's opportunity to mention her
hopes of moving, but he had left her to speak to a
customer before she could formulate the words. There
was almost never a chance to speak to him in private.
Even on Friday nights when the staff received their pay-
packets he always called her and Jim into the office
together. Then one afternoon he came up behind her as
she was replacing a cut-glass vase on a high shelf and
said quietly, 'The two fifty-five on Sunday afternoon.
Same as before. I'll meet you,' and it all happened again.
So it went on, scarcely planned in advance, never with
any certainty, but gloriously enjoyable once they were in
Warne Bay. The comforts of the hotel combined with
Will's being his real self, lively and full of interesting
talk, made Lilian feel like a queen, or at least like a
married woman. In spite of the changed manner which
he adopted after their return to Culvergate she could
live in the after-glow for a week or two, scarcely considering the future. Then the anxiety would begin. Had he
tired of her? Was there someone else? Once she was
kept in suspense for nearly three months. Each Friday
morning she would awaken with the thought that
perhaps today would be the day, that by evening she
would have something to look forward to, she would
know that he still loved her. She had no thought for the
course her life might take, except for the vague belief
that some day they would marry. Apart from Sylvia she
thought of little other than the visit to Warne Bay just

past, or the possible excursion to come. Admittedly
there were occasions when she was forced to worry
about the non-arrival of her period but invariably the
flow of blood started before the situation became
desperate. A private conversation with Dollie had
yielded the fact that there were such things as 'French
letters', but as Dollie had pointed out, Will's religion
would certainly preclude their use. In any case Lilian
could hardly see herself recommending such a pre-
caution; it would make her seem too worldly wise, too
experienced.

So the cycle of anticipation, then pleasure and its
aftermath, followed by slowly growing anxiety was
repeated, while life in other areas, in Shelley Street and
visits to Mabel, went uneventfully along.

Sylvia grew into a self-willed toddler, enchanting
when she got her own way, which was most of the time,
since everyone at Shelley Street adored her. Even Dollie,
the sworn hater of babies and children, made an exception for fair-haired, blue-eyed Sylvia. She and George
were peaceful playmates, since George always gave in.
He was too docile for his own good, and certainly for
Sylvia's. Nearly four, he was still pale and podgy,
though sweeter smelling now that he was out of
nappies. Rosie bathed them together most evenings in a
small oval tub in front of the kitchen fire. Rosie herself
changed too. She had begun to care about her appearance again. Her hair, washed more often, was softly
arranged, and she made herself one or two dresses in
the new simple style that even a beginner could run up
on a sewing machine. Sometimes she and Lilian would
walk out together on a Sunday afternoon, with Sylvia in
the big pram, and George walking until he grew tired,
when he was crammed in at the opposite end. She

bought a new hat, deep-crowned, trimmed with whirls
of braid, like limpets, and found a decent coat in a
church jumble sale. She looked quite a trim little figure,
and if old school friends or acquaintances of Lilian's
approached, her presence discouraged their starting
conversations which might have proved embarrassing.
They usually walked down to the front, and along as far
as the Fort, because Rosie always liked to look in
Fitzgerald's window and Lilian would tell her the prices
of the different pieces of jewellery that glittered behind
the protective grille. When darkness fell the stock would
be further protected by heavy wooden shutters which it
was Charlie's job to take down and put up, even on
Sundays.

Both women enjoyed these strolls. For Lilian they
helped to pass the time between visits to Warne Bay, but
this was not her real life. Walking along with the
children and Rosie was merely marking time, although
she was pleased when passersby glanced admiringly at
her pretty little daughter. But she knew that for Rosie
these afternoons were something to be looked forward
to, and remembered with pride. She would lay a
proprietary hand on the handle of the big pram as Lilian
pushed and exclaim loudly over the display in Fitzgerald's window, letting anyone nearby know that Lilian
was employed in the establishment and that therefore
she too was linked with this temple of luxury. Sometimes, in summer, they paid for deckchairs, and sat
down to listen to the band. Once they saw Will walking
towards them along the promenade, with his wife and
daughter, fashionably dressed, one on either side of
him. Rosie would have walked boldly ahead but Lilian
insisted on escaping up a side road. It was not
surprising, everyone in Culvergate walked along the

promenade on summer Sundays, but usually it was so crowded by visitors that it was easy to pass unnoticed.

'You ought to have faced him out,' said Rosie. 'You've got nothing to be ashamed of.' But Lilian knew better.

Because she was happier, and had a little more money than before the advent of Lilian, Rosie appeared to have more energy. She polished the kitchen range and whitened the front step. The floor of the lavatory was scrubbed and rolls of coarse crinkly paper took the place of newspaper for use in that noisome closet. She could not train her sons to refrain from dripping onto the floor, and Nance always wet the seat because she waited until the last minute, but still, it was better than before. Sometimes Lilian marvelled at herself. A couple of years ago the place had seemed appalling, now she was quite at home there. She could not be on easy terms with Ned or Albert, but they were seldom in the house. She knew that Rosie liked and admired her but it was the company of Dollie that she most enjoyed. Full of racy chat and lively anecdotes, Rosie's eldest never returned from her work at Collingham's without some fresh proof of the idiocy or snobbery of some customer in the millinery department to which she had recently been promoted, or some example of the way she or another assistant outwitted the unpopular buyer, Miss Wiles.

'And all the time she'd got it on back to front. Laugh! I nearly wet myself. And she puts on this special face whenever she looks in the morror, with her eyes wide open and her mouth screwed up small. Must think she's Clara Bow, or something. And there's old Wily, blooming near kissing the ground, since she's so glad to have got rid of a hat she's had in stock since the year one. "What did you say about where it was faded?" she says. "Oh, I told her it was shaded," says I. "Oh deah,

Ay don't think you ought to tell lies," she says, the silly cow. "Not really a lie," I told her, "I only changed two letters." It took her about an hour and a half to see what I was getting at, and then she nearly smiled. Not quite though, she didn't want to crack her face. Well, they say there's a customer for everything and it must be true, that hat had been through two summer sales to my certain knowledge. And d'you think they'll give me double commission? I said to her, "I reckon I ought to have double commission on that, seeing we couldn't sell it at a discount, and now I've got full price for it," and d'you know what she said, the old cow? "Your job is to sell, Miss Timms. That is what you are paid for, and very well paid too, if you ask me." "Well, you could ask," I said. "I mean, it'll help the department's figures, a good sale like that." "The department's figures are my concern," she says, all snooty-like, "selling hats is yours. We don't dock your pay every time you lose a customer, so you can't expect extra when you make a good sale. And now perhaps you'll tidy that counter. Really there are hats everywhere, I don't know why you can't put them away as you go along." Ha! I know her, she'll tell old Hardcastle *she* sold it and get a few bob extra herself.'

Really, Dollie was as good as a book. They all said so, Lilian and Rosie and Nance, as they drank their tea, sitting round in the kitchen with their elbows on the table. So when Dollie stopped amusing them and became subdued, morose even, it was very noticeable. She snapped at everyone and had no stories to tell. Rosie worried, and confided her worries to Lilian, but neither of them dared to ask questions of this changed Dollie, whose bad moods had hitherto been so transient. The evening tea-time lost its savour, and Lilian, tired in any case from the long day on her feet and the hurried walks back and forth, took to going up to bed early with a novel from the library.

On that Saturday evening in early autumn she was not actually reading. The book, chosen for her by Rosie, failed to hold her interest. Sylvia had a cold, and snuffled in her sleep. She was restless, throwing off her blankets. Lilian rose quietly, to cover her. Having tucked her in firmly she stood, looking down at her little daughter and thinking of the approaching winter, with all the depressing difficulties and ailments it would certainly bring. The kitchen and scullery would be festooned with damp washing for most of the time, with not only the drying rack above the range but the clothes horse and the high fire-guard all pressed into service. There would be constant anxiety about the proper airing of sheets and underwear, and a choice would frequently have to be made between clean, but possibly damp garments, and dry but grubby ones that had been worn for a week or more. The summer just past had been a poor one. Sylvia had not been 'built up' as she had hoped, and now this cold would drag her down, giving her a bad start. And Georgie caught cold so easily, invariably passing his germs on to Sylvia, coughing all over the place.

You could not expect children to go all winter without colds, there was no hope of that, but to succumb so early in the season was worrying. The child coughed, chestily. Supposing it was whooping cough? Not yet, please God, not yet. Let it wait until she's older. Of course she was bound to catch the dreaded illness sooner or later. A few children escaped it, but then they would have no resistance to it as adults, which was even worse.

Lilian remembered having whooping cough herself, at the age of seven. She had been nursed, for some reason, in her parents' bedroom. Perhaps because it was warmer there, or so that her mother could be with her at night. She saw herself standing up at the foot of the big bed, grasping the brass rail as the paroxysm came upon her. She had tried to call out, desperate to cling to her mother for reassurance while she fought for breath. Would Sylvia have to suffer the endless choking cough, that racked and exhausted; make those agonizing efforts to draw breath and hear the fearful sound of the whoop as she tried to suck in air that somehow could not reach her lungs?

And each time there would be, if she was old enough to understand, the conviction that she would die, that this time the coughing would never stop.

Usually the paroxysms had ended with vomiting, followed by exhaustion from which the child Lilian had only begun to recover before the onset of the next bout. Her mother had run up the stairs to hold her as soon as she heard the coughing begin. Once, only once, as far as Lilian could remember, had she failed to do this. Forced to go out shopping, she had left Harold in charge during his dinner-hour, with firm instructions to go to Lilian as soon as he heard her. Perhaps it was her strangled cry of 'Mummy' when she knew perfectly well that her mother was out of the house that irritated him. He did go to the bedroom, but once there, instead of offering her the physical and moral support she so needed, he stood watching her with an expression of disgust, while she coughed and retched and struggled for breath. Finally, because he was too late offering her the bowl, she was sick on the floor.

When Alice returned she found Lilian sobbing and

calling for her, while Harold, in his black overcoat, walked up and down the path in the back garden. As she cleaned up the rug and the patterned linoleum she promised the child that she would not leave the house again until the cough was gone.

Lilian wondered if she had remonstrated with Harold. Probably not. He was like that and you had to accept it. Alice had kept her word, and remained at home for the next three weeks.

But if Sylvia caught the whooping cough she would have to leave her to Rosie, and Rosie would have Georgie, they were bound to be ill at the same time. Lilian sighed, told herself that the child had nothing more than a bad cold, tucked her in gently, and returned to her own bed. With her own blankets, snowy sheets, and a white embroidered spread that had been Alice's, it looked inviting. The cracked basin and ewer had been replaced by a pretty set with pink flowers, and though the street outside was as squalid as ever, the room itself was clean and reasonably comfortable, if cold. The high bed creaked as Lilian climbed in and settled herself luxuriously in the middle. It was nice to have a double bed all to one's self. She was about to blow out the candle when there was a soft tap at the door. Lilian expected to see Rosie. It was not unusual for her landlady to visit her for a late night chat about life and the difficulties it brought, but it was Dollie who entered the room, shivering, in her pink artificial silk nightdress.

'Doll! What's wrong?'

'I should have thought you could guess that. Oh, Lily, I'm blowed if I know what to do.'

Could this be the worldly-wise, cynical Dollie, not knowing what to do?

'Oh, Lord, you're not ...'

'If you mean have I caught on, of course I have. It was bound to happen sooner or later. I've been going with Arthur Leeson for four years, you can't be lucky for ever.'

'But you said ... I mean ... I thought ...'

'Well it doesn't always work, does it? Look, you're not to tell Mum about this. Poor old Ma, she's got enough on her plate as it is.'

'But what are you going to do?'

'Get rid of it, of course, what d'you think?'

'How?'

'Hot bath. Drop of gin. Jump off the kitchen table a few times.'

'Supposing that's no good?'

'Then I'll have to go round to old mother Alcock in Keats Passage.'

'What can she do?'

'Never you mind. Look, I want you to get mum out of the way tomorrow afternoon. She'll heat up the copper in the morning, ready to put the washing in soak, and I've bought some gin. I'll have a boiling hot bath and with any luck it'll bring me on.'

'Doll, Arthur Leeson isn't married, is he? Well, couldn't he ...'

'Him? Marry me? He's too bloomin' comfortable as he is, with all his money to spend and his old mother to look after him.'

'But if you told ...'

'No. He's not got to know anything about it. I can look after myself. Though I'm not saying if Mr Right came along I might not think otherwise. I suppose I'll have to give Artie the chuck one of these days, but not just yet. He's good fun to go out with, and he's not close-fisted, I'll say that for him. You'll get Mum and the kids out on Sunday afternoon so that I can stew myself, will you?'

'Well, if it's not raining we'll go for a walk, though Sylvia's got a rotten cold. Won't she see that you've used all the hot water out of the copper?'

'I'll worry about that when the time comes. Do your best Lil, it's got to be soon or it'll be no good.'

Dollie was sitting beside Lilian, on top of the bedclothes. She shivered. 'I suppose I'd better get back,' she said, but she didn't move.

'You're cold. Come in and get warm.'

Lilian moved over and Dollie slid in beside her.

'Oh, Lord, ain't it rotten being a girl?' She sniffed, brushing the back of her hand across her eyes. Lilian felt under the pillow for her handkerchief.

'Don't cry, Doll. I'll help you. I expect it'll be all right. Though ...'

'Though what?'

'Well, Sylvia's all right. I wouldn't be without her now. Perhaps ...'

'Go ahead and have it? No fear, not me. I hate kids. And anyway, you've got your old Will Fitzgerald behind you. He's rich. I know what Artie'll do. He'll drop me like a hot cake if he hears I'm in the family way. And I like him, blast it. Oh, damn everything!'

Lilian put her arms round Dollie, and laid her cheek against her hair. 'I know, dear. It's not fair.'

Dollie drew a long shuddering breath and snuggled closer.

'I say, this is nice, Lil,' she said with sudden cheerfulness, 'what say we do without men altogether? What do we need them for?'

'Well. I suppose we do need them.' Lilian gave an embarrassed giggle.

'Get on with you. Anything Will could do for you I could do better. After all, I'd know what it felt like, wouldn't I?'

'But we couldn't. We're both girls. How could we?'

'Easily.' She pulled down Lilian's nightdress and laid her head on the bared shoulder. 'There's two girls at work who live like that. Well, we call them girls. Miss Francis must be at least thirty-five and Miss Fisher's even older. We call them Fanny and Finny. The other girls laugh at them behind their backs, but I think it's not such a bad idea.'

She replaced her head on the pillow and lay looking up at the ceiling, her arms behind her head. 'What about it, Lil? We could be like a married couple. You can stay at home and look after the babies, and I'll go to work. At least we could be sure of not having any more kids.'

'Don't be silly, Doll, people don't really do that.'

'Don't they just.'

Lilian felt Dollie's hand travel gently down her body and start to pull up her nightdress. A wave of heat swept over her, and she was also aware of the weak dissolving sensation that Will's touch brought about in her. She sat up. 'Dollie, stop it. I don't like it. Stop.'

'Cowardy cowardy custard.' Dollie sang the words softly, but Sylvia stirred and began to grizzle. The two young women in the bed were immediately quiet, but it was too late. The child having been thoroughly disturbed and feeling far from well, the grizzle developed into a wail, and the wail into a howl. Lilian had to take her up.

Dollie swung her feet out onto the cold lino. 'You'll get Mum out of the way, will you, tomorrow afternoon?'

'If I can. But I think you ought to tell her.'

'No. And you're not to either'.

'Goodnight, then.'

Dollie laughed sardonically and closed the door quietly behind her. Lilian sat Sylvia on her little enamelled chamber pot, waited for what seemed hours for her to produce a few drops of urine, replaced the towelling napkin and rubber knickers the child still wore at night, and took her into the big bed before at last blowing out the candle.

Sylvia, warm and comforted, fell asleep at once, but her mother lay for nearly an hour, thinking about Dollie, and the extraordinary things she knew and talked about. Of course women couldn't marry each other, but still, if they could it might often work out quite well. Women were easier to be with than men. You didn't have to try so hard, and it didn't matter all that much what you looked like. She wouldn't have to worry nearly so much about her nose, either its largeness, or its propensity of turning red in cold weather. But on the other hand you wouldn't be anybody, just a pair of spinsters, though Miss Watts and Miss Timms would hardly qualify for that title.

She imagined them growing elderly together, two funny old things like the Misses Porter who lived at the top of York Road. Their meanness, which was really their poverty, was a byword, and their hats which they retrimmed every season, a joke. In any case she must marry Will. It was only a question of time. She must be married to Sylvia's father, thereby acquiring status and respectability. She saw herself sitting on committees, organizing charity concerts, opening bazaars and graciously receiving bouquets of flowers. Doing everything, in fact, that Louisa Fitzgerald did. She knew that people whispered about her now, as her parents had whispered gossip when she was a child. Understanding in retrospect, she had learnt that gossip could be lived down, and as the fast Miss Pilbeam whose parents owned the York Hotel had married well and settled down to be a pillar of society, so could she. No, she must not give up, because in the end it would be all right, because overriding everything was the simple fact that she and Will loved each other. But Dollie's case was different and Lilian sincerely hoped that the hot bath and the gin would serve their purpose, although it seemed wrong. She held Sylvia a little closer and stroked the damp fair hair. Please God, she thought, don't let it be whooping cough.

Sunday afternoon did not go according to plan. Sylvia seemed slightly better, but the wind was cold. She could not possibly be taken out, even in the pram.

Dollie sulked unreasonably when this was explained to her, but the situation was saved when Rosie announced her intention of going to call on her sister, Violet. This she rarely did, conscious of her social inferiority to the successful boarding-house keeper, but today she felt equal to the project. She had lit the fire under the copper as she always did on Sunday morning, so she could soak the washing overnight, and as soon as her mother was out of the house Dollie stoked it up, increasing the draught so that it roared away. Nancy was bribed to keep the children amused, and Ned and Albert went to hang about in the market place or down by the harbour among their friends.

With Lilian's help Dollie took the zinc bath from its hook outside the back door, and dragged it into the scullery. Long unused, it was grimy and inhabited by several spiders. She screamed and giggled as Lilian tried to catch them in a piece of rag. Finally she bailed the near-boiling water out of the copper with a saucepan while Lilian added cold from the tap by means of the enamel washing-up bowl. When the water in the bath had been reduced to a bearable temperature she began to throw off her clothes and Lilian retired tactfully into the kitchen, only to be urgently recalled. Dollie had forgotten the gin, which she believed it necessary to consume, diluted with very hot water, whilst actually in the tub.

'Cripes, this is hot! Look at me!'

She pulled herself up, showing that the lower half of her body was bright red, whilst the top was a slightly mauvish white. Lilian averted her eyes. Such immodesty made her uncomfortable, particularly after their strange conversation on the previous night. She went quickly to fetch the gin, poured some into a cup, added water from the kettle that was permanently on the back of the kitchen range, and delivered it to her friend.

'Why don't you keep me company? It's bad manners to drink alone.'

'Oh, I don't know. I've never had gin.'

'Course you have, you've had cocktails, haven't you, at that posh hotel you go to? Well, they're mostly gin. Help yourself.'

'Oh, well, if it's just the stuff they put in cocktails . . .'

Lilian fetched another cup and poured herself a rather small drink. This time she remained in the scullery, leaning against the copper where she had no view of anything more indelicate than Dollie's back.

'Cheers!' said Dollie, raising her cup.

'Cheers!' responded Lilian. She sipped the neat gin carefully but soon began to feel warm and relaxed.

'D'you come here often, Miss Watts?' Dollie drank eagerly, her little finger sticking out in mock refinement. 'Charming place, this is. And so many well-known people. Why, I do declare here's Lady Fitzgerald dead drunk under the table ...'

They exploded with laughter as Dollie went from outrage to outrage. Lilian lounged against the sink, feeling strangely carefree.

'Who else is there?' she asked, eager for more.

'Well, of course that's the Prince of Wales over in the corner, spooning with the honourable Lilian Watts. They say she's to be his next mistress, you know. Personally, I wouldn't have him if he was served up on toast, but then she always did like the upper classes. Oh, she's very ladylike our Miss Watts, though what she gets up to ...' Dollie paused for a gulp of gin and water. 'What I like about us is, we're so refined. It's terribly important to be refined, don't you think so, deah? Perhaps you would care to wash my back, in a very refined way?'

'Oh, Doll you are a scream, honestly!'

Wiping her eyes with the back of her hand, Lilian took the soapy flannel that Dollie offered her just as the door opened and Rosie appeared.

'What's going on? Have you gone and used all my hot water? What are you doing having a bath at this time of day?'

Then she saw Lilian's cup on the draining board, picked it up and sniffed gin. She knew what that meant.

'My gawd, Doll, you're not ... you're never ...'

'Oh, mind your own business, Ma, can't you? I didn't want you to know.'

'Didn't want me to know? What are you trying to do, drown it? Get out of that bath. You can boil yourself all you like, it won't make any difference. I know, I've tried. And what d'you think you're doing Lilian, out here in all this steam? Your clothes'll be damp through. That'll be a

great help, you getting rheumatic fever. Get upstairs and
get out of that frock.'

Startled and ashamed, Lilian pushed past Rosie and
did as she was told. When she returned to the kitchen
she could hear Dollie bailing out the bath water and
went to help her.

'You stop here. Let her get on with it.'

Obediently Lilian closed the scullery door. She picked
up Sylvia from the grubby hearthrug and wiped her
nose. The child protested vigorously and struggled.

'Put her down for God's sake,' said Rosie.

Again Lilian did as she was told. Where was the
politeness, the touch of deference, with which Rosie had
treated her hitherto? Yet she was not affronted. She was
virtually a member of the family and Rosie was within
her rights.

'How long has she known?'

'Oh, not long. I think it's only a week or two.'

They should not be talking like this in front of Nance,
but Rosie seemed past caring.

'That fool Leeson. I thought he was looking after
her. They'll have to get married. I'll go and see his
mother.'

Lilian wondered what Dollie would have to say about
that, but when she entered the room, half-dressed,
flushed from the hot water and alcohol her mother said
nothing about such a plan, merely saying that neither of
them was to go out into the cold, and the bath was to be
left for the boys to take outside.

They had their tea in silence, all sitting round the
table. The cloth was laid, and plates and knives. Saucers
were provided except for the children who used enamel
mugs, but there were no plates of thin bread and butter
such as Lilian would have liked to see. Instead the loaf

was placed on the breadboard, beside the dish of Blue
Band margarine, and they cut slices and spread them as
required. There was jam, Tickler's, the cheapest you
could buy, popularly supposed to consist of boiled
vegetable marrow, colouring, and chips of wood for
pips. Still, it was sweet, and all right when you were
hungry. Rosie could have afforded something better,
now, with Lilian's money coming in, and Albert in
work, but the habit of poverty was strong upon her, and
though some small comforts had appeared, good quality
jam was not one of them, for she was saving up for a
rainy day. When tea was finished Rosie told Nance to
take the crockery into the scullery, and put the kettle on
for the washing-up. Sensing that Dollie was destined for
a good talking-to, Lilian said she might as well get
Sylvia ready for bed.

'You can stay where you are,' said Rosie, and it was
more of an order than a giving of permission. Lilian sat
down again, forced to listen while mother questioned
daughter. Eventually castor oil was prescribed. Dollie
protested, saying that she already had pains, that the
hot bath and the gin would do the trick, but Rosie went
over to the corner cupboard, took out the lethal bottle
and poured a thick and generous measure.

'I can't drink the blooming stuff like that,' groaned
Dollie. 'It's effin' awful. 'Avn't you got a drop of
brandy?'

'You watch your tongue, my girl. You needn't think
I'm wasting brandy on you. Get it down you.'

Rosie stood threateningly over her daughter.

'Oh Christ,' said Dollie, swallowing most of the stuff,
'I'm going to be sick.'

'And keep it down,' added Rosie. 'You can if you
make up your mind.'

So Dollie made up her mind, and kept it down, and spent most of Monday in the lavatory, instead of at Collingham's. She was still there when Lilian arrived home from work. Rosie was ironing in the kitchen.

'Is she . . . has she . . .?'

'She hasn't come on, if that's what you mean. She's like me. Once it's there it's stuck for good and all. I was just the same.'

Rosie spoke with gloomy pride, and Lilian, thinking of Dollie sitting out there in the dark smelly outhouse, her bottom sore from the rough cheap paper, was filled with pity. Rosie banged the iron down angrily on a flannelette shirt.

'I shall go round and see his mother. He'll have to marry her, that's all. Dollie's never been with anyone else, that I do know.' Just then Dollie staggered in through the scullery.

'You'll do nothing of the sort Ma, so shut up.' She sat down heavily, white faced and dishevelled. 'Give us a cup of tea, for Gawd's sake. This time next week it'll all be over.'

The next day she went to work, and was late home. Rosie was putting on her hat to go and look for her, when she returned, whiter-faced than ever, and said she felt poorly. She went straight up to bed, and Lilian took up a bowl of bread and milk Rosie made. She was momentarily shocked at the shabbiness and undisguised poverty of this room which she had never before had occasion to enter. The other rooms, her own, the kitchen and the front parlour had all been made brighter and more comfortable during the two years of her stay, but this one was apparently unchanged. She stood looking down at Dollie, saw how her hand trembled as she raised the spoon to her lips.

'I s'pose I'll have to eat some of this muck to keep Mum quiet.'

'Don't do anything else to get rid of it, Doll, you'll only make yourself ill. I'll help you. You can have all Sylvia's things. That'll help a lot.'

'Thanks, you're a real pal, but I shan't need them. I'll be all right now.'

'What d'you mean?'

'I've been round the corner.'

'Round the corner?'

'To old mother Alcock. Where all the bad girls go.'

'Doll! It's dangerous, you shouldn't have. What did she do?'

'You really want me to tell you?'

'No ...'

'Well, you lie there with your legs apart on her filthy old sofa, and she gets this thing ...'

'No ... don't ...'

'And she sticks it right up you, and Christ, it hurts, and then she says go home, it'll start in a few hours, so I'm waiting. And don't you tell Mum, either. It won't be much worse than usual.'

It was considerably worse than usual. When the clotted blood started to flow from Dollie about two o'clock that morning she and her mother were both frightened enough to call Lilian.

She scrambled out of bed and put on the dark blue silk kimono that had been a present from Will in the Victoria Lodge days. The metallic gold flowers and dragons glowed with incongruous luxury in the crowded little back bedroom. Light was provided by a single candle in a chipped enamel candlestick that stood on a chair. The landlord's munificence had not extended to putting in the gas upstairs. Dollie lay in the middle of the bed, white-faced, her hair damp with sweat. At the foot sat Nance, in her winceyette nightdress, her bare grubby feet dangling. Georgie slept odoriferously in his cot in the corner. These three items of furniture, with the addition of a yellow-stained chest of drawers, virtually filled the little room. To reach the window it would be necessary to climb over the bed, since the cot was jammed between it and the wall. There was a six-inch space on the other side, just enough to stand in, if you were slim, when you made the bed. Narrow porridge-coloured curtains were drawn over the dark space of the window, inadequate to keep out the night. The blankets were old grey ones with red borders, but the calico sheets were very white. Rosie was always proud of her washing. Dollie had been sick on the flowered quilt, which was now bundled into a corner.

Rosie pulled back the bedclothes, revealing the pool of blood in which Dollie lay, despite the fact that she had padded herself well with an old towel.

'The mattress is ruined.'

'Never mind that, Mum, I'll get another.'

Dollie looked up at Lilian. 'Bit of a mess, innit? I don't know what she wanted to wake you for. I'll be all right in the morning.'

There were steps on the stairs. Albert, sleeping fitfully on the couch downstairs, had been roused by the sound of people moving about over his head. He squeezed into the room, his hair on end, a stubble of beard fuzzing his jawbone. Lilian noticed that he was wearing the same shirt he had worn all day.

'What's up?'

'It's Doll. She's been to Keats Passage, the fool.'

'Shall I go for the doctor?'

'No, no, I don't want no doctor. Go back to bed,

Albie, and mind your own business.'

Dollie gasped as a spasm of pain gripped her.

'We can't get him now, I've got no clean sheets. What will he think if he sees us like this?' But Rosie went to the chest of drawers, and searched through it as if hoping to find bed linen whose existence she had not hitherto suspected.

Lilian took Dollie's sweating hand in hers.

'That doesn't really matter. In any case I've got some in my trunk, though they might be damp. We'd have to air them. But we ought to get him.'

'No!' Dollie pulled away her hand. 'You keep out of it, Lily Watts. It's nothing to do with you.'

'Dollie, don't speak to Lilian like that.'

'Never mind, Dollie dear. You aren't well, I know you aren't. You must let Albert get the doctor. Something might have gone wrong.'

'Gone wrong! You're right there. My whole bloody life's gone wrong. Give us a drink of water, and shut up.'

'Get some water, Nance.'

Nancy demurred, pulling her feet up under her.

'It's cold, and I ain't got no slippers. Can't Albie go?'

'Can't you see when somebody's ill, you little cow?'

Rosie tried to push the girl off the bed but Albert had already gone downstairs, glad of an excuse to leave the room. She beckoned Lilian out onto the tiny square of landing, closing the door.

'I don't know what to do for the best. It's against the law, what she's done. And I haven't had a chance to get ready for the doctor. What shall I look like? I reckon she'll be all right till morning, don't you? If it hasn't stopped by seven Albert can go round. I don't think she's feverish, her forehead's as cold as stone.'

'She's lost an awful lot of blood ...'

'But in the middle of the night? I reckon we should hang on till morning.'

Albert came back upstairs with water in a cup. 'Shall I run for Doctor Bradley? What do you say, Mum?'

Wide awake now he seemed to be enjoying the excitement, perhaps imagining himself as he ran through the dark streets and banged on the door of the doctor's house. Lilian took the cup and went in to Dollie.

'If you get the doctor round here I won't see him. I'm not letting that horrible old man get his hands on me. Give us a drink.'

'Dollie, I really think ...'

'The pain's going off now. The blood'll get less soon. Find a towel or something will you, Lil, there's some in the chest.'

Lilian opened the bottom drawer. To her surprise it was full of clean-folded towels and tablecloths. Dollie raised herself on one elbow.

'Don't touch those things. That's all Mum's best stuff. Try the next drawer up.'

Lilian found what she sought and closed the drawer. Nance, huddled at the bottom of the bed, shivered and Lilian took pity on her.

'You go and get into my bed, there's no sense in you sitting there all night. Don't wake Sylvia.'

Nancy obeyed at once, and Lilian, thinking of the unwashed feet sliding between her own sheets, shuddered inwardly, but there was no help for it. Rosie re-entered.

'I've put the kettle on. Thought we could all do with a cup of tea. That's not one of my best towels you've got there, is it? I don't know what we're going to do about the mattress. Have to burn it. Make a bonfire in the

yard. That's a good way of telling the whole street what
you've been up to.'

'Mum ...' Dollie turned her face away, tears on her
cheeks. Lilian wiped them away with her own handkerchief.

'It's all right Doll, your Mum's just upset.'

'Upset. Yes, I should think I am upset. Just when I
thought we were getting on top of things, you go and do
this. I knew it would happen all along. That Arthur
Leeson, I knew he was no good to you. All show, him
and his stuck-up old mother ...'

Dollie gave a shaky sob, and Lilian turned fiercely on
Rosie.

'Shut up! What's the good of saying that now? Look,
go into my room, and go to sleep. I'll stay here.'

'But what about you? You've got to go to work. I
shouldn't have wakened you. It's our trouble, not yours.
You've had your share.'

'It's all right, honestly, Rosie. I don't mind. I stayed
up nights with my mother, it won't hurt me. And you'll
have the kids round you tomorrow.'

'Yes, go on, Mum. Lilian will stay with me.'

'Well ... I'll make the tea first, that'll warm us all up.'

Gratefully, she went downstairs. Georgie stirred and
mumbled, half awake, but Lilian soothed him and he
quietened, much to her relief. She had no desire to
transfer him to her own bed as well.

Dollie's face was sticky with sweat. Lilian, carrying
the candle, crept into her own room, found her flannel,
dipped it into the cold water in the big jug on the wash-
stand, squeezed it out, and returned to wipe Dollie's
damp forehead. Then she pulled back the bedclothes
and wiped some of the blood from her legs and
buttocks, dried her gently, arranged her on the clean

towel and was straightening the clothes when Rosie
returned with two cups of tea.

'I'll put these in soak.'

Rosie bundled up the blood-soaked towels and the
vomit-stained quilt and took them away. Lilian fetched a
blanket from her trunk and her own pillow, substituting
Rosie's under Nance's sleeping head, and made herself
more or less comfortable beside Dollie.

'Thanks, old pal,' Dollie groped for her hand. 'I'd do
the same for you.'

'Let's hope you'll never have to.'

'Don't you be too sure!' Dollie smiled faintly, and
soon drifted into sleep. Lilian pulled the blanket up
round her shoulders, and closed her eyes. Apart from
comparing her present competent down-to-earth self
with the Lilian of before her mother's illness and the
subsequent events, who would queasily have removed
herself from this situation as fast as she could, her
thoughts were all of Dollie. It occurred to her that she
was fonder of the sick girl at her side than of anyone
else in the world, excepting Sylvia. Perhaps if she had
agreed to the crazy plan of making their lives together
her friend would not now be lying ill. But Dollie had
such funny ideas! Then there was the question of
money. How could one woman earn enough to support
a family? And that seemed wrong, for her own work
was as valuable to Fitzgerald's as Jim's, yet he intended
to marry and have a home and family of his own, and
would just be able to afford it on his earnings, while on
her own lesser wage it would be impossible. It was not
fair, but it was a fact of life; women were paid less for
the same work.

When morning came Dollie seemed rather better. The
bleeding was less and a little colour had returned to her

cheeks. If anything she was slightly flushed. Lilian went
to work at the usual time, leaving Rosie to cope with the
invalid and the mess. She would not be home at
midday, she said. Rosie would have enough to do
without preparing a meal for her and Elsie would give
her a sandwich and a cup of tea, if nothing else offered.
Nancy, it was decided, should stay and look after the
children. Ned, who worked intermittently as a window-
cleaner, would carry the soiled bedding to the rubbish
tip. A bonfire, being slightly more private, would have
been preferable, but the back garden, a tiny area of
rough grass beyond the coal-shed and the lavatory, was
really too small. Then another mattress would have to
be bought.

The day dragged. Lilian told Will that there was
illness at Shelley Street, though not its nature, and he let
her go home early, giving her five pounds, a huge sum,
to buy anything she felt was needed on the way home.
She bought, among other things, a bottle of tonic wine
and some Valentine's meat juice, hoping that these
items would help Dollie to regain her strength.

Turning the corner from Keats Road, she saw Doctor
Bradley leave the house, mount his bicycle and ride
away. She hurried to the door, entered the narrow
passage and went through it to the kitchen. Nancy was
there, giving Sylvia and Georgie their tea. They were
eating boiled eggs, dipping in strips of bread and
margarine. Rosie was making lemonade, slicing lemons
into the big jug.

'How's Dollie? I saw the Doctor. What did he say?'

'She's got a fever. Albie went round before dinner,
but he didn't come till now. He said she had to drink
plenty. Well, I needn't have got him here to tell me that.'

'I'll go up.'

The room was clean and very tidy, as it had been ever since Rosie decided to send for the doctor. Dollie's damp hair streamed over the clean starched pillow case and the white honeycomb bedspread which was one of Rosie's treasures concealed the shabby blankets.

'Doll?' Lilian stood by the bed. Dollie stared at her with suffused eyes, but obviously did not know her. She mumbled some gibberish and turned away. She was burning with heat, seeming to radiate it, with the sick smell of fever.

'I'm to sponge her down with cool water,' said Rosie, following her into the room. 'At least that's what he said, though I should have thought it'd give her pneumonia. I don't know. I never thought I'd see a girl of mine go to Keats Passage. I did my best to bring her up right. I'd like to go round and give that Ma Alcock a piece of my mind. I've got some sausages for your tea, I sent Nance down to Burton's for them.'

'Never mind about that. I'll help you with Dollie. Perhaps we can get her to take a drop of that meat-juice; it did my mother the world of good.'

'We could try, though she hasn't kept anything down all day.'

They tried the meat-juice, they tried the tonic wine diluted with water in a spoon. They sponged Dollie gently and dried her, sprinkling her with Sylvia's baby powder, and changed the sweat-soaked nightdress for a clean one. That night they took it in turns to sit up with her while Nance slept in Lilian's bed for the second time. In the morning she seemed very slightly better, a little cooler and knowing who they were, though very weak.

With many misgivings Lilian left for work. They were busy in the shop that afternoon. A big wedding was

imminent, one that would unite two of the town's
leading families, and three or four of the people privi-
leged to be guests came to Fitzgerald's to purchase gifts.
Jim was delighted at having sold their most expensive
canteen of cutlery, though the cut-glass, silver-rimmed
fruit bowl and the Royal Doulton tea-service from
Lilian's department added up to more money. When
their employer returned from one of his mysterious
errands and received the good news they all felt happy
and successful. Lilian, who had eaten a good midday
meal upstairs, wondered whether she could request
permission to leave early for a second time, and decided
that she could not, but Jim offered to take over her share
of the closing procedure, so that she could leave the
moment they actually shut the shop. Even so, it was
getting dark when she arrived back at number nine
Shelley Street. The house showed no lights, but this was
not unusual. They would all be in the back of the house
and there was no gas in the passage. But the street lamp
showed her that the curtains were all drawn. Lilian
remembered opening her bedroom curtains that
morning, and in the scarcely-used front room downstairs they were never closed. Who had been into these
rooms to draw them across? And why? She knew the
reason, recognized the fear that had prevented her
hurrying home as soon as she could. Entering the front
door she stood for a moment in the dark stuffy passage
that was always redolent of boiling clothes, because
there was never time for the smell to fade between one
wash-day and the next. There was no sound. No sound
of children playing or quarrelling, no clatter of teacups,
or noise of the range being raked out. No voices from
the kitchen or smell of Ned's Woodbines. Without
taking off her outdoor things Lilian opened the door

facing her. The kitchen was empty and cold because the
door to the scullery was open and so was the back door
beyond it. Going to close the outer door she heard
Rosie's voice, and saw her, a blurred shadowy form as
she leant against the fence talking to their next-door
neighbour, a fat sluttish woman whom she usually
avoided.

'Rosie?'

Rosie turned and followed Lilian back into the
kitchen. She stood and stared at her accusingly.

'She's gone,' she said.

'Gone? Dollie? Gone to hospital?' That's what she
must mean, she must mean that Dollie had gone to
hospital, perhaps to the fever hospital at Bantring, a
dreadful place by all accounts. 'Have they taken her to
Bantring?' But she knew they hadn't

'Bantring? No, they haven't taken her to Bantring.
Bantring couldn't do my girl no good, not now.'

Lilian stood looking down at the old green cloth on
the kitchen table. She noticed a new patch of stickiness
where a child had dropped some jam.

'You going up? Nurse has been in to see to her. Looks
like a child, she does. An innocent little child.'

'Why didn't you let me know?'

'What could you have done? I'd got my hands full,
what with the kids and Nance carrying on something
awful, and getting the doctor. Albie doesn't know yet,
Ned's out looking for 'im. Thank goodness 'er father
didn't live to see the day.'

The range was out. Lilian took the kettle, filled it, and
put it on the gas stove in the scullery. She stood
watching the blue flames for a moment, thinking of
nothing, then she took the matches and lit the two
gauze globes under their glass shades in the kitchen.

The cold yellow light showed dirty plates on the table, the bottle of tonic wine, half-empty. She collected the crockery and took it out to the sink.

'Don't you bother, I'll do that.' Rosie's voice was flat, exhausted.

'You sit there, I'll make some tea.' Lilian found clean cups, and milk, and took down the teapot.

'You'll go and see her, won't you?'

'Of course,' said Lilian.

There would be time while the kettle boiled. She went out into the passage, and slowly, very slowly, climbed the stairs.

It was a long time before the Timms household recovered from Dollie's death. The lack of her racy cheerfulness, her pretty face, even her outbursts of bad temper, made for a dull family. Lilian remembered how much she had looked forward to the brief periods when Dollie was at home, and realized she had been her friend in a way that Mabel could never be. Then she felt disloyal to dumpy Mabel who regularly set aside every Thursday afternoon for her visit, who adored Sylvia, and spent a great deal of time making dresses for her, and a great deal of money on buying toys for her. These toys, however, could only be played with once a week because Mabel would not let Sylvia take them back to Shelley Street, and there were sometimes ugly scenes when Sylvia had to part with a new teddy or picture book on leaving the house. On occasions Mabel suggested that the child should stay for the night, but this suggestion always induced in Lilian a ridiculous feeling that she was in danger of losing her little daughter altogether. So she preferred to pack her, half-asleep, into the push-chair that had replaced the big

pram and push her back home. In the winter months
Mabel and Jack always accompanied her through the
allotments, where it was dark. After that the streets
were well lit, and in any case her friends scarcely
wanted to penetrate the Poets' Corner area, where most
of the hard-up, the menial workers, and the petty crimi-
nals of the town lived.

CHAPTER 6

In the spring of the following year a slight improvement in living conditions was brought about by the marriage of Albert, who went to live with his wife's family. He now worked as a railway porter, and his hands were never clean. Lilian wondered how anyone could want to marry him, and was thoroughly pleased when he moved away, but she became on easier terms with Ned, who sometimes cheeked her as he had once done his elder sister, and she found that she could give as good as she got. But she never became comfortable with Mabel's husband Jack; in fact she felt more and more that he was jealous and disapproving of his wife's friendship with her, while at the same time sometimes weighing up his chances of getting to know her better himself. She believed he looked on her as a loose woman, and didn't see why he shouldn't stand as good a chance as the next man. She wanted to tell him that she wasn't immoral, that there never had been, never would be, anyone for her but Will.

Yet she had to admit that Jack was an attractive man. He smelt of tobacco and tweed and had a vaguely outdoors look, in spite of his dull office job. Sometimes when he and Mabel said goodnight and turned to walk home together Lilian envied his wife hanging onto his arm, cuddling up to him every single night.

On these evenings Rosie was often out when she arrived home, since she now spent an hour or more each night at the Lord Byron. Once she would have scorned the idea of sitting there among the 'old biddies' of the neighbourhood, drinking port and lemon and getting more and more raucous with every gulp, but now it was what kept her going, enabling her to fall into bed without thinking, and sleep till morning. If her awakenings were wretched, she evidently thought it worth while to put up with them. Sometimes, about nine o'clock when supper was cleared, Lilian would offer to make a cup of tea, but Rosie always preferred to 'pop up the road for a minute or two'. She had her hair bobbed, and took to wearing lipstick. You could see she had once been a pretty little thing, but she looked thin and fragile, as well as, Lilian thought, rather common.

The year wore round, punctuated by brief stays at Warne Bay and one memorable trip to London. Phyllis produced a baby girl, and Lilian reflected on the difference between the love and luxury which surrounded this infant, and the meagre amounts of both that came Sylvia's way. Little Gillian had two loving parents, and two sets of grandparents to lavish care and attention upon her. She proved to be rather a plain baby, with small beady eyes quite unlike her mother's, and Lilian tried not to feel glad about this.

She was invited to the christening, for old time's sake apparently, since she and Phyllis had met seldom and only casually for over three years. She wondered if Phyllis knew of the relationship between herself and

Will, or suspected the existence of Sylvia. Refusing the invitation she nevertheless knitted a tiny white jacket as a present. Seeing her at work on this small garment Mabel became depressed at her own failure to conceive. She spoke tearfully of her devotion to Sylvia, making Lilian nervous. It might be wise, she thought, to cut down the Thursday visits, but she could not think how to do so without hurting her friend's feelings, and so they continued.

Even so, it was rare for her to go to Millmead Road on any other day of the week and on one isolated occasion when she took Sylvia there on a Sunday afternoon she was to wish she had stayed indoors. Mabel had been forced to put her off on her usual day. Her explanations were copious, and included the birthday party of a young niece by marriage at which she must help, a cool-ness on the part of Jack's mother who had asked her to tea on the previous Thursday and been refused and an inability on the part of Jack to understand that Thurs-days were sacred to Lilian and Sylvia. So Lilian must come on Sunday, whether Jack liked it or not. Yes, they usually went to his sister's or she and her family came to them, but since they would all have met at the birthday party, and she knew how Lilian looked forward to it after the whole week in that awful place at Shelley Street, and when Lilian said they could quite easily wait till next Thursday, Mabel shed some more tears and said she didn't want Sylvia to forget her Auntie Mabel. So, in the end, they went on the Sunday, at half-past three.

Rosie was left alone in the kitchen with the *News of the World*, disappointed because the Sunday afternoon walk with Lilian was a high-spot of her week. She made the best of things in her usual way, saying it would be nice to have a bit of peace. Nance had taken Georgie for a walk.

With Sylvia, dressed in her best blue velveteen coat
and tam, both presents from Mabel, in the pushchair,
and looking very smart herself in her bottle green
costume and matching cloche hat, Lilian went briskly
along Shelley Street and through the park to the more
salubrious district where Mabel and Jack lived. It was a
surprise, altogether unwelcome, when Jack opened the
front door.

'Hello, Jack.'

She hesitated on the doorstep. Indeed there was little
else she could do since the big man was blocking the
doorway. He was an imposing figure, and she wondered
for the hundredth time what such a man could see in
Mabel. But then her friend, dowdy, dumpy, bespec-
tacled, had always been able to get the boys.

Lilian was close enough to Jack to smell his tweedy,
tobaccoey smell, quite different from Will's expensive
cologne. She would have drawn back a little, but since
to do so would have necessitated retreating down the
steps, therefore seeming rather too pointed a gesture,
she stayed where she was.

'Mabel's out.'

'Oh, I'm sorry. I thought she was expecting us.' Lilian
was taken aback.

'It's all right. The tea's ready.' He stood aside, adding,
'Enter at your peril.'

Lilian stood still. She couldn't have tea alone with
Jack.

'Well, perhaps if Mabel's not here ... I'll pop up on
Thursday.'

'She said you were to stay. She'll be back soon,
anyway. She had to rush round to her mother's. Some
sort of crisis, you know what they are. Mabel wouldn't
let *you* down. Come on in.'

Still Lilian hesitated doubtfully, but Sylvia, whom she
had lifted out of the push-chair before ringing the bell,
now dived past Jack's legs into the house and her
mother was forced to follow.

'I want my dolly's pram, and my dolly, and Bobbie,
and . . .' Bobbie was a wooden dog on wheels. Supplied
with these objects Sylvia announced her intention of
taking them for a walk in the garden. Not wishing to be
left alone with Jack, in whose presence she had never
felt truly at ease, Lilian pretended that it was too cold,
though in fact it was a mild spring afternoon.

'Why don't you play indoors today? You could
undress your baby and put her to bed in the pram.'

'No, she wants to go for a walk. If I don't take her out
she'll scream and scream . . .'

'Then you must tell her not to be naughty,' said Lilian
desperately.

'Let her go.'

Jack followed the child into the kitchen and sent her
out into the garden through the back door. Lilian went
into the dining-room at the back of the house, which
Mabel and Jack used as a living-room. It had a french
window overlooking the garden, through which she
could see Sylvia. The room was overwhelmingly comfortable. Entering it, Lilian thought, was rather like getting
into bed. The brown-and-orange patterned carpet square
that covered most of the floor was further softened by a
thickly piled hearth-rug. On either side of the fireplace
was a large easy chair, with wooden arms and an adjust-
able back, padded with thick soft cushions covered in
brown velvet. There was a large round pouffe uphol-
stered in the same material, and heavy brown curtains
which Mabel changed for beige flowered cretonne in late
spring. An upright piano stood against the wall facing the

window, and the stained wood surround of the fireplace
with its several shelves and niches added to the dark
heaviness. An oak-framed mirror did little to add light-
ness. The room was warm, comfortable and safe or
merely claustrophobic, according to the mood of the
occupier. A square dining-table with twisty legs occupied
a large proportion of the available space, the chairs being
set back against the walls.

It was on one of these, conveniently near the window,
that Lilian seated herself. This position had two advantages, the first being that she could keep a watchful eye
on Sylvia as the little girl pushed her doll's pram
solemnly up and down, pausing occasionally to adjust
the pillow and coverings with a busy maternal air. The
second advantage was that it was as far as possible from
Jack's chair on the other side of the fireplace. Here he
invariably sat, listening to the wireless, while Mabel and
Lilian chatted or prepared a meal.

Lilian had brought her knitting, a jumper for Nance,
and she now took it out and set to work, hoping that
Jack would ignore her as he very often did.

'If you want to listen in, don't bother about me,' she
said hopefully, but Jack was approaching, not his own
chair, but Mabel's, which he now turned, heavy as it
was, away from the fireplace and toward the window
and Lilian before he sat down.

'Your life must be a bit boring,' he said conversationally.

'Oh, I don't think so, no more than most people's.'

'I mean just going to work every day, and looking
after her,' he jerked his head towards Sylvia.

Lilian's head was bent over her knitting. What could
he mean? He knew there was more to her life than that.

'I enjoy my work.'

'Work's not enough, though, is it?'

'It can be. I've got a very pleasant job.'

'And a very pleasant boss, eh?'

'Mr Fitzgerald's very nice to work for.'

Of course Mabel knew all about Will, and must have told Jack, but the subject of Lilian's relationship with her employer was never mentioned in his presence. What was he getting at now? She must change the subject.

'I'd have thought working at the town hall was rather dull, but I don't suppose it seems dull to you.'

'Why do you think that? Why are you so sure?'

Lilian who had never before given any thought to the subject of Jack's work sought for an answer.

'Well, I don't suppose you'd stay there if you didn't like it.'

'You can't walk out of a job just because you don't like it. I've got Mabel to think of, a home to keep going.'

'Yes, of course.'

How on earth had she and Jack reached this oddly personal level so quickly? She glanced out of the window. Only a few daffodils graced the narrow borders. Their insignificant presence was not really worth commenting upon, but she tried.

'Your garden will soon be nice.'

'Will it?'

'The daffodils are coming out.'

'They usually do at this time of the year.'

'I suppose so.'

She took her knitting pattern out of her bag and pretended to consult it.

'Put that thing away.'

'I want to see what I have to do next.'

'Stop fiddling about. I want to talk to you.'

'If you'd rather listen to the wireless, Jack, I shan't mind. I'm quite happy with my knitting.'

'I wouldn't rather listen to the wireless. I've just said I want to talk to you.'

'Well, you usually do listen to it when I'm here.'

Why had she said that? It sounded deliberately provocative.

'I don't want to listen to silly women's chatter. I dare say you're quite intelligent when you're on your own.'

'Thanks.'

What was the matter with him? What could he possibly have to talk to her about? He went on. 'Some men wouldn't be so keen on their wives making such a friend of you. You should be grateful to me.'

'Mabel and I have been friends since we were children. Why should I be grateful to you?'

She spoke with some acidity, but she knew what he meant, and it was true. She was an immoral woman with an illegitimate child, if that was how you wanted to see her situation. She remembered suddenly that it was Jack's money that Mabel was continually spending on Sylvia. She would have to put a stop to that; it placed her in an impossible position. She said rather feebly, 'I think Sylvia gives Mabel a lot of pleasure.'

With a sense of relief she heard a tapping sound on the window and turned to see the child with her nose pressed against the glass.

'I want my teddy, and my other dolly,' she yelled.

Normally Lilian would have told her to ask properly, and then kept her waiting until she came to the end of a row of knitting, but now she rose eagerly.

'Mummy will get them for you,' she called, and said to Jack, 'I think I know where Mabel keeps them. Do you mind if I have a look?'

'Please yourself.' He leaned back, picking up the newspaper.

Lilian left the room wondering how long she could make this errand last, and how soon Mabel would be home. When she found a big gaily coloured ball among the toys in the bottom drawer of the chest in the spare bedroom she decided with relief that she could use it as a pretext to stay out in the garden with the child until Mabel returned. If Sylvia could be prevailed upon to play ball, of course, which was doubtful. She looked at her watch. It was barely four o'clock and they never had tea until five. How on earth could she fill in the time if Mabel did not return? She thought of taking Sylvia and walking in the direction of Mabel's mother's house to meet her. Carefully she replaced in the drawer the collection of toys that Mabel had amassed, leaving aside the doll, and teddy and the ball. There were fluffy animals that Sylvia no longer played with, even a rattle she hadn't seen for a couple of years. There were picture books suitable for an older child which Mabel was evidently saving, and some new dolls' clothes. Lilian felt that she was prying; she had expected to find only familiar toys in the drawer. The extent of Mabels obsession with Sylvia was rather frightening.

She closed the drawer carefully, gathering up the doll, the teddy and the ball and left the room. Jack was waiting for her at the top of the stairs.

'I've found a ball,' she said. 'I'll keep her amused for a while in the garden.'

She moved to go past him but he grabbed her fiercely. Holding her tightly he pressed her against the wall as he tried to kiss her. She turned her head aside, feeling his moustache on her cheek.

'Don't, Jack. What do you think you're doing? Stop it. Jack . . .'

'Don't you play the lady with me, my girl. I know you

like it. Sitting there as though butter wouldn't melt . . .'

He put his hand on her breast, squeezing none too gently. Dropping the ball, she gave him a violent push which sent him reeling back against the newel post.

'For God's sake, you nearly had me down the stairs.' He seized her arm in a painful grip.

'No, I didn't. Let me go, Jack, please.'

Calm politeness might be the best policy. She stood rigid, making no attempt to free herself.

'You're a cool customer, aren't you? But then you're used to this sort of thing, eh?'

Indignation gathered in her but fortunately at that moment Sylvia's voice floated up to them. Tired of waiting, she had come in search of her toys.

'Mummy, where are you? Mummaay!'

'I'm coming, darling.' Lilian glared at Jack. 'Let me go, you fool.'

He did let her go and she descended the stairs, trembling.

On reaching the bottom she took her jacket from the hall-stand, glad that Sylvia was still dressed for the street. 'We're going home. Leave those things, darling.'

She had placed the doll and the teddy on a chair, from which Sylvia collected them. 'I've only just started playing. I don't want to go yet. I want to see Auntie Mabel.'

'Well, you can't.' Hasily Lilian crammed on her hat. Should she fetch her knitting-bag from the dining-room? No, best forget it.

'My pram's outside. I've got to fetch my pram.'

'Be quiet.'

'But you said I wasn't to leave things in the garden, you said I . . .'

Holding Sylvia by the wrist, Lilian opened the front

door as Jack came down to them.

'What do you think you're doing? You mustn't go yet. What about Mabel?'

'Of course I'm going. We can't stay here.'

Quickly Jack bent down and picked up Sylvia. Lilian tried to take the child from him, but he held her firmly.

'Let go, Jack. We're going, I tell you.'

'No. You've got to stay. Mabel will want to know what's happened.'

'Don't you tell me what I've got to do.'

Sylvia, frightened now, began to scream and wriggle, clamping one arm round her mother's neck, though Jack still held her. They struggled in the doorway, to the accompaniment of her hysterical sobbing. A passerby looked at them curiously.

Unfortunately both parties realized simultaneously that this situation could not be indefinitely prolonged, and disengaged themselves from the child at the same moment, so that she slithered rather quickly to the floor between them.

Lilian bent to pick up her daughter as Jack stepped back into the hall.

'I'm sorry, I don't want Mabel to find us like this.'

'I don't care how she finds us. It's not my fault.'

'Look, I made a mistake. I'll never touch you again. Just don't tell Mabel, that's all. She's got enough to be miserable about without that. If she loses you two I don't know ... Come back in and I'll make you a cup of tea. Please. I'm sorry. Please.'

'Well, I'll stay, but only for Mabel's sake. And if anything like that ever happens again I shall tell her at once.'

So she hung up her hat and her jacket, soothed Sylvia, and took her out into the garden with her toys.

She lingered outside, wondering whether she had done
the right thing in agreeing to stay, but it was chilly in
her thin blouse. To sit down in the living-room with Jack
would be impossible, but she could wait in the kitchen
until Mabel came. To her great relief she heard her
opening the front door almost immediately. She greeted
Lilian with explanations and apologies and began the
final preparations for the elaborate tea that she always
provided for any visitor, especially for Lilian and Sylvia.
Lilian helped her to carry in the dishes of fruit salad and
jelly, the cream, the plates of bread and butter, the
sponge cake, the fruit cake and various other items. Jack
did not raise his eyes from his newspaper. When all was
ready and with Sylvia seated on two cushions, Jack
decided to exercise his prerogative of taking tea in his
easy chair. Mabel was her usual self, pressing food on
her guests, fussing over the child, teasing Jack. Like an
old grandfather, she said he was, sitting by the fire. Set
in his ways.

'Never mind love, you suit me all right. But don't get
old before your time, that's all.'

Spreading plum jam for Sylvia she went on cheerfully, 'Mum and I thought we'd go to London on
Tuesday. Meet Auntie Gertie and go to the pictures. If
you catch the nine-fifteen it gets you in by half-past
eleven. Pity you can't come with us, Lily, you never get
away, do you, not even on your summer holiday?'

'I don't really need to, living here. So long as I can
take Sylvia on the sands she's happy. And we went to
Sturry for the day last year. The woods there are lovely.'

'Not much change for you though. Tell you what,
why don't you come to Torquay with us? You could
book your holiday the same time as Jack and we could all go
together.' She beamed at Sylvia, delighted with her idea.

'You'd like that, wouldn't you lovey, you'd like to come on holiday with your Auntie Mabel? Go in the puffer train, all the way to Devon. And we've found a lovely place to stay, not too dear. You can't see the sea, but that doesn't matter to us, we can see the sea any time. Mrs Bunting, that's the landlady, was ever so funny. "I'm afraid you can't see the sea from this room," she said, "That is, not unless you stick your lead up the chimney." Laugh! "That doesn't matter to us," I said, "We can see it any time at home." But still it's nice to have a change, isn't it? Does you good. Wouldn't that be nice Jack, if Lilian and Sylvia came to Torquay with us, then you could go off fishing, and I wouldn't be alone, I'd have company.'

Jack stirred his tea with deep concentration and said nothing. Lilian tried to sound appreciative while still rejecting the suggestion completely. 'It would be lovely, dear, but you know I have my holiday in May, before we get too busy in the shop.'

But Mabel was not to be deterred. 'Oh, I'm sure if you wanted to you could fix it up a bit later in the year. And Jack could have his just a bit earlier, couldn't you Jack? Jack, are you listening? And we wouldn't need to go out in the evenings, there's always plenty doing at Park Lodge. You can play cards, or have a sing-song. It's really a very friendly place. You might even meet some-body, you never know.'

Mabel went too far sometimes. Lilian said coldly, 'I don't want meet anyone. I'm all right as I am.'

'Perhaps you're all right now, dear, but it's your future I'm thinking of. What about the future?' This was a subject that Lilian had no wish to discuss with Mabel at any time, since her friend had expressed grave doubts on the subject of Will's ever being in a position to marry

her. And as for talking about it in front of Jack, what
could be more embarrassing?

She tried to change the subject with a joke, saying,
'I'm training Sylvia up to marry a millionaire, so we
shall both be able to live in the lap of luxury,' but Mabel
went on relentlessly.

'What I want is to see you in a nice little house like
this with Sylvia having a proper family life. Why, she
hardly knows her father; Jack's more of a father to her
than that Will Fitzgerald.'

'Mabel!' Lilian felt her face grow hot. How could she
refer to Sylvia's dubious parentage, so casually, in front
of a third person?

'Well, there's no one here but ourselves, is there?
Why mince matters? Good heavens, Lily, you're
blushing! You wouldn't mind being Sylvia's father
would you, Jack?'

Fortunately Jack had just picked up the Sunday paper
and was able to pretend to be absorbed in what he was
reading, but Sylvia, though she could not have understood the conversation, having heard Jack's name chose
to announce clearly, 'I don't like Uncle Jack.'

Mabel paused in the act of apportioning the fruit
salad.

'Ooh, what a naughty thing to say. Of course you like
your Uncle Jack.'

'No, I don't, do I Mummy? He ...'

'You're a very rude little girl. I think I'd better take
you home,' Lilian scrubbed at Sylvia's sticky mouth
with the embroidered linen napkin that Mabel had
tucked into the neck of the child's dress, effectively
silencing her, though at the same time grateful for an
excuse to cut short the visit.

'She gets silly when she's tired. We'll have to go soon

in any case, dear. I always do my ironing on a Sunday
evening, and I like to get her to bed early.'

'But aren't you staying to supper? I've got a lovely
piece of ham. I thought you'd be staying to supper as
usual.' Mabel's disappointment was genuine.

'It's sweet of you dear, but I think we'd better be
running along after tea. I always get a lot of odd jobs
done on Sunday. I have so little time during the week.
We'll come up Thursday as usual. That is if you'll have
us.'

'Of course I'll have you. Don't be soft.'

When at last Lilian was strapping Sylvia into the
push-chair Mabel decided to walk part of the way home
with her. Being barely six o'clock it was still broad
daylight so Jack was not called on to provide an escort,
but as Mabel was putting on her best coat and hat in the
bedroom he came out onto the front step.

'You won't say anything to Mabel, will you?'

'Of course not. Don't be so idiotic.'

'I don't want her upset.'

'Pity you didn't think about that before.'

'I'm going to . . .'

Whatever Jack was going to do was never revealed as
at that moment Mabel appeared in the hall wearing her
best brown winter coat with its fur collar and deep
crowned velour hat that nearly rested on the top of her
spectacle frames. Her husband moved down the path
and opened the gate. 'Cheerio, then. Don't go too far,
Mabel.'

'I'll just go past the allotments. Shan't be long.'

'Off you go then. Cheerio.' He went back into the
house.

As they set off down the road Mabel said, 'What's up
with you and Jack?'

Lilian was appalled. What had made her suspicious? Could she possibly imagine that Jack's advances would be welcomed? She was reassured by Mabel's next words.

'Did you fall out about something? He's a funny old thing, you know.'

A funny old thing. This seemed a strange way to describe a handsome man in his thirties.

'I just don't think he likes us coming on a Sunday. He likes to have you to himself.'

Was this a lie? If so it was a thoroughly justifiable one. Mabel was pleased.

'Well, I know what he's like, but I tell him I've got to have my friends. I can't devote myself to him entirely. Of course he never wants anyone but me. Just the two of us. One thing, he'd never look at another woman. At least I can be sure of that.'

Would this afternoon with its lies and treachery never end? Lilian was thankful when at last Mabel turned back, after renewing her assurance that they would be welcome as usual on the Thursday.

'Can't miss seeing my baby, can I?' she said, bending down to kiss Sylvia.

The park closed at six so Lilian was forced to go the long way round by the road which gave her time to think. She began to feel that perhaps she had been hasty, had handled the situation with Jack clumsily. Mabel herself, she thought, would have been able to make a joke of it, to push him away laughing with a cry of 'ohh, aren't you awful?', such as Lilian had heard her utter when they were girls together, at the dance in the church hall. Perhaps by taking his action too seriously she had deepened the awkwardness that had always existed between them. Perhaps it hadn't been such a

tremendous insult after all, perhaps it was only her own
awareness of her ambiguous position that made it so.
But what had he said? 'I know you like it.' No, it had
been deeply insulting. 'Don't pretend to be a lady.'
Something like that. Her face burned again at the
memory. At least he had appeared to be ashamed of
himself, and anxious that she should never tell Mabel.
Feeling more at peace she began to walk a little faster,
looking forward to a cosy evening by the kitchen fire.
Mabel's house might be more comfortable and attractive
but by this time Shelley Street was home, where she
could sit with her knitting or her novel, or both at once,
not bothering to talk if she didn't feel like it, making a
cup of tea if she fancied one, sharing a bag of pear drops
with Nance. She had lied about the ironing. In fact
Sunday evening was one of the few periods in the week
when she had some leisure.

Beneath these reflections she recognized a thread of
something positive, some more pleasing aspect of what
had happened. It was reassurance. The worrying
thought that no man of her own age, except perhaps
Jim, who hardly counted, had ever desired her, was
gone. She had been forced to defend herself from the
advances of a man who was after all very handsome and
presentable, and she had done so very firmly indeed.
She certainly could not tell Will, but she might tell Rosie,
and they would have a good laugh together about how
she had nearly pushed Jack down the stairs.

Then as she turned into Shelley Street from the top
end she saw Will. Tall, spare and elegant in his dark
Sunday suit, he left number nine, putting on his trilby
hat as he closed the door behind him, then with his
gloves in his hand he marched jauntily off down the
road. She hurried after him, calling his name, but he

was too far away, and soon turned into Keats Road and out of sight.

She was anxious and puzzled as she went in. He must have come to see her, but for what reason? She lifted Sylvia out of the pushchair, and stowed it away in the front room. The sun was setting now and the little kitchen with its one window was gloomy. The fire in the range was almost out, there was no sign of Nance, or Georgie, and there were no tea-things on the table. She took off her fashionably deep-crowned hat, glancing as she did so into the spotted mirror that had so often reflected Dollie. Her hair, pressed to her head by the hat, sprang back to vigorous life. It was bobbed now, and freed from its own weight, more vital than ever. She moved about quietly, getting Sylvia ready for bed. She lit the gas, washed the child in the scullery and finally took her upstairs. Where could everyone be? Why had Will called? He must have only just arrived, and finding the house empty, left at once. Perhaps he had come to see Sylvia as she had long wanted him to do. He had not seen her for months, and then only in passing. Where was Rosie? Gone to tea with her sister, perhaps. But it was not long since her last visit, and while it was customary for Ned to be missing after tea on Sunday, Nance and Georgie were invariably at home.

Upstairs, in the last of the daylight, she settled Sylvia to sleep with the usual difficulty. The child had a game, much enjoyed by her but not by her mother, in which she began by demanding a drink of water. When it was duly fetched she would hide under the bedclothes until Lilian gave up in despair, only surfacing to scream for water again as Lilian left the room. This manoeuvre she would repeat several times. Lilian wondered what her own father would have done with such a child. At last the game was over, Sylvia took a small sip of water for form's sake and said firmly, 'Go away now.'

Lilian did so. A creak of the bed from the room opposite arrested her as she took two steps necessary to cross the landing. Was Rosie ill? Or Nance? Cautiously she opened the door. In the half-light she could see Rosie's small shape in the bed.

'Rosie?' she whispered, 'Rosie?'

The humped figure did not move, and thoughtfully, she went downstairs.

By means of the old-fashioned bellows she revived the kitchen fire and sat down in the wooden armchair beside it.

Will leaving the house and Rosie in bed. Really, if she didn't know Rosie better . . . and Will, of course.

She had been sitting there in unaccustomed solitude for nearly twenty minutes when she heard a step on the stairs. The door opened and Rosie stood blinking in the gaslight. She too had bobbed her hair, and wore it parted on the side and secured by a slide, but now the slide was absent, her hair falling forward, and she was still fastening her best grey flannel skirt, over which she wore a blue knitted jumper. The loose, shorter clothes gave her a girlish appearance that was belied by the lines under her eyes and round her mouth. But there was something different about her, a warmth, a languorousness that was new.

'Oh, I didn't hear you come in. I must 'ave dropped off. Where's Sylvia?'

'In bed.'

'Isn't Nance back?'

'No. Where's she gone?'

'She took Georgie round to see Nellie, 'cos Vi was going out somewhere. They must have stayed for their teas.'

'They must have.'

'So I thought I'd stop here on me own and have a bit of peace. You have a nice time with that Mabel?'

Lilian ignored this question. As Rosie sat down in the chair opposite her and leaned towards the fire she said, 'What was Will doing here?'

'Will?'

'Yes, Will, my Will. Don't pretend you don't know who I'm talking about. I saw him going off down the road.'

Rosie flushed scarlet. Then she covered her face with her hands. Lilian stood up, took the poker and poked the fire noisily.

'Rosie, you've got to tell me what happened. Did he try to kiss you or something? Did he come upstairs? How long was he here?'

Rosie kept her hands over her face. Through the muffling fingers Lilian caught the words, 'Sorry, Lily. I'm truly sorry.'

'What for? What are you sorry for?'

'I ought to have stopped him, I know, but he was in that mood, you know what he's like. He came here to see you. If you hadn't gone out it would have been all right. I could have turned a blind eye, and Nance was already ...'

'Rosie, what do you mean? He didn't ...you didn't ...?'

'It wasn't me, Lily, honestly. I never led him on nor nothing. It's just that, well, he's such a nice man, and he put his arms round me, and told me how brave I was, with Arthur dying, and bringing up all the kids, and then Dollie. I couldn't push him away, not without being rude, could I? And I'm not made of stone. I like to go with a man just as much as anyone else and fat chance I've had the last few years. And I didn't think you'd ever know. Why the hell did you have to come back early? I suppose you'll never speak to me again now.'

Lilian turned away and stood hugging herself, staring down into the fire. Her main thought was that she was not very surprised. This was something that part of her had always known, That Will would go with anyone, or nearly anyone. That what was for her a sacred act of love was for him just a physical release that he could find almost anywhere. The whispers she had half-heard as a child, the suspicions she had stifled since he had become her lover, gathered round and overwhelmed her. It was all true. Almost she could laugh. Will being, as Rosie had said, in that mood, had taken the unprecedented step of visiting Shelley Street. He'd been lucky in finding the children absent, unlucky in discovering the wrong woman at home. But he hadn't let that worry him. A woman was a woman after all. So he'd got round Rosie with his smooth talk and they'd gone up to bed together. Lilian wondered what he'd thought of the poorly furnished back bedroom and iron bedstead and the grey blankets, and the faint smell from the red rubber sheet that inadequately protected Georgie's unappetizing bedding.

'It's you he wanted, Lily. It's just that he'd got himself all worked up.'

'The idiot. Coming here on a Sunday afternoon. What does it look like?'

'He never seems to care about that.'

'Never! What do you mean, never?'

'I don't know. Nothing.'

'Wasn't this the first time? Has he been here before?'

'No. No he hasn't been here before.'

'What then? Rosie, this wasn't the first time, was it?

You've got to tell me.'

'It was so long ago.'

'When? How long ago?'

'Years and years. I was only seventeen. He hadn't been married that long. Phyllis was about three, I suppose. I went there as maid after Vi left. I ought to have known better seeing what happened to her, not that she hasn't done all right. I couldn't resist him. Well, you can't, can you, and he was young then too. So when I fell for Willie, he gave us a hundred pounds to set up with and Arthur and I got married.'

'You mean, Willie . . . your son . . .'

'Yes, my Willie that got killed.' Rosie stood up and want to the dresser. After a few moments fumbling at the back of a drawer she became back with a framed photograph showing the head and shoulders of a young man in army uniform. She held it out to Lilian. 'I put it away, see, when you came, because, well, you'd have known, wouldn't you?'

Lilian stared at the picture. Yes, she would have known. The young face in the cheap studio portrait smiled with Will's charming smile, looked at her with his eyes. In spite of everything she felt a pang of sorrow. Will's son, and he was dead.

'I've given up everything for him.' But as she spoke Lilian asked herself if this were true. She'd had no home, no love to sacrifice. All she had relinquished was a little money which she supposed that, if she really tried, she could get back. Some last remaining shred of prudence had made her keep the scribbled I.O.U. she had received five years earlier. And he had given her passion, some luxurious weekends, the delight and stimulation of his company, and Sylvia, a beautiful and infuriating child.

No, Rosie had told her something that for all this time she had been trying very hard not to know. That her darling Will who was only waiting for his elderly wife to depart from this world so that he could marry Lilian was a rake, a womanizer, a more-than-philanderer who took his fun where he could find it. Bold grubby gypsies, shopgirls, maidservants, wives, he had to try his luck with them all. And being a man of charm, good looks, intelligence and sensitivity he usually overcame any half-hearted objections they might have. He enjoyed himself, and so did they. And unless they fell deeply in love with him, or had a child which could be attributed to an unobservant husband, little harm was done. But it was different for her: she loved him, she was alone, she had Sylvia. He was the most important thing in her life. And now she saw clearly that if she had any pride at all, she must give him up. 'But I love him,' she said aloud.

'More fool you,' said Rosie.

Yes, thought Lilian, more fool me.

There seemed to be no more to say. The only sound in the room was the small steady hiss of gas from the light fittings. After a few minutes Lilian broke the silence. 'Shall I put the kettle on?' she asked.

'Might as well,' answered Rosie.

CHAPTER 7

Walking to work the next morning, deep in thought as usual, Lilian decided that the time had come when she must alter her way of life. Firstly, no more weekends at Warne Bay. She could not sink to knowingly sharing her lover. In the mood of searing honesty that now possessed her she had to admit that the knowledge was not new, but then she had been able to pretend it didn't exist, or at worst didn't matter. Now the thought of Will's arriving at Shelley Street and going up to bed with Rosie was so crude, so sickening, that it devalued the whole of the last five years. Previously, she had been able to convince herself that she, whatever was true or untrue, was the one that mattered. She was the one who would become the second Mrs Fitzgerald, she who had his child. Now she could no longer believe this. She saw herself as one of a procession of cheap women, the mother of a by-blow who was herself one among many. Sick with shame and anger she imagined herself storming into his office, having it out with him and finally reminding him of the money he owed her.

She must move out of Rosie's, find a flat, ask Mabel to

take care of Sylvia in the daytime. She knew her friend
would jump at the chance, would see it as a step
towards having the child for her own, but Lilian would
not let that happen. It would only be a temporary
measure, until Sylvia was old enough to start school.
Then Will would have to pay for her to go to St Hilary's.
If he was difficult about it she would threaten to tell
Louisa everything she knew. Louisa and other people.

Drinking her cup of tea at the shop, her resolve weak-
ened a little. Once or twice she had seen Will lose his
temper. Still, two could play at that game, she wasn't
red-haired for nothing.

As usual he came downstairs while she was dusting
the china, and as usual he went through her department
to the office. Trembling, she put down a Worcester
figurine and nerved herself to follow him. But he
departed from his custom. Ignoring the little pile of
letters on his desk he snatched his hat from behind the
door, reappeared immediately, and with an even brisker
tread he left the shop.

'He's in a hurry,' observed Jim.

'Yes.'

Why hadn't she been in more of a hurry herself. Why
hadn't she waylaid him? Had he looked a bit shame-
faced, a bit sheepish? Was he afraid to face her? It was a
cheering thought and she almost smiled. Perhaps the
others didn't really matter after all, perhaps she was
important to him. She decided not to act precipitately.
After all, there was a great deal at stake. If only Louisa
seemed a little more frail, but really the woman hardly
seemed to age at all. She was as majestic as ever. The
shop was busy, and Lilian scarcely saw Will again until
the afternoon. Then, at a moment when Jim was
working away in his cubbyhole, and there were no

customers, he approached her. She stood rigid, wondering what he could be going to say.

'I came up yesterday afternoon, to see Sylvia, but you were out.'

Here was her opportunity. Here was her chance to say, 'I may have been, but couldn't you have left Rosie alone? Must you grab at every woman you see ...' It was a moment of decision. If she brought his unfaithfulness out into the open, then she could not continue the affair, must relinquish her hold on him for ever. All the morning she had been telling herself that she must do that very thing, that no alternative was possible. Now he presented her with one. They looked at each other.

At nearly sixty, he was still a handsome man. His hair had faded to pepper and salt and his green eyes had lost a little of their brightness, but those things hardly mattered. He smiled. An uncertain smile.

'It's about time we went to the Granville again,' and Lilian said yes, perhaps it was.

In a way it was a relief. She did not really want to entrust Sylvia to Mabel, to have to plan the future afresh. What could she put in the place of the happy ending she had always envisaged for herself – marriage to Will, a respected place in Culvergate society, and the provision of a background against which Sylvia would be able to finish her growing up? What else was there? She might marry someone else, but who? Apart from the fact that she met few people socially, few men would want to marry a woman with her reputation. Yet marriage seemed her only chance. Could she launch out into business on her own? If Will returned her money perhaps she could but a tiny house and set up as a seaside landlady, letting rooms in the summer. Mrs Denning was very prosperous, could not she do like-

wise? What a dreary prospect. A little shop of her own
would be better, but the only trade she knew anything
about was jewellery and fine china, which needed far
more capital than she would ever have. No, it was best
this way. In any case, she still loved him, must take
what he offered, little as it was for the moment.

Yet her outlook was changed by the incident. Having
lived from day to day, scarcely ever looking further
ahead than the next visit to Warne Bay, she now began
to be anxious about the future. And when, as they
strolled along Warne Bay High Street, she saw a small
neat shop, between a baker's and a newsagent's, with a
'To Let' sign, she casually guided Will towards it.

'What a nice little place! Wouldn't it be just right for a
china shop?'

Will peered in through the plate glass window. 'Not
much room.'

'Lovely position though. It's a busy street.'

She chose her words carefully, not saying too much.
They walked along, pausing to look in the window of a
jeweller's, and to compare prices.

'They've got some nice things,' said Lilian with
professional interest.

'Must be quite a bit of money about.'

'They get a good class of visitor.' Lilian felt that things
were going her way. 'Look at the people at the
Granville.'

At dinner on that Sunday evening they did look at the
people at the Granville, and they seemed to be a well-to-
do section of society. All were in evening dress, as they
were expected to be, and the older ladies were in expensive, fashionable gowns, decorated with rings and necklaces. One or two of the younger women were much
more cheaply dressed, and it was easy to guess in what

circumstances they had come to the Granville. On the
Monday morning they took another look at the little
shop. Lilian noted the words 'Living Accommodation' at
the bottom of the 'To Let' poster, but she did not point
this out to Will. They walked up the street, assessing the
other shops, and all seemed prosperous. Will did not say
much, in fact the idea that Fitzgerald's might open a
branch was not mentioned between them, and Lilian's
own idea that she might move to Warne Bay, manage
the shop, and live in the flat was not even hinted at, but
over lunch there was a new excitement in the air. As
they ate whitebait and drank sherry their conversation
sparkled. Will actually said that he wished it was
'always like this' adding, 'But you're all right, aren't
you, my darling? It's not too bad at Rosie's?'

Lilian seized her chance. 'It's all right. I suppose I've
got used to it. Though it's not the same since Dollie
died.'

Lilian paused a moment remembering the silk camisole that Dollie had lent her and the way Dollie had
arranged her hair when she was preparing for her first
visit to the Granville. Then she said, 'I want to get away
before Sylvia starts school. She can't go to school with
the Shelley Street children. She's a lovely child, Will, so
intelligent. A pity you missed seeing her last week.' Had
she gone too far? Will sat silent and after a moment she
continued. 'If only you could have a bit to do with her.
Girls need their fathers, I think.'

In fact she did not think so at all. She had been far
happier without her father. But still, it might be true of
Sylvia.

Will answered 'Yes,' slowly, and then, 'We'll have to
see what we can do.'

No more was said on the subject, as at that moment

the waiter came to remove their plates and take their order for the next course. Will chose a strawberry sundae, and Lilian was able to tease him about his sweet tooth while she herself ate biscuits and cheese. As she made her separate way back to Culvergate she felt excited and happy, half convinced that the little shop and its living accommodation would soon be virtually hers.

In the 'Ladies Only' compartment of the three-fifteen she sat by herself, so there was nothing to prevent her rising and taking stock of her appearance as reflected in the oval mirror set in the panelling above the seats.

Her jade green cloche hat was pulled down over her bright hair, her face was powdered, and she wore a little lipstick. Her dangling earrings were designed to draw attention away from her nose. She looked, she thought, quite striking and Will had been calling her 'The Girl in the Little Green Hat' after the popular novel, and this made her feel successful and up-to-date. She took out a cigarette, fitted it into the holder she had just started using, and sat back, crossing her legs. Nice legs, she thought cheerfully. How on earth could poor little Rosie possibly compete? She opened the *Sunday Express* Will had bought her and thought how she had very nearly made an awful mistake. Will had probably just been very sorry for Rosie. He was like that.

The next two weeks were uneventful. Rosie, still feeling guilty, tried even harder to make the little house comfortable, made an effort to take the children for a walk each day, and kept Sylvia from playing in the street which, though barely four years old, she now wished to do. They had fewer meals of greasy stewed mutton and more beef casseroles, but she still went

along to the Lord Byron most evenings, lipsticked and
short-skirted.

One evening she brought a man home with her, a
local butcher. He was big and red-faced, a widower with
several children. She made tea, and they all sat round
the kitchen table, Rosie and her man friend laughing too
loudly, and making what Lilian considered unseemly
personal remarks about each other. Rosie teased Ben, as
she called him, about his weight, adding conciliatorily
that she liked big men. He answered with a leer that
he'd be plenty big enough for her, winking at Lilian as
he spoke. Rosie said, 'Oh, aren't you awful,' and
slapped his arm.

Lilian thought she would like to go to bed, but
decided it would be unwise to leave Rosie alone with her
friend.

He did not on that occasion stay very late, but it was a
worry just the same. Was Rosie hoping to remarry, or
was she about to abandon her much-prized respectability and embark on a career of loose living? Either
course would make Lilian's position in the house impossible.

How Rosie had changed in the last few months. She
was more cheerful than at any time since Dollie's death,
but it was the alteration in her appearance that was
most striking. It was doubtful, in Lilian's opinion, if
Dollie, returning to earth, would recognize her mother.
The shabby, untidy little woman who had greeted Lilian
on her arrival at Shelley Street had vanished, and Rosie
was trying to recapture her lost youth, at the unlikely
age of forty-seven. She wore shiny rayon stockings and
a fashionably short skirt, and her hair was now
shingled. Unfortunately this severe style exposed her
thin neck, and emphasized her haggardness, but the

lipstick and rouge she wore when 'going out', though
inexpertly applied, made dimly visible the pretty young
woman she had once been. Lilian saw that Will could
have found her attractive, thirty years earlier. But she
still wore old slippers in the house, saving her smart
uncomfortable shoes for the Lord Byron.

Days passed, and nothing was said about the shop at
Warne Bay. Was the fact that Will had been absent all of
the Friday following their visit a hopeful sign? Had he
been to Warne Bay? If so, a week later he had still said
nothing to Lilian about it. Perhaps he had not given the
matter another thought. On her walks to and from work
she had plenty of time to worry about the future. That
Saturday evening she arrived home tired and depressed,
to be appalled by Rosie's greeting.

Dressed for the Lord Byron, she was applying her
make-up in the kitchen mirror. Patting her face ener-
getically with a small powder puff she said, 'Oh Lily, I'm
not half glad to see you. I've invited Mr Wallace ... Ben
... round for dinner tomorrow. Do you think you could
make us a nice jam tart? Your pastry's ever so much
nicer than mine.'

Lilian sat down wearily. 'All right. I suppose I can.
What about his kids? They're not coming as well, are
they?'

'Well, of course, they are. He can't leave them at
home, can he? It'll be really nice for him to have his
dinner cooked for him, for a change, and he's given me a
lovely piece of beef. You have a look at it, and tell me
what time to put it in.'

'All right. How many children are coming?'

'All of them. Four. Boys.'

'Four boys? Oh Lord.' Tired and longing for a quiet
Sunday, Lilian visualized the kitchen filled with the

butcher and a crowd of boisterous schoolboys.

Rosie said appealingly, 'I want it to be nice, Lily, as a lot depends on it. He's not your sort, I know, but he's nice and kind, and in a good position. And I've got Nance and Georgie to think of.'

So it was out. She hoped to marry again. During all the four years she had spent with the Timms family Lilian had dreamed of the day when she would move on to better things. But it was Rosie who was going to move on to better things, namely the flat in the High Street, and she was supposed to ease her path towards this goal by helping to cook the dinner. Well, of course she could not refuse. If only Will would say something about the branch shop. How ironic if Rosie were to go up in the world while she and Sylvia were left, miserably searching for lodgings.

Will would have to do something. He must.

The Sunday was not quite as bad as might have been expected. Dinner was a success, and the four boys, all scrubbed and shiny in grey flannel shorts, grey shirts, and navy blue school pullovers, were remarkably well-behaved. Indeed they hardly spoke during the meal. Fortunately the afternoon was dry, and Lilian and Nance at Rosie's suggestion took Sylvia, Georgie and the butcher's youngest for a walk, while the three older boys went home. The oldest was at the grammar school and had homework to do, and the other two, it seemed, were anxious to play with their Meccano. Rosie and her admirer were left sitting cosily in the kitchen, one each side of the fire that burnt brightly in the range. Lilian wondered whether she would arrive home to find an engaged couple.

On this occasion she did not do so. Certainly when

she and Nance returned the pair had transferred to the couch, where they were rather solemnly sitting side by side, but Benjamin Wallace was not the man to rush things. It seemed he had further tests in mind for Rosie before asking her to become his wife. She was invited to spend the following Sunday in the home above and behind the butcher's shop in the High Street. She would be expected to 'give a hand' with the dinner and receive Ben's elderly mother to tea in the afternoon. Nance and Georgie were invited, but Ned would stay at home to have his meal cooked by Lilian.

'You don't mind for once, do you dear?' asked Rosie, as though Lilian did not play a major part in the production of all their Sunday dinners.

Lilian said she did not mind, but she feared for Rosie. Her cooking had improved a great deal, but she was still incapable of organizing things so that the various items were all ready at the same time, so that the meat grew cold while they waited for the potatoes, or the cabbage was served underdone to catch up with the Yorkshire pudding. Lilian invariably made the gravy according to an old recipe of Alice's. Lessons in gravy making would have to be enforced before the next Sunday or the whole enterprise could fail. Rosie's voice was brightly confident but her eyes were anxious, and if success depended on her cooking she had some reason for anxiety.

By the following Friday there was still no mention of the Warne Bay shop, but Lilian had become convinced that negotiations were taking place. The buying, for one thing. When a commercial traveller called, Will placed orders that were considerably larger than usual, and twice his solicitor telephoned when he was out, and Lilian replied as she normally did on those occasions that Mr Fitzgerald was not available and could she take a message. Supposing he had not thought of making her manageress. He might have decided to take on someone new, or even to send Jim there. But no, they had envisaged it as a china chop and Jim was on the jewellery side, as well as doing the watch repairs.

She wondered if Will had realized how much it could facilitate the pursuit of their affair. Why, if he were to buy a car and learn to drive he could cover the distance in under an hour, without all the bother of catching trains. In desperation Lilian disregarded their tacit understanding that private matters were not to be mentioned in the shop. While they were discussing stock replacement she interrupted him to say quietly, 'I think Rosie will be getting married soon.'

'Rosie? Good Lord!' His surprise was not exactly complimentary.

'Why shouldn't she?' said Lilian, thinking that she had been good enough for him so why not for Ben Wallace. 'Sylvia and I will have to move.'

'I wouldn't worry about that if I were you. Something will turn up by then.'

'Well, I hope it will. I shouldn't be surprised if it's quite soon, once they make up their minds.'

'Lilian, don't worry.'

It would be useless to press him further. She would have to trust him. He obviously had something in mind but suppose it was not Warne Bay at all, just another version of nine Shelley Street? She tried to concentrate on her work, ticking off the sold items in her stock book, but it was hard to concentrate, and she was glad when a customer arrived to absorb her attention.

It was at about this time Miss Bethune first made her appearance; Miss Dorothea Bethune, which Lillian spelled Beaton until corrected by the lady herself. In the following two weeks she returned to the shop no less than five times, perhaps because on the second occasion, when she was accompanied by her brother, Will sensed an important new customer and emerged from his office to chat while Lilian instructed Charlie in the packing of the Doulton dinner service they had purchased.

They had recently moved into a house at Palmer's Bay, and evidently wished to join in the social life of the town. Miss Bethune was perhaps a little under forty and had retained a girlish flirtatiousness which Lilian found decidedly irritating, but to which Will responded with enthusiasm. Her clothes were expensive, her somewhat brassy blonde hair was marcel waved, and her pearls were real. After that second occasion it seemed as though she was always in and out, though she did not visit more than twice a week. She would bring a watch or a piece of jewellery to be repaired and then call far too soon to see if it was ready. On these occasions she generally found time for what she called 'a little look round' and would allow her eye to be taken by a pair of earrings or an Art Nouveau photograph frame and with many laughing protestations of guilt at her own extravagance, would purchase something at the small discount which Will assured her he allowed to all 'regular' customers.

She was rather a plain woman, but had the rare knack of behaving as though she were beautiful, a knack which seemed to be remarkably successful in taking in certain people. Lilian considered her middle-aged and over made-up, and thought her girlish manner absurd, but she knew better than to voice these feelings and served her, as she served all customers, with well-simulated enthusiasm. In return, Miss Dorothea Bethune was friendly enough, if a shade patronizing.

'I must ask Miss Watts what she thinks,' she would cry, as she sailed through into Lilian's department wearing a rope of amber beads or a pair of paste earrings.

'Are they quite me, dear?' she would say, and Lilian thus appealed to would give an honest opinion, sometimes saying the trinket was exactly right, or perhaps suggesting that something larger, more important looking, might be better.

'You know, dear Mr Fitzgerald, that young lady is a treasure. You must never let her go. She has such perfect taste,' and Lilian, who thought she did have rather good taste, was almost won over. But not quite. Miss Bethune had a way of laying her beautifully manicured hand, with its perfect pink fingernails, on Will's arm which was certainly too intimate for a mere customer, however regular. So when at last Will announced that Seventy-four High Street, Warne Bay was to become a branch of T. Fitzgerald and Son Ltd and that he was relying on her to become its manageress, she heard the news with mixed feelings.

She would have the flat to live in, an adequate salary, and a say in the choosing of stock. She would be single-handed to begin with except perhaps for a lad to help with unpacking and deliveries, part-time, but later, if things went well she might need an assistant in the shop. All exactly what she had hoped for but how, from that distance, could she keep an eye on her lover?

It seemed to her that Dorothea Bethune was only waiting for her to have departed to throw herself at Will with redoubled fervour. Lilian wondered if she knew of the existence of Louisa. At least that was something she could make sure of.

The next time Miss Bethune made her usual somewhat theatrical entrance through the shop door, wearing
a hyacinth blue tussore silk dress and an exactly
matching deep-crowned hat, and declared that a necklace to match the outfit was absolutely necessary to her
well-being, Lilian was able to tell her that she was sorry,
but Mr Fitzgerald was not in the shop, having accompanied Mrs Fitzgerald to the dentist.

'Poor dear lady, having trouble with her teeth, is she?
Of course, I believe she's much older than dear Mr Fitzgerald, is she not? It always tells in the end. But he's
such a kind man, I'm sure he's very patient. Well, now,
I'm in quite a rush this afternoon, so I'll leave you this
little pattern of the material, and you can take your time
looking out for exactly the right thing. You'll do that for
me won't you, dear. You know I trust your judgement
implicitly.'

Lilian, forcing a smile, promised to do her best.

She was busy for the rest of that afternoon, but the
next day she took the first opportunity to fulfil her
commission. Jim was rather disapproving of Lilian's
invading his department, but after all she knew where
things were as well as he did, and with the pattern on
the counter she drew out several trays of necklaces,
hoping to find an expensive one in the right shade of
blue but the only perfect match to be found was among
the cheaper strings of beads that hung on a display
stand. She would have suggested the long rope of artificial pearls, but not to anyone who possessed the real
thing, and the cornelians made a pleasant contrast, but
the quite inexpensive blue glass beads were the right
ones, they so perfectly reflected the soft mauvish-blue,
and yet with a faint silvery sheen. She would have to
forgo the commission on the higher price that would

have been readily forthcoming. It was, after all, a matter
of integrity. Turning, rather pleased with herself, to try
the necklace round her own neck, she saw, reflected in
the mirror on the counter, the front door open, and a
woman enter. Ruth Smith, the gypsy woman, had not
called for several weeks. This time she did not pretend
to have anything to sell.

'I want to see him,' she said, putting the word into
capital letters. 'He's in there, is he?' Tall, stately in spite
of her shabbiness, she moved towards the office.

'You can't go in there.' Lilian looked round for Jim,
but he had retired into his cubby-hole.

'And who's going to stop me?'

'Tell me what you want. I'll see if he's there.' Lilian
stepped quickly across the gypsy's path, not knowing
herself why it was imperative for her to be kept away
from the office. If she was merely begging . . .

The woman stood still then, and Lilian felt that she
herself was the one who had lost dignity. 'Wait here a
minute.'

If Will came and spoke to the woman in the shop,
then they could be seen and heard. Lilian would be able
to judge whether the rumours that had reached her were
true. No shame would attach to this eavesdropping. She
had a right to know.

'Tell him it's Mrs Smith.'

In the office Will was smoking and reading a newspaper. Lilian closed the door behind her, something he
did not allow. If ever they were in the office together it
was with the door wide open. To protect her reputation,
he said. He looked up sharply.

'What it is? Why have you shut the door?'

'It's that gypsy woman.'

To her relief Will said, 'Damn. Can't you tell her I'm out?'

'She wouldn't believe me. Come out and speak to her, Will, I don't think she'll go away unless you do.'

'Lilla,' he said, and he had rarely called her Lilian during business hours, let alone this pet name. 'Lilla, get rid of her for me. You can do it somehow.'

Appealed to in this special way, Lilian thought perhaps she could. Certainly she was ready to try. He trusted her, she was his Lilla, and he wanted her to get rid of the gypsy. She turned away, feeling strong and determined, only to see the tall figure of Ruth Smith framed in the doorway. Will rose to his feet.

'What do you want? I told you ...' He broke off, remembering Lilian's presence. 'Miss Watts, go back into the shop please.'

The woman, with a little triumphant smile, stood aside for her to pass. Will closed the door behind her.

There were two glass panels in the top of the door, but these had been covered with a coloured translucent paper, patterned with red and green, presumably in the hope that it would be mistaken for stained glass. She turned to peer through this, but only the vaguest shadows were visible. Without actually putting her ear to the door she tried hard to hear what was being said, but could make out no words. Jim left his cubby-hole and came to the six-foot gap between the glass-fronted showcases that formed the entrance to her department.

'Leave it alone, Lilian,' he said. 'Believe me, you don't know the half of it.'

An overweight, pale-faced little man, he looked at her anxiously. They had worked together a long time. He'd married Elsie, but she knew he had wanted her first. Perhaps he still did. She did not have to say, 'What do you mean?' because he had on more than one occasion hinted at areas unknown to her in the life of Will

Fitzgerald, but of course she had never encouraged him to tell her more. Now he said, 'Come through here,' and he led her towards the jewellery counter, away from the glass-panelled door, then turning to face her, he continued.

'You know I work late sometimes, to finish repairs. Well, twice last month I didn't get finished till after eleven, Elsie was worried to death, I was so late. Well, as I was going home up Invicta Road, I met that woman coming this way. Both times.'

Lilian stood silent, feeling sick. In listening to what he had to say she had somehow admitted to her relationship with Will, otherwise what business could this be of hers? But of course Jim had known for a long time, since before Sylvia was born. She remembered how he had received her on her return. Feebly she said, 'She wasn't necessarily coming here.'

'Of course she was. He comes down and lets her in. Why do you think he has that sofa in his office?'

This was too much, too open and too crude. She flushed.

'I haven't the faintest idea what you're talking about.'

Trembling, she walked back into the china department. Dazed and confused, she tried to find work to do. If this were true ... and of course it must be true. She had always known really.

More than twenty minutes passed before the door to the office opened and Ruth Smith emerged. As she passed Lilian she said, 'Don't worry, dear, you've got a lucky face.'

Lilian said 'Good morning' coldly, which seemed more dignified than ignoring her. Will remained in the office for the next hour, and only when Lilian was busy with a customer did he reappear and leave the shop by the front door.

Lilian thought of the dinner-hour with dread and distaste. By this time she had relinquished her habit of walking to and from Shelley Street between the hours of one and two-fifteen. Sylvia was no longer a baby, and the exhausting journey no longer seemed necessary. Dinner at Rosie's during the week was almost always some kind of stew, but nowadays fairly free from gristle and fat and, flavoured with an Oxo cube, really quite palatable. Lilian thought the mixture of meat and vegetables quite nourishing for Sylvia, and the child would eat it cheerfully provided everything was cut up small. But the joints, casseroles, or fish pies prepared by Winnie, the cook-general who had superceded Elsie in the Fitzgerald kitchen were really excellent, and normally Lilian anticipated them with pleasure.

Not today, however. She had become used, hardened she supposed, to sitting at table with her lover and his wife. Sometimes it was all she could do not to smile at the formal way he treated her, sometimes conversing at length with his wife whilst Lilian and Jim sat silent, remembering that after all they were mere employees. Louisa was kind, in her patronizing way, occasionally suggesting that Lilian must still miss her parents and expressing the hope that Mr Right would come along soon. Jim was helpful on these embarrassing occasions, jovially inclining to the view that she was 'too choosy by half', and changing the subject as soon as he could.

Often Lilian had cause to be grateful for the arrival of Winnie with the second course, when Louisa's chat would be interrupted as she served it. The puddings were good too, apple tart, jam roly-poly, they were all filling and delicious. Louisa would serve those seated at the table first then dish out a helping for Winnie which she would take down to the ground-floor kitchen to eat at the corner of the kitchen table. When the meal was over they would all enjoy a cup of tea, after Lilian had helped to clear the table. This was not expected of her, but she disliked sitting still while Winnie bustled around, and in any case it expedited the appearance of the tea.

The dining-room was a well-furnished but somewhat dark apartment with a depressing outlook over the small neglected back gardens beyond the Fort, which had in some cases degenerated into untidy back-yards. The heavy lace curtains which obscured this dismal view also deepened the gloom. The surrounding buildings were tall, three or four storeys, and effectively kept out the sun. Sometimes Lousia was forced to light the gas so that they could see to eat their dinner. Lilian tried to go out for a breath of fresh air after the meal, but this was only possible on casserole days, since the carving of a joint was a serious business over which Will took his time.

The meal that followed the visit of the gypsy woman was partaken of without any of the usual light conversation. Jim was silent, as if he had been personally offended, and Lilian was angry and upset. Also a new anxiety had risen to the surface of her mind: Dollie had long ago told her that there were illnesses one could catch from going with men who had caught them from bad women. Was Ruth Smith a bad woman? What were the symptoms of this painful disease and could she have passed it on to Sylvia? Such were the unsuitable thoughts that occupied her mind while she ate her roast mutton and Queen's pudding that day.

Either because of this anxiety or because of a common minor infection, a few days later she began to itch, and spent a week or more waiting for further, more

distressing symptoms to develop. Eventually, in desperation she confided in Rosie, who diagnosed a common
female ailment and described a course of homely treat-
ment.

'You needn't worry about that with him, duck. After
all he never goes with tarts, does he? Doesn't need to
with half the women in Culvergate falling over themselves to get him.'

Lilian told her about the gypsy. Could she be
described as a tart?

'I didn't think you knew about her, though everyone
else does. She's well-known, came here with a whole
tribe years ago, and he got hold of her. Then when the
others left she stayed on alone. Gave up everything.
Lived up near the allotments for a bit in her caravan and
then got it moved somewhere out Barling way. No, she
wouldn't go with no one else. Mad on him, she is, and
quite respectable in her way.'

So Lilian was able to stop worrying about that particular aspect of the matter and soon afterwards the
trouble cleared up. She mulled over the idea of
confronting him with her knowledge, and decided that
there was little point as he was obviously growing tired
of the woman and would soon finish with her for good.
When Will at last set a date for opening the Warne Bay
shop, which he naturally wanted her to manage, she
was too busy to think about anything else.

There were difficulties to be taken into account. Who
would look after Sylvia during business hours, and later
on take her to school and fetch her? How would she
furnish the little flat? The first anxiety she concealed
from Will, fearing he might think that after all an unen-
cumbered manageress would be preferable, but she did
ask him about furniture. As usual he told her not to

worry, and she understood this to mean that cast-offs from the Fitzgerald home might become available.

Sylvia remained a problem until she began to talk about it to Rosie, when Nance immediately expressed a wish to go with them to Warne Bay.

'Oh, do let me come, Lilian! I could be your maid, I could look after Sylvia and take her to school and do the housework – I wouldn't want any money.'

Lilian demurred. Nance had left school and was now a wage-earner. She had grown into a lanky quiet girl with a determined nature. Intending to become a shop assistant like poor Dollie, rather than a servant such as Nellie, she had sought long and hard for the kind of work she wanted, but lacking Dollie's looks and personality she had in the end accepted a situation in a rather sordid little giftshop near the harbour where her pale face and greasy hair did not matter. Lilian doubted whether she would be able to afford even the pittance that this establishment paid, but on the other hand surely Nance would have a better life. With an improved diet and the opportunity to bath and wash her hair at frequent intervals she might stand a better chance in many ways. She would be a great help with Sylvia, too, and company of a sort. So it was agreed. Rosie was delighted to see her daughter going up in the world, and glad to have only Georgie to take with her when she eventually married.

The second problem was also unexpectedly solved. A letter from a solicitor, delivered by hand to Lilian at the shop, informed her that her aunt, Miss Annie May Hewitt, had died, and invited her to call at his office without delay.

Lilian, feeling guilty, went that same afternoon. Aunt Annie, she was told, had died of semi-starvation among

other things, and had collapsed outside her own front
door where a neighbour had found her. Lilian explained
that they had lost touch, and bore the accusing looks as
well as she could. She had been so anxious to keep the
knowledge of Sylvia's existence from this strange sister
of her mother's that it had never occurred to her that
she might be needed.

The terms of the will were explained. Aunt Annie's
small capital, left to her by her parents, plus half the
value of the house, was to go to the church she
attended. The rest would be Lilian's.

'Though I don't think there's much in the way of
furniture,' said the solicitor. 'Miss Hewitt was a lady
who lived very simply, I understand.'

Lilian scarcely heard this warning. Half the value of
the house and all her grandparents' furniture! There
might be some valuable antiques. These she would sell
for she wanted no old furniture in her flat. In this first
home of her own she intended everything to be new, to
have been owned and used by no one but herself. But
antiques fetched good prices. She made up her mind to
visit an auctioneer as soon as possible to make arrangements for a sale. That money, plus half what was realized on the house, would set her up nicely and leave a
little over for emergencies.

Rosie helped Lilian to make the modest funeral
arrangements and when this was done they walked
together to the tall narrow house in the quiet street
where Lilian's grandparents had brought up their
family. Five stone steps led upwards to the front door,
and seven more went down to the kitchen entrance in
the basement. To their right was the bow window of the
room that had been the front parlour and above this
rose the similar window of the best bedroom. Beyond

that was the dormer belonging to the attic. Lilian, glad of Rosie's company, put the key in the lock. The musty stuffiness that she expected was absent, and the only smell was that of floor-polish.

'The hall-stand's gone,' she said, remembering childhood visits to her grandmother. She opened the door into the front room. It was dark, and she moved quickly across to part the red plush curtains, confirming what she already guessed from her uninterrupted passage across the room, that it was totally bare of furniture.

'I suppose she needed the money.'

Lilian was disappointed. The best things would have been in that room. But still, she might yet find something saleable.

They went straight down to the basement kitchen. A scrubbed deal table, an upright chair, and the minimum amount of utensils that would satisfy the needs of one person were all it contained. Mystified, they climbed the stairs to look into the dining-room, then went on up to the bedrooms and up again to the top floor. Six rooms and all of them empty. Not an article of furniture anywhere, not a pair of curtains except those at the downstairs front window, not a forgotten mat or empty vase. Not so much as a piece of paper. Everywhere the old wood-patterned linoleum was polished to a brightness that the thin veil of dust scarcely dimmed. The back rooms were filled with brilliant sunlight, unfiltered by lace or net, and the patterns of flowers and ribbon on the old-fashioned wallpapers had faded into pastels.

At the top of the house they stood in the attic room which Alice's two brothers had once shared.

'She must have slept somewhere.'

Rosie opened a narrow door in the corner which looked as though it led to a cupboard. More than that,

but less than a bedroom, the narrow space beyond must
have been intended as a boxroom. Here they found an
iron bedstead, covered with a dazzling white spread.
There was a kitchen chair, a small shabby chest of
drawers, and that was all. The walls had been patchily
whitewashed, and over the bed, from a nail banged into
the plaster, hung rather precariously a plain wooden
crucifix. On the chair lay a prayer book.

Lilian sat down on the smooth white bed, while Rosie
hovered uneasily in the doorway.

'I reckon she was a kind of nun, all on her own. Come
on Lily dear, it gives me the creeps.'

In that cruel light Rosie, in the shabby black coat and
skirt she kept for funerals, looked tired and old. She had
shortened her skirt to fit in with the current fashion, and
perhaps she had overdone it a little. The cupid's bow
that she had, none too successfully, superimposed on
her lips, the smart shoes that hurt her feet suddenly
seemed to Lilian not just pathetic, but brave. Rosie had
lost a husband, a son, and a daughter, had suffered
miscarriages, struggled against poverty, and was still
soldiering on, believing that life would improve,
intending to do her best for the butcher and his family.
Aunt Annie had withdrawn from life, lost nothing
because she had nothing to lose. She had drawn inward,
to a narrowing space until in the end she had disappeared almost without trace. Lilian stared at the wooden
cross and hoped it had given her aunt some comfort.
She herself scarcely gave a thought to religion. When
she did it was only to feel surprise and some irritation at
Will's adherence to his faith.

She looked at Rosie who had not been to church since
Dollie's funeral or for years before that, and wanted to
tell her that she thought her a truly good woman. But

she knew that such a statement would only embarrass them both.

'Come on, then,' she said, rising to her feet. 'I'm not going to be rich after all.'

Together they went down the echoing stairs and out into the sun.

CHAPTER 8

Closing time. Thankfully Lilian bolted the shop door and pulled down the blind. She was tired and the day had been full of frustrating incidents, lost sales and difficult customers. An elderly woman with a shopping bag had smashed a cut-glass vase, knocking it off the shelf as she turned to leave the shop. Lilian had seen earlier in the day that it was in a dangerous position and had meant to move it. Now it was too late, and there had been an unpleasant argument, during which Lilian had been forced to admit that the customer was not entirely to blame. At last she was free to go upstairs to the flat where thirteen-year-old Sylvia was doing her homework with the wireless on. Bing Crosby was crooning a popular song and Lilian switched him off irritably.

'Oh, Mum!'

'How can you possibly concentrate on your home-work with that row going on?'

'I like it. It helps me. And anyway, I'm only doing my French translation. I don't need to concentrate.'

Sylvia was good at languages, as at most other

subjects. She was tall for her age, with smaller, neater features than her mother. Fair, in spite of her two red-haired parents, she was pretty as well as clever, but moody and difficult. Lilian hoped this was just a phase, though she could scarcely remember a time when her daughter had been easy to get on with.

'Feel like making a cup of tea?' she asked hopefully as she sank into the blue velvet easy chair and kicked off her high-heeled shoes.

'Oh, Mum, can't you do it? I've got this to finish.'

Sylvia leaned over and switched on the wireless again. She sat chewing the top of her pen. The dark-green of her box-pleated gym-slip and the green-and-white striped shirt she wore underneath it suited her fairness. Lilian looked at her more closely.

'Have you got lipstick on, Sylvia?'

'It's only Tangee. That doesn't count.'

Sylvia named a brand that was reputed to be not only kissproof, but invisible in wear.

'You're too young. Don't you dare go out with it on.' But Lilian, as she waited for the kettle to boil in the neat kitchenette, reflected that Sylvia certainly would go out with it on. When her homework was finished she would change into her grey pleated shorts and her short-sleeved jumper and run down to the sands to play hide-and-seek with her friends, girls from her own school who lived nearby, and a handful of boys from the grammar. These games were a constant worry to Lilian, who felt that a good deal more hiding than seeking went on as the sun set over the sea, and the shore, cleared of visitors, scattered with bathing-huts, became a play-ground for the local girls and boys.

When she carried the tray back into the sitting-room Sylvia was packing her books into her attaché case. The girls at St Margaret's School for Young Ladies did not use satchels, though the miniature suitcases were awkward to carry, and did not hold enough, so that there was always an armful of books as well.

'Is Uncle Will coming tonight?'

'I don't know. He might.'

In fact Lilian was not expecting him, but if a visit was likely Sylvia might decide not to go out. Though she knew him only as a family friend and her mother's employer she liked him, enjoyed his lively company, and always accepted his half-crowns with unembarrassed grace.

'Did he say anything about coming tonight?'

'No. But sometimes he just comes.'

'Well, I don't suppose he will. It's only Tuesday. I think I'll go out.'

Ten minutes later Lilian stood at the sitting-room window and saw Sylvia appear from the side entrance and run down the main street, soon crossing the road and disappearing down a turning that led to the seafront. She had tied a pale blue ribbon round her head, with a bow on top and the grey shorts showed off her bare sun-tanned legs. With pride and anxiety Lilian watched her disappear out of sight, then turned to look at herself in the fashionable frameless mirror that hung over the mantelpiece. Her own hair was still bright, her thinness no longer mattered because she had become elegant. In the shop she always wore a tailored suit or dress, her nails were painted with bright varnish chosen to match her dark-red lipstick and her shoes were always smart. The few people she knew in Warne Bay understood her to be a widow, but in spite of this fictitious respectability her social life was non-existent. She had joined the local amateur dramatic society, but in three years she had played only two parts, both of maids, so she had given up. On early closing days she invariably took the train to Culvergate to visit Mabel or Rosie, and occasionally on Sundays Mabel and Jack, still childless, would drive over to tea.

During the week her day was occasionally enlivened by the advent of Miss Dorothea Bethune, who with her brother would sometimes come to spend a few hours in Warne Bay. She invariably called at the shop and would sometimes chat to Lilian for nearly an hour before concluding her visit by making some sort of purchase and departing to meet her brother for lunch at the Granville. Though their conversations were somewhat one-sided, and the main topics were Miss Bethune's clothes, Miss Bethune's possessions and Miss Bethune's holidays, Lilian was nevertheless quite pleased to see her sweeping in and to hear her cry of 'My dear! Have you anything exciting to show me today?'

It seemed rather a pity that she never brought her brother Victor into the shop. Sometimes Lilian thought it would be nice if she were invited to lunch with them in the hotel. She wondered if Victor would ever marry. But the pattern of Dorothea's visits remained unchanged, and because she was lively, amusing, and a good customer, Lilian enjoyed them.

She had few other distractions, apart from Will. There ought to be more in life for a woman who looks like that, she thought, for tired as she was, her reflection pleased her.

Nine years earlier she had been delighted with the move to Warne Bay, to give Sylvia a proper home, to get away from Culvergate. In comparison with Shelley Street her present circumstances should have been blissful, but so often things happened to make her feel dissatisfied with the limitations of life. A week ago the Culvergate paper had shown a photograph taken at a local Chamber of Commerce dinner. Will, the president, sat at the centre of a long table, distinguished in evening dress. On his left sat Phyllis, dark, plump and pretty, with her husband on her other side, and on his right was Louisa, still full-bosomed and imposing though long past her allotted three score and ten. Her silver hair was elaborately coiffeured, and she was expensively draped in chiffon.

Lilian took the cutting out of the drawer and looked at it for the tenth time. It was so good of Will! If only she could have been beside him, with diamonds or an orchid pinned to the shoulder of her evening gown, taking part in the conversation, drinking wine. Feeling depressed she put away the picture and returned to the window. She supposed she would soon put her little pekinese dog on her lead and take her for a walk along the promenade. At least the dog gave one some sort of purpose. Walking on her own would otherwise have made her feel conspicuous.

It seemed a pity to do so little with the beautiful evening by the seaside. Tomorrow being Friday she would close the shop later, and on Saturday evening later still, so that the evening would be gone before she was free. Some people, she thought gloomily, would be getting into cars and driving round the countryside, calling in at picturesque little pubs, or visiting friends. Or playing tennis, or watching cricket, or just dawdling along the shore hand in hand. The two youngish sisters who ran the hairdressers next door would be out with their young men and the couple from the shoe-shop on the other side of the road would have gone home to their bungalow, where no doubt they were already busy gardening. They were a friendly but dull pair, who quite often invited Lilian round to 'see the garden'. On these occasions they always gave her an enormous bunch of flowers, but since they had no other interests and Lilian, though liking flowers and gardens, had very little to say about them, they found each other heavy going.

Lilian would have liked to discuss the novels she took out of the tuppenny library, the Sheila Kaye-Smiths, and the Ernest Raymonds, or the political news that she read in the papers, but apart from Will she knew no one with whom to share an interesting talk. So tonight it must be a stroll along the promenade with Tiger Lily, informally known as Tig, on the lead. And she would remember to avoid the area where Sylvia and the others were playing, or her daughter would come home angry, demanding to know why she was being spied on.

She was in her bedroom changing her linen dress for a brown and white patterned silk when someone pressed the bell on the side door. Who would be calling? Perhaps Mabel and Jack had decided to pay a surprise visit. Fastening her belt she went to the window to see if a car had been parked in front of the shop, and was surprised and pleased to see Will's big maroon Austin. After fifteen years of love, pleasure and disillusionment she was still made happy by his arrivals. She ran down the narrow stairs, not bothering to do up the top button of her dress. Sylvia would be out for a good hour.

Will came quickly into the tiny lobby, taking off his trilby hat. He was wearing his black jacket and striped trousers, with a dark tie, though he usually changed into something less formal when he came to Warne Bay. His face, still handsome, was ruddy and lined. He was tense and unsmiling.

'Will! What's the matter?'

Louisa! Had Louisa died suddenly?

'I want you to come with me. Straight away. It's important.'

'What's the matter? Is someone ill?'

'Yes. Come on. You don't need a coat.'

'But who is it? Tell me.'

'No one you know. Are you ready?'

'But Will, if it's no one I know ... what about Sylvia? She's out playing.'

'Leave her a note or something.'

'She won't be able to get in. She hasn't got a key.'

'Then tell her to go next door. Only hurry.'

'Will, come upstairs. You've got to tell me what it's all about.'

She preceded him up the narrow staircase and into the sitting-room. 'You look rotten. Shall I get you a cup of tea? Or a drink? There's some sherry.'

'No. I don't want anything, there isn't time. Lilla, I need you. You've got to come with me. Now!'

Lilian went to the window and looked along the street as if by some extraordinary chance her daughter might be visible on her way home three-quarters of an hour before her usual time, but of course there was no sign of her.

'We'll have to find Sylvia and bring her home. Then I'll come.'

She spoke decisively. More decisively than she felt. It would not be easy to persuade Sylvia to leave her friends before the game was over.

'Have it your way then, only come on.'

'Look, I can't leave her wandering round the town for Heaven knows how long. For God's sake, Will, she's your child as well as mine.'

'She's got friends hasn't she? She'll go home with one

of them. Pin a note to the front door.'

'I'm not going anywhere until Sylvia's indoors. We'll go and fetch her. She's somewhere on the sands. I'll just get my bag.'

She picked up her smart cream leather bag, shut Tiger Lily in the kitchen, and followed Will down the stairs.

Sylvia was not pleased when her mother interrupted the game, and Lilian abandoned the idea of taking her home. Instead she gave her the key and instructed her to be indoors by nine, deploring her own weakness as she did so.

'And stay with the others. Don't go off alone.'

'Of course I won't. Where are you going?'

'Just out to have a drink with Uncle Will, I won't be long. But don't go to sleep, you've got my key, remember.'

Anxious already, Lilian got into the car, and they drove off. 'Where are we going, Will? What's happened?'

'It's Ruth.'

Ruth? For a moment she could not think of anyone called Ruth, then, 'Not Ruth Smith?'

'Yes.'

'But I've got nothing to do with her. I haven't seen her for years and years. Will, you can't expect me to do anything for her. I thought you finished with her when I came here. You can't expect me to do anything for Ruth Smith. When I think . . .'

She could not bring herself to say, 'When I think I shared you with that woman.' For years she had put the knowledge at the back of her mind, determinedly kept her imagination from dwelling on it. Now Will was forcing the realization upon her.

'You've got to stop, Will. Take me home. I don't know what you think you're doing.'

They were in the open country now, speeding along between the flat Kentish fields.

'Lilla, for God's sake don't waste time behaving like a silly girl. You've known about Ruth all along, don't pretend you haven't. You know the kind of man I am. And I've been fair to you, haven't I? You're all right, you and Sylvia. You've got nothing to complain about, but now someone's got to help me, and you're the only one.'

'The only one.' Lilian laughed sardonically.

They drove in silence for several miles, then she said, 'What do you want me to do?'

'Ruth's ill. That is, she's hurt. There was an accident. I want you to see if it's really bad, get a doctor perhaps. I don't know. We must think.'

We! It's nothing to do with me, thought Lilian. There's no 'we' about it. I want nothing to do with that woman. What did he mean, an accident? Would there be blood? What could she use for bandages? Why hadn't he told her this before so that she could have come prepared?

The car turned up a narrow side road, towards a little copse. Just beyond it, concealed from the main road by stunted bushes and a few thin trees was the shabby gypsy caravan. Will turned off the track and drove over the rough ground for a few yards, so that the car too was hidden. Not the first time, thought Lilian. The evening was still beautiful. The setting sun shone with a mellow, peaceful summer evening light. The freshness of the sea breeze mingled with the pungent smell of the cabbage fields. Lilian felt cold, and shivered as Will led her up the steps of the van and opened the door. Inside it was nearly dark. The windows were tiny. Will struck a match and lit an oil lamp that stood on a small table, carefully replacing the pink glass shade.

The first thing that struck Lilian was the cleanliness and order of the place. The curving roof and the walls were of dark stained wood, the steel of the little stove was burnished and the table was covered by a red plush cloth, with a white crochet mat under the lamp. The floor and the rugs upon it were clean, the brass ornaments and pieces of pottery shone, the white lace curtains were pristine. It was crowded, cramped and dark, but it was a home.

'Come in,' said Will irritably. 'Come in and shut the door,' for Lilian was still hesitating on the steps. Entering the confined space she was aware of a sour smell, despite the cleanliness. Should she have to clear up the woman's vomit? Why couldn't she just walk away?

He moved to the far end of the van where a figure lay still on a bunk bed, covered by a grey blanket. 'Ruth,' he whispered urgently, 'Ruth.'

Carefully so as not to knock over the lamp, Lilian squeezed past the table and stood beside him. The woman's head rested on a pillow that was snow white where it was not stained with blood, and heavily trimmed with crochet lace. A thick braid of coarse greying hair snaked across it. Blood was caked round a wound on her temple, the dark gypsy eyes were open and the jaw was too.

'She's dead, Will. For God's sake, she's dead. Come away.' She saw now that there was a pool of vomit on the grey blanket. Surely Will didn't expect her to do anything, to touch this appalling object? He stood beside her, looking down at the dead face, then he lifted his right hand and very gently closed the eyes, afterwards pulling up the blanket to cover the head. He crossed himself, and murmured something that might have been a Latin prayer.

'Will! You can't do anything. Come on, we must get away!'

She stumbled down the rickety steps and hurried to the car. Shivering she sat in the front passenger seat. If she had not been too far from home she would have run there. Supposing somebody came? What if they had been seen? Leaning over, she wound down the window on the driver's side and called, 'Will! Come on!'

At last he appeared. He got into the car and sat there beside her, but he did not attempt to start the engine.

'I thought ... you could get a doctor. I couldn't, but you could have said something. She was alive when I left. I'm sure she was alive when I left.'

'What happened?'

'I'll tell you later. Not now. Lilla, we can't leave her like that.'

'Of course we can. We must get right away, quickly.'

'Somebody's bound to find her sooner or later. There'll be an inquest.'

An inquest. People asking questions. Why had he brought her here, got her mixed up in it? Could she go to prison for shielding him?

His hands on the steering wheel, he leaned forward, resting his head on them. He said, 'It'll be the end of everything.'

The end of everything. The end, probably, of her cosy flat and pleasant job, the end of lovemaking, the end of all her hopes.

In the gathering dusk she saw a glimmer of the lamp through the caravan window.

'You didn't put the lamp out.'

'What does it matter? We'd better go.'

He was gripping the steering wheel, trembling convulsively. A dark vein at his temple was distended, pulsing.

She opened the door of the car.

'Where are you going?'

'I won't be a minute. I'm going to turn out the lamp.'

'What the devil for? Get in.'

'Wait.'

At the foot of the steps she picked up a heavy stone, a flint, such as were common in the area. Standing in the doorway she thought perhaps she should look at Ruth's body once more, to make quite certain that she was dead. But she had been certain. So had Will, he had closed the eyes. She hesitated with the stone in her hand, then she lobbed it carefully at the lamp. It shattered the pink shade and the thin glass chimney inside it, but the base was broad and heavy, the thing remained obstinately upright. She took three steps into the van, and laid the lamp on its side, expecting the oil to flood out, and burst into flame, but it did not. It seeped out slowly, and the flame burnt upwards, not catching it. What had been an impulse, something to be done quickly and immediately put out of her mind, had become a considered, deliberate action. Something she would never be able to convince herself had been half accidental, the result of a moment's panic. Carefully she moved the lamp, still on its side, towards the lace curtain. The flame, licking up through the broken glass, caught it at once, flaring quickly up to the varnished wood above. She left then, not quite closing the door. She ran towards the car, turning her ankle, stumbling in her high-heeled shoes.

'Quick, we must go.' She clenched her trembling hands together on her lap, tried to be calm, to breathe slowly and deeply. But suppose the car would not start? Suppose they were marooned here among the cabbage fields and had to walk away, mile after exposed, treeless mile, on to Culvergate, or back to Warne Bay? But the car started, rocked over the field and down the track, and was speeding back the way they had come. Neither of them spoke. On their right the sun was setting over the distant sea in a glory of peach and gold.

When they drew up outside the shop, Lilian saw thankfully that the light was on in the sitting-room. Sylvia was home. Not in bed, as she should have been. She looked at Will. His face was a peculiar, worrying colour, greyish under his normal ruddiness.

'Are you coming in?'

'No. I'd best get home. And you've got Sylvia to see to.'

For God's sake. What 'seeing to' did a girl of thirteen need? Surely they were beyond the need for excuses?

'Just as you like,' She paused. 'Will. You'll go straight back, won't you?'

She was afraid he might stop at the caravan. Perhaps it would be burnt out by now, perhaps the fire brigade would be there, or the police, or both. 'Why don't you go home through Grange and Winham? It's longer, I know, but ...'

'Best not to do anything unusual.'

'But the police might stop you. They might ask you if you came that way earlier tonight. Even if they don't recognize you they'll want to know who you are and where you live. They're sure to stop every car that passes.'

'Why should the police be there?'

Did he really not know? What did he think she had been doing? 'Will, go the other way. Please.'

He covered her hand with his, and she was glad it was his left hand, not the right hand he had used to close the dead eyes.

'Thanks, Lilian. I'll be over in a few days.'

'No. No, don't come for a while. Stay in Culvergate. Ring me up.'

She got quickly out and slammed the door. By the time Sylvia came down to the private entrance to let her in Will had turned the car and was almost out of sight. Her daughter preceded her up the stairs and when Lilian reached the sitting-room she was curled up on the settee, her feet in canvas shoes resting on the blue velvet.

'Why aren't you in bed? And take your feet off the cushions.'

With an exaggerated sigh Sylvia moved her legs. 'You told me not to go to sleep, so what was the point in going to bed? Why don't we get another key? If I had a key of my own you wouldn't have to worry about me. Anyway, where's Uncle Will? Why didn't he come in?'

Lilian glanced at herself in the mirror, saw her own pale face, and her hair, usually set in regular undulations by June next door, now untidy where she had pushed through the bushes. Looking down she saw the mud on her heels. Why had she not anticipated these questions?

'Uncle Will was worried about something, he wanted to have a talk. It's all right now.'

'He always comes to you when he's worried. I think he ought to get a divorce and marry you.'

'Don't be ridiculous. It's not like that at all.'

But it was like that. How many times had she not had the same thought? And others. Others that made her feel ashamed and guilty.

'Your shoes are all muddy.'

'Yes, I'm just going to take them off.'

'You've got mud on the carpet.' Sylvia sounded

pleased. Lilian removed her shoes, fetched the brush and dustpan, and cleaned away the mud.

Sylvia, her feet back on the velvet cushions, watched her. 'I don't see why he shouldn't be divorced. Film stars get divorced. It's nothing to them. Franchot Tone, Cary Grant, Robert Taylor, they've all been divorced.'

'Well, you should know all about that.'

Most of Sylvia's pocket money went on *Film Weekly*, and *Picturegoer*. The walls of her room were covered with portraits of the stars that she had cut out of these periodicals, in her mother's opinion ruining the effect of the pink taffeta eiderdown, the rose printed curtains and carefully matched bedside rug. But still it was her room, she must be allowed to have it as she wanted it. Lilian had too many memories of her own girlhood, cramped and limited as it had been, to fail to understand her daughter's need for some sort of freedom. After all she expressed herself in her surroundings, so why not Sylvia? The cool blues of the sitting-room, very modern, with bare pale grey walls, a few but beautiful ornaments, and everything clean, clear, what was called streamlined, fulfilled a need for order and restraint that her way of life lacked. Sometimes it was the sheer untidiness of it all that irked her most. Never knowing when Will would arrive, having no legitimate father for her child, being known as Mrs Watts when she was really Miss Watts and ought to have been Mrs Fitzgerald: it was all so messy.

She took the dustpan out into the kitchen, emptied it, and put it away in the cupboard under the sink. In the tidy white bathroom she ran warm water into the basin, submerged her hands, and stood motionless, looking down at them. She had done a stupid thing. She should have touched nothing, made Will drive her home: it wasn't her business. But if Will were put in prison, what then? She was glad he had not told her what had happened, and she would not ask him again. If he and Ruth quarrelled, and why they had quarrelled, whether she had fallen or been pushed when she hit her head against the corner of the stove as she presumably had, these were things she did not want to know. She knew too much already. She must fear the police ringing the bell or coming to the shop. She must dread the arrival of the Culvergate paper. She thought of phrases like 'accessory after the fact', she remembered about finger-prints. As she meticulously washed and dried her hands she hoped the caravan had burned to the ground. But supposing the fire had failed to take hold? The wood might well have been damp. Then things would look bad. Had anyone noticed the car parked near the trees? Few passed that way in the evening, but there was no comfort in that, it was all the more reason that they might have been noticed there on the outskirts of Culvergate. Everyone knew Will's car. They knew her, too. Old Fitzgerald's fancy woman, one of several. That was how they spoke of her. She sat at the kitchen table with a glass of sherry, the only alcohol she had in the place. She could have done with a brandy. Her thoughts went back to the day when she had first seen Ruth, and accepted the sprig of white heather from Will. That was the first step on the road that had led her to this situa-tion. You got what you asked for in this life, she thought. Got it and paid for it. She could have been married to Jim for years and years now, living in the little terraced house in Station Road, overworked, shabby and bored stiff. Not that Elsie seemed bored, on the contrary she seemed quite happy on the rare occa-sions when they met. It had been quite amusing to see dumpy Elsie's patronizing attitude towards elegant Lilian.

When Sylvia called goodnight Lilian poured herself another drink and carried it back into the sitting-room. Sinking into her velvet-covered chair, Lilian decided that she would not change places with Elsie, not yet. But of course she would not be given that chance.

CHAPTER 9

For weeks she was jumpy and nervous, sleeping badly, irritable with Sylvia. When a policeman walked into the shop she broke out in a cold sweat, but he was only delivering a description of some stolen porcelain in case the thief tried to sell it to her. A young friendly constable, he was often on the beat in the centre of the town. In the late evening he would religiously try the door of every shop, and had once called her down when she failed to lock up properly.

The caravan fire and the discovery of Ruth's body were reported in the *Culvergate Gazette*, which was sent to her every week by Rosie. For years there had been little in it to interest Lilian, but she knew that folding it neatly, tying it with string, labelling and posting it, was something that Rosie found worth doing. Now it was not just interesting, but frightening. Anxiously she awaited the account of the inquest. Supposing they brought in a verdict of murder? Murder by a person or persons unknown? Of course, Will was not guilty of murder, but he had a temper. She tried not to think about the scene in the caravan, but it kept recreating itself in her mind. She thought that if Ruth's lover had been some other man she could have pitied her, giving up family and friends to die alone in the end.

The coroner's verdict was death by misadventure, and she began to feel more secure. Before Christmas, Will resumed his visits, and even accompanied her to Sylvia's school prizegiving. Lilian hoped people would take him for her brother, or possibly even her uncle, and hoped she would not be forced to introduce him to anyone, but it was pleasant to be escorted, and to share her pride in her child. Sylvia was loaded with prizes and certificates and afterwards Will gave her a crisp five pound note, telling her it was not to be saved, but spent at once on something she wanted. It was all very like being married until Will took his leave as soon as Sylvia had gone to bed.

'You're not staying? She'll be asleep in a few minutes, she's tired out.'

'I'd better get off. Lou's not too well. She likes me to be at home.'

And I like you to be here, thought Lilian, but I'm not your wife. Aloud she said, 'Just a little while, let's finish the evening properly.'

She put her arms round him but he removed them gently. 'Don't worry, my darling. Our time will come.'

Lilian did not ask what he meant by that. Time to go to bed together? Time to be married and together always? Standing on the dark landing they kissed fondly enough, then telling her he would let himself out he hurried down to the side door.

Lilian put the kettle on to make herself a cup of tea. Standing in the kitchen she wished that they were married, could have drunk the tea in quiet companionship and gone to bed, without feeling anxious because of

Sylvia, or unsettled because he would have to get up in an hour or two and drive home.

Thinking of the millions of wives preparing for the beds they shared with their husbands Lilian was envious, yet when she projected her imagination towards the morning she felt differently. Supposing she and Will were married and he lived here with her and Sylvia in the little flat. The place would be crowded for a start, there was not enough room for a third person as a permanent resident. Then after breakfast, which she supposed in Will's case would have to be bacon and egg rather than the cornflakes and toast with which she and Sylvia were contented, he would be the one to go down into the shop, to open the mail, and greet the customers and commercial travellers, rearrange the window display and count up the takings at the end of the day. She would be up here in the flat, cleaning, preparing meals, shopping, washing, doing all that Nancy still did even now she was married, since she was busy on Lilian's behalf from nine till four-thirty every day. Will, not she, would go to the meetings of the Warne Bay Chamber of Commerce, deal with the bank account and the insurance. She would not even know how well or badly they were doing in the shop. It was not at all an attractive picture and for the first time Lilian saw some advantages in her situation. Did she then still want to marry Will when the time came? Well, of course, she must do so, for Sylvia, and to justify her years of waiting, to prove to herself and everyone else that Will was the one man for her, the love of her life, and to make the years of illicit love retrospectively legitimate. And in any case, she and Will would not live here together, but in Culvergate, where she would be kept busy being Mrs Fitzgerald, sitting on Committees such as Friends of the Hospital, organizing charity bazaars, and probably being Mayoress, for Will had twice been Mayor, and would almost certainly be chosen again. Then there would be receptions, and At Homes, fittings for the special dresses she would need, and perhaps before many years were out a grand wedding for Sylvia. Sylvia Fitzgerald she would be by that time, because Will would adopt her legally, though everyone would know he was her real father. They would see a lot of Phyllis who would say, 'I'm so pleased about all this, Lilian, it's what I always hoped for. You've made Dad so happy.'

Then surely Will's retirement was not far away. Perhaps she would take over the business herself, making it even more successful. This flight of fancy was a great solace to Lilian, and one which she repeated at frequent intervals, so when Jim phoned one morning to say that Louisa Fitzgerald had been taken ill in the night and was not expected to live she was forced to pretend a concern she did not feel. She did try to feel pity for the seventy-six-year-old woman who had always been gracious and pleasant to her, but after all Louisa had lived a good long life, and a comfortable one, she'd been lucky in most ways, and even now she was being cared for in Culvergate's most expensive nursing home. During the three weeks that she remained there Lilian's greatest fear was that she would make a startling recovery and return to the Fort.

'She's thirty-six years older than me.' thought Lilian, 'and it's my turn now.'

When death finally claimed Will's wife she sent flowers, feeling somewhat hypocritical.

From Lilian Watts, she wrote, *with pleasant memories.*

That she could truthfully say. The music evenings had

always been enjoyable.

That done, she began to prepare herself for Will's next visit, when he would undoubtedly propose. They would have to wait a few months, but not too long. She went to the hairdresser's and had her still brilliant hair set in a new style with a half-fringe. She bought new clothes, and experimented with make-up. She and Sylvia tried out mud-packs and astringent lotion, coloured nail varnish and new shades of lipstick, which Sylvia was supposed to remove before going out, but usually did not. Lilian was indulgent, because for once they were enjoying each other's company. She bought flowers for the flat and made sure that the sitting-room was always tidy, with Will's favourite cigarettes in the box on the low table, the Swan Vestas always to hand. Even so, she was not surprised when several weeks elapsed without a visit from the man who was the cause of all these preparations. When Sylvia said, 'It's ages since Uncle Will came, isn't it, Mum?' she explained that it would be tactless for him to appear soon after his wife's death. He had to do the right thing, he was a man in the public eye. She hinted nevertheless that the future might hold some very exciting changes for them both, although they could not expect to see him for a week or two yet.

But he could have telephoned. He had an extension in the flat, as she had herself. He could telephone any evening without fear of being overheard, but she did not really think he would. It was more likely that he would arrive as he often had, unexpectedly, with a bottle of sherry for her and some sweets for Sylvia. Only this time it would be different because they would at last be able to make plans for their future together.

Spring came, and with it Sylvia's fourteenth birthday. Lilian remembered giving birth in Nurse Tebbitt's

cottage, and how confident she had been of marrying
Will in the end. Well, she was still confident, though she
hadn't expected to wait fourteen years. Seven, perhaps.
Stupid, really, to assume that Louisa would depart this
life punctually on reaching the age of seventy. After all,
she might easily have lived to eighty or eighty-five. Lots
of people did, or Will might easily have gone first.
Things were turning out quite as well as any sensible
woman could possibly have expected, and now it was
just a matter of waiting.

As the weather improved Warne Bay came to life.
Visitors strolled up and down the promenade and
shopped in the High Street. Lilian wondered when Miss
Bethune would next make an appearance. She and her
brother often went abroad for the worst months of the
year, but it was unusual for them to delay visiting
Warne Bay until nearly May. Any day now they would
come. Lilian decided to show Dorothea a lifelike statuette of a cocker spaniel in porcelain that bore a marked
resemblance to Victor Bethune's dog Tess. As the weeks
passed Lilian wondered quite anxiously if all was well
with the Bethunes, and hoped that no misfortune had
overtaken them.

Every day she considered telephoning Will herself,
and every day she decided to wait a little longer. After
all, what could she say? Now your wife is dead, please
can we get married? Dusting the china she tried hard to
think of acceptable phraseology, and found none. She
snapped at Sylvia when she asked repeatedly if Uncle
Will was coming soon and forgot her usual letters to
Rosie and Mabel.

She considered taking the train to Culvergate on an
early closing day, but by now she was filled with
doubts. The shop would be closed, she might easily not

find Will at home. Would he be glad to see her? Would he embrace her at once and then lead her upstairs to the big heavily furnished room he had shared with his wife? Would she want to go to bed with him if he did? To lie with him on that connubial couch? Though perhaps if they were in bed together she would be able to ask him how soon they were to marry.

Unbelievably, over five months had passed with no more than the briefest business communication between them, no more than a pencilled note at the bottom of an invoice.

'Hope you are keeping well. Business here very quiet. Give S. five bob out of the petty cash. W.F.'

She knew he had to be careful, but surely he was being unnecessarily punctilious? Most people in Culvergate had known of their association for years.

During the last week in May Rosie came over on the afternoon train, and tried to be reassuring, though her expression was anxious. Three days later Mabel and Jack arrived for Sunday tea on the sands, but Mabel's gift of a new dress was ungratefully received by Sylvia who thought the Peter Pan collar and puffed sleeves far too babyish. Mabel was upset, and Jack was annoyed and they left early. Lilian rebuked her daughter, who was insolent in return and they both went to bed miserable.

Waking early the next morning Lilian was depressed. Nothing seemed to be going right, except the business, which was thriving.

When the telephone rang after Sylvia had left for school she expected nothing unusual, but hearing Jim's voice she was frightened. In all these months she had never really entertained the idea that Will might be ill, now she feared it. Jim, who rarely telephoned, bellowed into her ear.

'Have you seen the paper?'

'No. I don't get it till Friday. What's the matter?'

'Its Mr F.'

'Mr F?' The old name came strangely to her lips.

'Yes.'

'Is he ill? Has there been an accident?'

'No. Nothing like that. He's getting married.'

She was silent. What could he mean?

'Are you there? Lilian, are you there?'

Her voice shook as she said yes. But wait. Will must have told Jim that he intended to remarry, without divulging the identity of his bride-to-be. Of course that was it. The cheek, to tell other people before he had even asked her properly. But of course he was sure of her after all these years. She would forgive him.

Jim was speaking. 'I thought you ought to know. Only fair to tell you.'

'It's very kind of you, Jim,' she laughed a little 'but I've got to know sometime, haven't I?'

It was Jim's turn to remain silent for a moment, then he said, 'I thought ... I was afraid you might be upset. After so long. I'm sorry if I've made a mistake. I don't suppose you remember Miss Bethune, do you?'

Dorothea? What had she got to do with it? 'Oh yes. She and her brother come over here sometimes.'

'Lilian, you do understand what I'm driving at? Mr F's got himself engaged to her, to Miss Bethune. They're getting married in June. I told Elsie and she said I ought to ...'

There was a click and a hum as the receiver was replaced. Jim had evidently been interrupted.

She returned to the kitchen and sat down at the little table. Sylvia had already left for school, and Lilian had been looking forward to a quiet interval with a cup of tea and her newspaper before opening the shop. The tea was cooling, but she did not raise the cup to her lips. She sat there, staring at it, while time passed. She noticed the gingery skin forming on the surface of the liquid. She saw how this skin thickened and contracted, leaving exposed some of the paler liquid beneath. She was interested by the creamy line that bordered it, and repelled by the patchiness that began to appear like a disease. No other conscious thoughts occupied her mind, it was as though the skin on the tea covered a bottomless pit, a huge blackness, and for the moment prevented it from overwhelming her. Nearly half an hour passed before she became aware that Nance was banging on the side door, banging and shouting with alarm in her voice, for Lilian was invariably in the shop by the time she arrived.

Nance had to be admitted. The shop had to be opened. Slowly, stiffly, Lilian went down the stairs and did both of these things.

It was late morning before she was able to think at all clearly. She longed for Rosie, her true friend with whom she had shared so many cries. She would have liked to leave the shop to her part-time assistant and go straight to the flat over the butcher's in Culvergate High Street, but that was unthinkable. If you were a shop-keeper you attended to business, whatever happened. But tomorrow, on early closing day, she would go. Rosie would help her to decide what to do. Because of course the whole thing must be stopped. As she considered the situation she came to believe that Will had no intention of breaking with her, merely wishing to avoid her temporarily until he was settled with his new rich wife. But she couldn't let him get away with that. She'd played second fiddle long enough. Now she must have her rightful place, publicly, at his side.

The *Gazette* arrived the next morning, a day earlier than usual. Rosie could not have had time to read it herself. When Lilian opened it a note fell from between the pages.

> *Dear Lilian,*
>
> *I know you'll be upset about the news. I would have come over but you know what it is. I will try next week. I did not think he would play such a rotten trick, but we live and learn.*
>
> *Yours affectionately,*
> *Rosie.*

No mention of putting a stop to it. No suggestion that there was anything to be done. Oh, Rosie, Rosie. But she would do something.

She spread the newspaper out on the shop counter and searched the closely printed columns. The brief paragraph was much as she had expected. Alderman W.D. Fitzgerald was to marry Miss Dorothea Bethune of Oak Tree House, The Avenue, Palmers Bay. He had expressed his intention of retiring from business but would continue with his public work. Alderman Fitzgerald had twice been Mayor of Culvergate. A prominent Roman Catholic, he was well-known in the town for his interest in civic affairs and various charities. His wife, Mrs Louisa Fitzgerald, had died in January.

There seemed to be a hint of criticism in the reminder of Louisa's too recent death. Well, it was too soon for him to remarry, and everyone would say so. Lilian herself had never imagined that he would consider marrying before the following spring. That woman must

have got round him somehow. Lent him money,
perhaps. But her fools' paradise was to be shattered
because no one but Lilian Watts was likely to marry Will
Fitzgerald, for a number of very good reasons. Did he
really think that a fifteen-year love affair, a daughter,
and complicity in some sort of crime left him free to
marry anyone he chose?

Luckily business was brisk and absorbing until closing
time. Lilian spent the evening making arrangements and
preparing her clothes for the next day. She still intended
to go to Culvergate as soon as the shop was shut at one
o'clock, but not to visit Rosie. Rosie would offer consola-
tion but that was not what she wanted. Her resolve had
hardened. She would go to Will and demand that he
break with Dorothea Bethune at once. He could not
refuse. But if he did refuse she would then go straight to
Oak Tree House and tell her story. It was hardly likely
that Dorothea would wish to marry him after that. Lilian
felt the strength and fearlessness of one with right on
her side. She almost looked forward to the battle.

Yet as she pressed her silk blouse and washed her silk
stockings that evening she would not have been
surprised to hear the door bell ring, and to find Will,
ready with an explanation, brimming with promises,
waiting to be admitted. In those circumstances her fury
might easily fade away, he might be able to persuade
her that it was all for the best.

It did not happen. On the Thursday she closed the
shop very punctually, and leaving Sylvia to eat her
midday meal with Nance in the kitchen, she went
straight to her bedroom and changed into her best
outfit, which consisted of a straight skirt with pleats and
a fitted braided jacket. She put on her cream blouse and
a very smart little black hat, which had to be tipped

forward and sideways, anchored to her head by a band of elasticated velvet which pressed her hair down at the back. She debated over her fox fur, and decided to wear it, with her new black court shoes and best handbag. She had been able to afford good clothes for two or three years now, and enjoyed them. Surveying herself in the long mirror inside the wardrobe door she saw a tall elegant woman, suitably dressed for a somewhat formal visit to Culvergate which was a town where people had always dressed fashionably, and clothes mattered.

She caught the one-fifty with time to spare, having asked Nance to stay on and get Sylvia's tea. Nance agreed eagerly, and offered to wait until Lilian returned. She could slip home in the afternoon and leave a note for Leonard. Poor Leonard. He worked long and awkward hours as a bus-driver, but Lilian could not cure his wife of the habit of putting her employer's concerns first. She frequently suggested to Nance that she should consider her husband rather more, but today she was glad of her eager assistance. Sylvia could not be trusted to come straight home from school if left to herself. She would probably take the opportunity to go to the cinema, not allowed except on Saturdays, or stay out with her friends.

'I shan't be late. I just have some business to attend to, though I might go and see Auntie Rosie if I have time.'

It would be nice to go and tell Rosie that Will had changed his mind.

'We'll be all right,' said Sylvia, who enjoyed Nance's undemanding company, so Lilian was able to get off with a mind free of domestic worries.

During the half-hour journey in the stopping train to Culvergate, she went over her plans. She knew that Will

was in the habit of resting for an hour after the midday
meal, so he would certainly be at home. He might not,
of course, be pleased to see her. He might even be angry
with her. She remembered the death of Ruth Smith and
her heart sank unaccountably, for surely this was quite a
different situation. After all, he had loved her for years,
she would persuade, not threaten, and all would be well.
But what if she was forced to take her story to Dorothea? Was it conceivable that she might still wish to
marry him despite everything? She told herself that
these speculations were fruitless, that she must adapt to
the situation as it developed. At least they would find
that she was a force to be reckoned with.

Leaving the station she walked along the Esplanade in
the sun. There were taxis available but she had plenty of
time. This decision was wrong. Her new shoes were not
made for walking, and her feet were tired and painful by
the time she reached her destination. It being Thursday
she had expected to find the shop closed, but not to see
the shutters obscuring the windows and the grille bolted
into position across the entrance. What had happened to
Charlie, who had always returned in the late evening to
secure the premises? She noticed that the shop next
door had changed hands, and that the corner chemist
had become, of all things, a fish and chip shop. Because
of the grille she was unable to reach the front door bell
so she walked round the corner to the narrow passage
that ran behind the shops. The high gate that led into
the back yard of the jewellery and china shop was
unbolted, and the yard itself was as untidy as it had
always been. Packing cases littered it, bits of straw and
paper blew about. She knocked hard with her gloved
knuckles on the back door, and peered through the glass
between the bars that were fixed across inside. All she

could see was the lobby, the door to the china store which was closed, and facing her the door that led into the shop, also closed, and finally on her right the kitchen door, which stood ajar. Moving along, she peered in through the kitchen window. That cheerless workplace was much as it had always been, clean, tidy and dismal. It looked as though Will still kept a servant but where was she now? It did not appear that any cooking had recently been done there. Perhaps Will now took his meals at Oak Tree House. Or perhaps he was upstairs asleep.

She thought of the telephone. She would find a callbox and ring up, just saying she had something important to discuss, and if Will was there he would come down and let her in. She did not have far to go. There was a new call-box on the opposite side of the road in front of the shop. She found two pennies, inserted them, asked for the number and waited with her finger on Button A. From where she stood she could see the windows of Will's drawing-room, and she thought a curtain twitched slightly, but it might have been her imagination.

She waited, holding the receiver fastidiously away from her ear. She could hear the ringing tone, on and on and on. No one answered, no welcome click or voice saying hello. Staring in despair at the window above the shop it seemed to her that the curtain twitched again. She replaced the receiver.

Now there was only one thing to be done. The situation must be resolved today somehow. She must go to Oak Tree House, and confront Dorothea. If she were alone it would not be too difficult. She would be upset of course, but Lilian felt that Will's fiancée was a fairminded woman who would understand her situation. If

Will were with her it would be different. She would need all her reserves of dignity and authority to face them both, but she thought she could do it. She set off along the front, but the new, high-heeled shoes, uncomfortable from the start, soon began to cause her real pain. There seemed to be a blister forming on one heel, and all her toes were savagely cramped. Absurd to wear shoes she had not 'broken-in', and then to walk when she could have taken a taxi.

The afternoon was warm. People sat outside the hotels on shaded verandahs, the women in bright sleeveless dresses, or shorts and sun-tops, the men in open necked shirts, although it was still only May. She began to feel conspicuous in her black tailor-made and her fox fur. Culvergate had changed, become less formal, and she had not realized. She would arrive at Oak Tree House and find Dorothea sitting in the garden, coolly dressed in pale blue shantung or apple-green linen, and she would feel clumsy and old-fashioned.

By the time she reached the corner of the Avenue, a good twenty minutes walk from the Fort at the best of times, her feet were like balls of fire. At every step the back of her left shoe scraped savagely at the raw place on her heel. She wondered if Victor Bethune would drive her back to the station. She could hardly expect Dorothea to be grateful to her, but Victor might be pleased that he was not going to lose his sister.

But she could not take another step, and there was still a hundred yards to go. She sat down on the low wall that surrounded the garden of the corner house and took off her shoes. Her heel was bleeding and the silk stocking had worn through. She sat there, shoeless, undignified and wretched. Well-dressed women did not sit by the roadside in their stockinged feet. She could have wept.

A car turned the corner and drew up outside the next house. An elderly man and woman climbed out and when money changed hands she realized that it was a taxi. Glancing curiously at her, the couple passed through the front gate followed by the driver carrying a suitcase. When he returned Lilian stood up.

'Would you take me to the station?'

'Certainly, Madam.' He saw her shoes in her hand. 'You women will wear these damn silly shoes. My wife's just the same.'

Lilian wanted to tell him that she was a successful business woman, not at all like his wife, but she leaned back and closed her eyes.

The walk from the car into the station was agony, but she hadn't long to wait for a train. The carriage that stopped in front of her was marked First Class, and though she had taken a Third Class ticket, she opened the door and got in. As the train began to move she settled herself in the empty compartment, thankfully removing her shoes again and putting her feet up on the opposite seat. She took off her hat, unbuttoned her jacket and leaned back. They served refreshments on this train, she knew, but she had never ordered anything on previous occasions because the journey to Warne Bay took barely half an hour and the service was slow. She lit a cigarette and watched the flat fields sliding by in the sunshine. She had never seen mountains, never travelled, and she thought she would like, some day, to visit a mountainous country, but she doubted if any scenery could be more satisfying than the wide horizon of her native landscape. The level fields

extending on either side as far as the eye could see
suffused her with a sense of space, freedom and light
that seemed part of a feeling of achievement that was
taking possession of her. But why? She had failed in her
object. She had seen neither Will nor Dorothea, she had
made rather a fool of herself, she had altered nothing.
She could always try again of course, telephone, write,
or go back to Culvergate. She could make appointments,
take taxis, wear comfortable shoes, instead of rushing
off idiotically in the wrong clothes and making a hash of
things. If she had been more sensible she could have
been the future Mrs Fitzgerald by now.

But sitting alone in her comfortable First Class
compartment, she found she preferred to remain Lilian
Watts. She would be all right and so would Sylvia. She
could earn a living anywhere if the present situation
came to an end, but she did not think it would. She was
making money for Will, probably the only real income
he now had. She remembered how run down the shops
of the Fort had appeared. The prosperous centre of the
town had evidently moved up towards Palmer's Bay,
and the area where she had once worked was now a
place where day trippers bought vulgar postcards and
crude models of bedroom china with the words 'A
present from Culvergate' painted in gold. Poor Will.
He'd be all right with Dorothea.

Perhaps she would leave Warne Bay in any case, take
a job as a buyer in a London store, or go to Bourne-
mouth or Brighton. Gazing out of the window across the
cabbage fields she thought what a lovely stretch of
colour these mundane vegetables provided, a sort of soft
blue-green. She would like a dress of that shade. It
would suit her.

The door slid open and a uniformed attendant asked if she would like some tea.

'Yes, please,' said Lilian. She smiled. 'But bring it as quickly as possible, will you? I'm getting out at Warne Bay.'

Read on for a taste of Valerie Maskell's absorbing new novel

THE WORKBOX

the tragic story of a woman haunted by a terrible secret . . .

Copyright © Valerie Maskell 1993

CHAPTER 1

MONDAY

Instead of getting out of her car when she had drawn up in front of the imposing Georgian portico of Easton Court, Dorothy remained in the driving seat. Just the moment for a cigarette. She imagined feeling in the glove compartment, finding a left-over packet, lighting up and drawing in the first sweet, relaxing puffs. She did not feel in the glove compartment, because she had given up smoking six months before. In any case they would be stale.

Four-twenty-five. Half an hour with Mum, and she could still reach home in time to persuade Angela into the bathroom with the baby, and tidy up the sitting room a bit before dashing out to meet Frank at the station.

There never seemed to be enough room for everyone these days, even with Mum here. When they had bought Jasmine Villa it was just the right size, and what an interesting coincidence that it had been built nearly eighty years ago by her own grandfather. Then when Angie had gone to university it had seemed too big, but before there was time to do anything about moving, there she was, back home again with a baby boy whose father she didn't want to marry. Fortunately, Angie got on quite well with her grandmother because, before baby Timothy was six months old, she, too, was installed at Jasmine Villa, having become too frail to live alone any longer. But then the fact that Jasmine Villa was once home of the Clarke family had turned out to be a disadvantage, adding to the old lady's confusion, and making her critical of the alterations they were having done. It was a relief, really, when she needed more nursing care than they could give and she moved, with surprising docility, into Easton Court.

Four times a week Dorothy visited. On Mondays and Wednesdays after school, on Saturday mornings and on Sunday afternoons. Now she sat in the car, nerving herself to be bright and affectionate. Poor old Mum! She'd been so smart and successful and confident, travelling up to London every week to buy for her three elegant shops, being wined and dined by sales managers, and coming home tired but happy after her busy, interesting day; and now all that business acumen and sense of style were gone, and the tall slim body they had inhabited had become hunched and gnarled, and was huddled in an incongruous pastel-coloured garment in the one-time drawing room of this eighteenth-century mansion.

How would she find her today? Sometimes she would be up, sitting in an easy-chair, with her hair done and wearing her rings. But on bad days she would be in bed, sleepy and muddled. Most of the time she seemed unhappy. Who wouldn't be, Dorothy thought, knowing they had come here to die? Presumably patients did improve and leave Easton Court for somewhere other than the chapel of rest; but Dorothy had not heard of any instances of this happening.

She crossed the well-kept gravel drive and entered the small entrance hall which led into an oval inner hall of considerable magnificence. It had a gallery at ceiling

height, beyond which you could look up to a glass dome
in the roof. The furniture was antique, of the same period
as the house, and there were great vases filled with chry-
santhemums, making splashes of warm colour against the
panelled walls. But Dorothy could take no pleasure in
these surroundings, being assaulted by the overwhelming
smell of urine. Most of the aged patients were inconti-
nent, and not even the latest hygienic appliances could
obviate this reminder of the failing flesh.

She approached the double doors of the old drawing
room. No screen barred her way. Its absence indicated
that she was permitted to enter. She saw at once that
today was one of her mother's better days. She was
propped up in a chair. Dorothy crossed the room quickly
and sat down beside her, taking her hand.

'Hello, Mum darling, how are things today?'

'Awful, of course, how else could they be?'

Yes, it was one of her good days.

'What did you have for lunch?'

'I don't know. I don't live to eat.'

'I see old Mrs Stanbrook's up and about again.'

'She's dotty.'

'Where's that nice nurse, the one you like?'

'She's off today. It's the other one. The fat one. She's
horrible.'

'How is she horrible?'

'She makes us all cry.'

'Oh, Mum, surely not.'

'She does. She hurts us.'

'Oh dear.' Dorothy was distressed. 'How does she hurt
you?'

'It's these catheter things.' The old lady moved her
dressing-gown, disclosing a plastic container on the
floor by her feet with a tube running into it. 'I don't

need it. I can control myself. It's just that it's easier for
them.'

Dorothy did not know what to say. Was it easier for
them?

'And it hurts. Makes me feel as though I want to pass
water all the time. If it wasn't for that, I wouldn't be too
bad, apart from being bored stiff.'

'We'll be getting more space at school soon. They're
letting us have a terrapin. That's an extra classroom. We
shall put the third years in there, they need a bit of peace
and quiet sometimes. Miss Fielding's been nagging for
years about it.'

'You wanted to be a teacher.'

'I still do.'

'You're always complaining.'

'I don't think I am. I like my work.'

'No money in it.'

'That's not everything.'

'It's nearly everything. You'll find that out one of these
days, when you're old and ill and nobody wants you.
Money's the only thing that can do you any good.'

'I expect you're right. I'm sure money is important. Or
what you can buy with it is.'

'That's your trouble. Buying things. Always has been.
Wasting money.'

The injustice of this almost brought tears to Dorothy's
eyes, exhausted as she was after her long day at school,
the tension at home, and the emotional effort of visiting
the nursing home. She was a careful spender; not even her
mother had accused her of extravagance for years and
years. Indeed, Angela's not always unwarranted cry was
that she was stingy.

She decided that it was hopeless to try and talk, but it
was too soon to leave. She looked round the room. The

floor was polished, there were flower-patterned curtains, and bedspreads in various colours, carefully chosen to tone. The beds were not hospital beds, except for one at the far end. There was the group of easy-chairs where she sat with her mother, and an arrangement of dried leaves and flowers on the table. Apart from the beds, and their ancient occupants, it was more like a hotel lounge than a nursing home.

A woman, round-shouldered and frail, shuffled along the ward and stopped beside Dorothy.

'I just thought I'd say goodbye,' she said, smiling.

'Oh, are you going home? How nice.' Someone was leaving the place alive! Dorothy felt considerably cheered.

'Yes, my son's coming to fetch me in a few minutes. I'm going to live with him. He's been trying to persuade me for so long, I thought I would.'

'How lovely.' And what a good son. He had not fallen short as she, Dorothy, had fallen short. Would it work? What about his wife?

'Yes, it's very nice here, but there's no place like home, I always say, with your own flesh and blood.'

'No indeed.'

'There are the grandchildren too. They're looking forward to having me, I know.'

'They must be.' Perhaps so, if they were small children. But what if they were teenagers?

'It's a very nice house. Plenty of room.'

'Is it near here?'

'No, it's a long way off. I must go and get ready. I mustn't keep him waiting.'

'You certainly mustn't.'

The old woman resumed her shaky progress down the ward and, after one or two attempts to find something to say that would enable them to part on a note of friendliness, Dorothy kissed her mother's forehead gently and said goodbye. In the hall she saw the old lady sitting in a chair, watching the door. A nurse approached.

'No, come on Miss Molyneux. You mustn't sit there in the draught, dear, come back into the ward.'

Protesting a little, she allowed the nurse to help her to rise and, now supporting herself with a walking-frame, set off slowly in the direction from which she had come. The nurse smiled at Dorothy.

'Always thinks her son's coming to fetch her,' she said.

'And ... and ... isn't he?'

'Oh, no. She hasn't got a son. She's never been married even. They get these funny ideas. You found your mother all right?'

No, thought Dorothy, since you've asked me, I didn't. There's a fat nurse that makes her cry. Why daren't I say that? Because you might be the fat nurse for all I know, you might be offended. Well, of course you would be and then you'd take it out on her in some way. No, if I'm going to say anything about that, it can't be to you.

'Yes, though she seems rather confused.'

'They get like that. So long as she's happy.'

'Oh, yes, I think she's quite happy.'

'You'll be in again soon?'

'Oh, yes.'

'That's right. She likes to see you.'

For a long moment Dorothy stood there. Through the double doors she could see Miss Molyneux slowly plodding down the ward towards her bed. Then she went out into the autumn afternoon and drove home faster than usual.

WEDNESDAY

Down the steep chalk-walled slope to the sea ran Addie,
her feet in their black boots gathering speed so that she
was halfway across the stretch of firm sand that bordered
the shore before she could stop. The tide was on the way
out, and the sands, deserted on this grey November afternoon, were damply brown and strewn with whitish stones
and black seaweed. On her right the view was bounded
by the chalky headland and on her left by the grey as-
phalt rise of the lower promenade.

Addie put her hands to her mouth, shouting with all
her might, 'Jay! Charlie!' Her voice faded away hopelessly
on the east wind. The boys could be hiding in the bathing
machines that were drawn up close together against the
cliffs. They were no longer dragged to the sea by horses,
but still served as changing cabins in the summer. Painted
white, each had a little balcony in front and wooden steps
down to the sand. Two at a time, Addie ran up the first
flight. The balcony being empty, she tried the door. It was
locked. Heaving herself up into a sitting position on the
wooden barrier, she swung her long legs over on to the
next machine. Empty again. She tried the door, and so she
went on down the line of twelve bathing machines, and
soon she was enjoying the rhythmic exercise for its own
sake. Heave up, legs over, jump down and rattle. Heave
up, legs over, jump down and rattle. She was only a little
impeded by her petticoat, her box-pleated maroon dress,
her white starched pinafore and her brown coat. Her tam-
o'-shanter, cleverly made by her mother from left-over
dress material, slipped back, and she crammed it down
over her ears.

Breathless, she arrived at the last balcony, and remembered she was looking for her brothers. How she wished

they would not come down to the sands in winter. She had often found them, as dusk gathered, fishing from the breakwater or scrambling over the rocks, in imminent danger, it seemed to her, of drowning or being cut off by the tide. She jumped down the last little flight of steps and ran along the sands and up the slope on to the lower promenade. Climbing on its ornate railings, she surveyed the beach, calling again, 'Jay! Charlie! Where are you?'

The sea was a thick, unfriendly grey, though to the west an edge of pale gold outlined the clouds. A dark figure stood far out on the breakwater. Was it one of the boys? Whoever it was evidently saw her, because it began to walk back towards the sands. When the figure reached dry land and jumped down, she saw it was far too tall for Jay or Charlie. The person was shouting something, and then Addie recognized him as the man known as Nitty Havergal, a grubby, slow-witted creature who was a byword in the town for dirt and stupidity. Unwanted by any relative, too limited mentally to do even the simplest work, he roamed about, lost and useless.

Once, to Addie's horror, he had exposed himself in front of her, and she was all the more appalled because she did not know then that he was constantly in trouble for indulging in this habit. Instead she held a guilty belief that she was partly responsible. Had she not, out of pity, smiled at him? Had she not, when he'd asked her, given him a sweet? After that she ignored him. Running home or to school as fast as she could.

Now she was frightened, for there was no one else in sight. She turned, and ran back along the promenade towards the gap. But there was a stretch of sand to cross before she could reach it. That was where he might catch her. He had broken into a shambling trot, shouting wordlessly. Breathless, terrified, and only a few yards ahead, she reached the bottom of the slope, but it was steep and endless. Her heart pounded, her chest hurt, her head was bursting. She was climbing through red mists and someone was reaching down to her. Someone with a kind voice, who said, 'You'll soon feel better, Mrs Castle. Just relax, just relax.'

With relief she realized that she was safe in bed; ill, obviously, but safe. Not being pursued. Her eyelids fluttered weakly as she tried to convey her gratitude to whoever was there. And then she remembered that she was eighty-four years old.

It was some time before she got it all straight in her mind again. She kept losing herself, on different places in her long past. They had gone back, of course, that was it. They had gone back to Jasmine Villa to live. She and Holly. But where were Mother and Dad, and Jay and Charlie? And Bella? No, wait . . . It was a different family. It was Dorothy, her daughter, and Frank, and Angela. Angela who was not Holly, though so like her. She must remember that. She knew she often called her Holly, but Holly was her elder sister, and Angela was her granddaughter.

Jasmine Villa! The house had lived up to its name. It was a villa and there was an abundance of jasmine. The name was engraved on a glass fanlight over the door. It had been built by Addie's father, a builder by trade, on a piece of land he had bought at a bargain price because it was an odd shape and at the back of the town.

Would the jasmine have been in bloom that day when she arrived home, sweating and exhausted, as dusk fell, her feet sore with pounding the grey pavements? She entered by the back way. Her anxiety for her brothers had returned when she left Nitty Havergal behind and she

waited at the kitchen door, wanting to hear their voices
before she opened it.

The scullery, where she stood, was dark, and smelled
damply of yellow soap, and scouring powder. There was
a duckboard on the stone floor in front of the shallow
sink. The walls were pea-green and the window was of
frosted glass. Under the sink was a noisome space where
Addie's mother, Nellie Clarke, kept a zinc bucket and a
scrubbing brush.

But the little room was a haven now to breathless
Addie. Her hand was slippery on the brass door-knob as
she listened for the boys' voices. It was her mother's she
heard, calling out of the opposite door, 'Jay. Charlie. Come
along, tea's ready.' Thankfully, she entered the kitchen.

In contrast to the bleakness of the scullery, it was warm
and homely. In the middle was the big scrubbed deal-
table, now spread with a white cloth, but the main feature
was the kitchen range, gleaming with black lead, friendly
with the glow of fire behind its bars. It was set into a
recess, below a high, wide mantelshelf on which stood a
clock, with some letters stuffed behind it, a pair of twisted
brass candlesticks, and a drawing of an elephant done by
Charlie at school. The walls here were dark green too,
except for a wainscot of embossed shiny brown paper
which protected the bottom three feet or so, but most of
one wall was covered by the dresser. This splendid piece
of furniture had been built by Addie's father, and with its
cupboards, its shelves, its hooks and its drawers, it played
an important part in the Clarkes' family life. The willow-
pattern plates were set out on the shelves, and the Coron-
ation mugs along the top, and when anything was lost or
misplaced in Jasmine Villa, whether hairbrush or ruler or
gloves or loose change, it would sooner or later be found
on the dresser.

This room, like the rest of the ground floor, could be lit by gas. The shaded white globes mounted on metal brackets at each end of the mantelpiece were already glowing, and by their thin yellow light Nellie was making the tea. She looked round sharply.

'Where have you been?'

'Playing with Lily Foster.'

Addie often lied to her parents, as did her brothers and sisters. The boys lied about playing on the deserted sands, and Addie, unable to tell tales even in her anxiety for them, went on her own to look for them. Then she lied about wherever she had been. Holly's lies were simply to get herself out of trouble or avoid questioning, and Bella lied all the time from force of habit.

'Hurry up,' said Nellie. 'Go and take your things off. And call Holly.'

Jay stared blandly at Addie. She knew he guessed where she had been and was thinking 'more fool you'. He sat down, poking Bella with his elbow as he did so, and the resulting scuffle was briskly quelled by their mother.

When they were finally all seated Addie looked round the table with satisfaction. Her mother she considered beautiful. Her soft fluffy hair, pinned into a high bun, was a pale gold, less red than Addie's own. She sat at the head of the table with her back to the range. Opposite Addie were cherubic Charlie, podgy little Bella, and dark-haired, glowering Jay. Beside her sat Holly, sixteen years old and a pupil teacher. But not grown up yet, surely, though she looked grown up, with her brown hair done in the same style as her mother's and her high-collared blouse.

There they were. All at home, safe and happy. Addie smiled at her mother.

'Shouldn't we wait for Dad?' she said.

'He's busy in the office, doing some accounts. When

you've had your tea, you can go over and help with the bills if you like.'

Addie, who loved her father and enjoyed arithmetic, said she would.

But it was not Dad she had missed, or Mother. No, it was her brothers and sisters: Jay, Charlie, and even Bella, but most of all Holly. What happy times they had all had together. Yet she could not think of Holly with joy. Why not, when Holly was so gay, so lively, with her piled-up brown hair and her full lips that laughed so often and pouted so sulkily.

Because of the Terrible Time.

She must not think of it, must not remember. For years it had scarcely entered her mind, why brood on it now she was old and ill? But still it would come back. And she, Addie, must do everything. There was no one else. She heard someone moaning and tried to raise herself. At once there was somebody in a white cap. Nurse. But Holly hadn't wanted the nurse. No, she had gone to hospital after all and then there was Timothy. Or was that Angela? But Angela was Holly and Holly was Angela and she had pushed down the bedclothes so that her shoulders were cold and it was starting all over again.

Waking in the night, uncovered. Rising slowly out of a deep sleep to find Holly sitting up, clasping her knees, with the bedclothes hunched around her.

'Holl,' whispered Addie, 'what's the matter?'

'You sleep heavily,' said Holly, accusing her.

'What is it, Holl? Shall I light the candle?'

'No.'

'Have you got a pain? You must tell me.'

'I can't.'

'You always do, Holly. You always tell me everything.'

This was true. Holly, nearly three years older, always

told Addie everything. Fears, guilts and hopes, she loaded them all on to her younger sister, and then turned away unburdened, while Addie feared, hoped and agonized in her stead.

So it was on this unforgettable night.

Holly told . . .

'I've done something awful. With a man. You know.'

But Addie didn't know. She had suspected and she had feared, but she didn't know. So Holly told her. Made crude by lack of vocabulary and her own youth and desperation, Holly told.

'I don't believe that,' said Addie. 'No one would ever do that.'

'Well, I have, you little idiot.'

'But the horrible stuff . . . it didn't come inside you did it, Holl?'

'Of course it did.'

'But it must have been awful.'

Addie moved away a little in the bed. A great many things that had puzzled and worried her were becoming clear. She said, 'But, Holly, suppose you have a baby? You might.'

'Well, I don't know yet, do I, stupid.'

'You'll have to tell Mum.'

'Tell Mum! Are you mad, Addie Clarke?'

'But if . . .'

'I'll run away, or perhaps I'll kill myself . . .'

'Couldn't you get married? Then it wouldn't matter, even if you . . .'

To her surprise, Holly gave a harsh sob. 'No, I can't get married. And you're not to ask me who it was because I shan't tell you, ever. So shut up.'

'I wasn't going to,' Addie replied truthfully. More knowledge, she felt, could only make her feel worse. She could see her sister clearly now, with the thin curtains letting in the moonlight. The room was small, nearly filled by the black-painted iron bedstead with its brass knobs. Holly was sitting with her knees drawn up, the white sheet and rough pale blankets held up to her neck, the honeycomb bedspread having been folded and placed on a chair. The dark bulk of the chest of drawers faced them. On it were a small swing mirror and two identical work-boxes of light-coloured wood, the lids inlaid with mother-of-pearl. These had been Christmas presents from their mother, too obviously chosen in the hope that the girls would thereby be encouraged to take up needlework. They both had to accomplish a certain amount of plain sewing and mending, but beyond this neither of them was interested. In the divided trays that rested inside each they kept different things. In Holly's were her hairpins and such small trinkets as she possessed, while Addie's contained her treasures, including her favourite sea shells, a skeleton leaf, and a golden curl of hair that she had managed to keep after she and her mother had taken Charlie for his first haircut.

But underneath these trays, the spaces that should have been occupied by dainty pieces of work in progress were stuffed with what Addie called their 'muddles': lengths of darning wool, sewing cotton, embroidery thread, bits of lace edging and ribbon, tape and knicker elastic inextricably tangled into a sort of ball. But the muddles were quite useful. Close examination would usually reveal a thread or end of the required colour and material and you could usually draw out almost as much as you needed before the tangle reasserted itself and refused to give up any more. Fortunately, Alice's regular inspections of her daughters' bedroom did not extend to opening their workboxes.

Addie fixed her eyes on hers now, so as not to look at

her sister. 'I don't see how you could do it, Holl. It must be horrible.'

'It's all right.'

'Well, I never shall, anyway.'

Addie curled up, trying unsuccessfully to take possession of her share of the bedclothes. But Holly had the last word.

'Perhaps you'll never get the chance.' She giggled suddenly. 'Except for Nitty Havergal.'

She lay down, turned her back to her sister, and slept. Addie stayed awake, the horror of it all overwhelming her. So that was what he'd meant. That was what he'd wanted. And she hadn't understood, not till now; and understanding brought with it a black cloud of guilt and shame that she felt would never leave her. It would never leave her because somewhere, deep down, her sister's words had awakened a trace of excitement. Unwanted, instantly denied, but excitement nevertheless. So while Holly slept, it was dawn before Addie fell into a troubled doze.

For the next few months Holly went her usual apparently carefree way, only with Addie in private was she irritable or taciturn. And Addie, sharing the bedroom, sleeping in the same bed, could not help knowing when her sister was menstruating, and therefore could not help knowing when she was not. Her carefully thought-out, desperately tactful enquiries elicited only accusations of nosiness and spying.

'Just you mind your own business, Addie Clarke. You've got babies on the brain,' and Holly, turning over after the candle was blown out and dragging the bedclothes away from Addie as she did so, would fall asleep immediately while her sister lay awake, worrying and making plans. It was Addie, pale and without her usual healthy appetite, who was forced to parry their mother's anxious enquiries, and to swallow laxatives she did not need. Even climbing scaffolding or walking round the top of the six-foot-high garden wall was not the fun it had been, though tomboyish games offered some distraction. Those, and the music evenings.

May Kingston, whom the Clarke children called Auntie May, was Nellie's old school friend who had, as Nellie said, done well for herself by marrying Tom Kingston. Musical evenings at their house were rather special occasions. Their daughter Bridget was a good pianist, but Addie preferred Holly's Strauss waltzes, played with dash and vigour and a good many wrong notes, to Bridget's classical pieces. Holly had a pleasant soprano voice, too, but Addie and her mother were the real singers. Bella was quite a good fiddler, and sometimes Jay could be persuaded to take his flute. Though young, he was a competent flautist, but the spindly chairs and thin china cups made him feel clumsy and awkward. To Addie's sorrow her father never went with them. He said the Kingstons were a different class and he believed in sticking to his own station in life. Nellie said this was silly, and that a builder was just as good as a chemist any day. Addie thought privately that her father disliked Mr Kingston, which was hard to understand, Tom Kingston being handsome, friendly and not a bit proud, for all his three shops.

So, though she enjoyed putting on her best velveteen dress with the lace collar and going round to the Kingstons' nearly as much as Holly did, it was the music evenings at home that gave Addie the most pleasure.

These were not arranged, they just happened. Somebody would start playing the piano in the front room. Mother would go in and say, 'If you're going to be in here I may as well put a match to the fire.' Then the others would follow and they'd be there for the rest of the evening.

Anything from 'Silent Worship' to 'Three little Maids from School', from Mendelssohn's 'Spring Song' to 'When Father Painted the Parlour', all were performed with equal gusto. Only Charlie was absent on these occasions. He preferred to stay in the kitchen, playing his mysterious games with lead soldiers, moving them about on the table and whispering to himself. Addie missed his pink-cheeked face and choirboy's voice, but still on these occasions she was happy and absorbed. After a music evening she would fall asleep quickly, and sometimes sleep till morning. But if she was unlucky enough to wake in the night, all her anxieties would come flooding inescapably back.

She put out a hand, under the bedclothes. No Holly. And the bed was strangely narrow. Opening her eyes she saw with a shock the high ornate ceiling, much too far away. Then she realized with her usual sensations of horror and relief that she was not thirteen, that it had all happened long, long ago, and that Holly was dead.

No wonder she had roused. In her half-dream she had been drawing dangerously near to the Terrible Time, and she did not want to think about that, not yet. Some day or night, quite soon perhaps, she would feel strong enough to go over it all again, but just now she did not feel up to it. And in any case it seemed to be tea-time, and teas at Easton Court were really excellent, with little savoury sandwiches, and pieces of very light sponge cake.

THE WORKBOX

TO BE PUBLISHED IN PAPERBACK BY
WARNER
IN 1993